FROM FAKE
TO FOREVER

T0345489

Laila Rafi has a degree in Criminology, which is gathering dust because she would rather spend her days dreaming of her characters falling in love. She has dabbled in Finance and Education, but realised her real calling was putting pen to paper, or more accurately fingers to keyboard and getting lost in a world of happily ever afters.

She lives in the heart of London with her boisterous family and when she's not writing or reading romance, she can be found watching almost any sport – though her preference is Formula 1.

From Fake to Forever is her first novel.

FROM FAKE TO FOREVER

Laila Rafi

First published in Great Britain in 2022 by Orion Dash,
an imprint of The Orion Publishing Group Ltd,
Carmelite House, 50 Victoria Embankment
London EC4Y 0DZ

An Hachette UK company

1 3 5 7 9 10 8 6 4 2

A CIP catalogue record for this book
is available from the British Library.

ISBN (eBook) 978 1 3987 0994 2
ISBN (Paperback) 9781 3 9871 060 3

Typeset by Born Group

www.orionbooks.co.uk

To Dad, Mum and my minions... sorry, siblings ;-)

CHAPTER ONE

Ibrahim

'I think it's high time we found you a good girl and got you married.'

And there it was. Just as it had been for the last six months or so. The same thing his older brother Zafar had gone through, and Ibrahim was fed up.

What his father failed to realise was that Zafar and his arranged marriage were part of the reason that Ibrahim had sworn off the entire bloody institution.

His older brother – like he always did – had followed their father's decree and married a girl of their father's choosing rather than his own. Apparently, that was 'the way it had always been', which as far as he was concerned, was a pathetic excuse to shackle yourself with a woman who would make your life miserable. Not that his sister-in-law made Zafar's life miserable as such, but by constantly giving in to the demands of tradition and duty to family, his brother had lost himself. Ibrahim was determined that he would not sacrifice himself at the same altar, no pun intended.

'It'll encourage you to get home at a reasonable time and having someone to welcome you home with a smile, a home cooked meal and all the comforts of a happy home will make you a happy man.'

His father's archaic thinking was yet another thing that always rubbed him up the wrong way. He had never seen his mother do much of the above, so for the old man to imagine someone would do it for his son was laughable.

Giving his father a few non-committal answers, Ibrahim made his escape, thanking his stars as a taxi pulled in at the rank near the office building in Central London. He had already been late for his catch-up with his brothers and being ambushed by his father had further soured his mood.

Trying to shake off the conversation with his father as he stepped through the doors to the restaurant, he made his way to the table his brothers were sat around.

'Glad you could make it.' Zafar scooted along to make space for him on the bench. Their youngest brother, Haroon, sitting opposite, threw out a casual greeting. Rayyan and Ashar still hadn't shown up.

'Where are the others?'

'Parents' evening and I don't know.'

'Ah.' Unlike Zafar and himself, Rayyan had chosen not to join the family business in any capacity, and much to their father's displeasure, had become a teacher. Ashar was a law unto himself and could be anywhere doing anything.

'What kept you so long?' Haroon waved a hand in the air, trying to get the waitress's attention.

'Four-letter word called work. You should try it sometime.'

'Ha! And end up like you? No thanks.' Being the youngest of the brothers, Haroon – aka Harry – was the definition of a spoilt and entitled brat. There was no fix his brothers couldn't get him out of when his charm didn't work and having all available attention on him was something he considered a birthright.

He waved his hand again at someone behind Ibrahim and catching his eye, he winked at him.

'I saw that. Don't start deliberately winding him up.' Zafar pocketed his phone and turned to give their youngest brother a pointed look.

'He needs to lighten up. He's so highly strung all the time.'

'I was caught by Dad as I was leaving the office.'

'Ohhh.' This was said by both of them, followed by silence. They all knew it was best to avoid their father most of the time but being caught by him unawares was the worst.

'*Ohhh* what?' Ashar arrived and unceremoniously pushed Harry along the booth to sit down.

Harry responded with one word. 'Dad.'

'Ah. So, what belter did he come out with today? It must have been a cracker because this one's knickers seem to be in more of a twist than usual, judging by his face.'

Ibrahim loosened his tie and undid the top button of his shirt. 'He made out like it was a complete coincidence that he saw me, when there was absolutely no reason for him to be on my floor whatsoever.' Harry scoffed and Ibrahim was about to carry on when the waitress came to their table.

'Jiya, sweetheart, where have you been?' Of course, Harry would start flirting first thing. 'I've not seen you for what feels like for ever. This place just isn't the same without you.'

'You saw me yesterday, Haroon Saeed. It seems you're mixing me up with someone else. Again. So, what can I get you gentlemen?'

'You break my heart, Jiya.'

'You'll live. Shall we start with drinks?'

Laughing at their baby brother being put down so beautifully by the waitress who obviously knew him given their level of familiarity, they placed their orders and in no time at all, their food and drinks were on the table.

There was silence around the table as all four of them savoured the first few bites of their meal until a few moments later, Ashar prompted him to continue.

'Apparently I need a wife who will welcome me with a smile and a home cooked meal so that I'm eager enough to get home on time. Ha, as though we need another Stepford wife in the house.' He felt a sharp pain in his shin as Harry kicked him hard and then glared at him. 'No offence, Zaf.' His older brother grimaced.

'He's got a friend's daughter who would be "just right" for me and he's invited them for the party. He's hoping to announce my engagement after our grandmother has blown out all eighty candles and cut the cake.'

'Congratulations,' Ashar said drolly.

'Shut up.'

'Ignore him. What else did he say?' Zafar had finished his food and turned to face him, his expression intent.

'He didn't say anything more because I left. If I had stayed there and let him carry on, I would have probably blown my stack and that would have set him off on another one.'

'You ought to go and tell him that you're not interested, just like I did. He can't force you.' Ashar looked like he actually believed what he'd just said.

'Do you not know who our father is? And just because you get away with certain things doesn't mean the rest of us will.'

'I'll talk to him. Just because I did as he said it doesn't mean that he should start doing the same thing with you as well.'

'No, Zaf, there's no point in anyone talking to him. He's like a bloody wrecking ball; he'll just ignore what others say and do what he wants anyway.'

The four of them sat back, thinking about their father's ability to dominate the conversation even when he wasn't present.

'What if you already had someone?' Ibrahim looked at Harry and raised an eyebrow in question.

'What if you tell the old man that you've got a girl-friend who you're serious about and ready to propose to? In fact, you can bring her as a guest to the party and that way, he'll lay off setting you up with his mate's daughter.'

Ashar ruffled Harry's hair, much to his annoyance. 'Since when did you get so clever?'

'Get off!'

'Quick question: where exactly am I going to find this saviour of mine? Besides, he'll know I'm not serious about her because I would have only known her for a month.'

'What happened to that legal eagle you were with? You could ask her.' Ibrahim scowled at Ashar's suggestion.

'Selina? Not a good idea. She was already expecting far too much from me when I called things off. If I called her back, took her home to a family gathering and introduced her as my *significant other*, she'll have sent out the invitations to our wedding before the evening's over.' He shuddered to emphasise his point and his brothers chuckled.

Just then, the waitress came back to their table. 'Can I get you guys anything? Coffee or dessert? And don't you dare say anything outrageous.' She pointed her pen at Harry.

He clutched his chest like a melodramatic actor of some bygone era. 'You wound me, Jiya. I thought we were friends.'

'We are, but only when you're not being a drama queen or a royal pain. And from what I can see, you've been a good mix of both this evening.'

Ibrahim noticed the way Jiya was responding to Harry, her eyes twinkling with mischief, and was amused by it.

In fact, now that he was actually paying attention to her, there was a lot more he was noticing. He was sure he'd seen her on previous visits to the restaurant but strangely, he'd never stopped and looked this closely before.

She had an open and happy face but he could sense her confidence and determination a mile off. She had very light make-up on, rather than a face caked with it. It highlighted her complexion, but didn't detract from her natural features and beauty. Her straight hair was tied up in a high ponytail and she was dressed all in black; the only colour visible was her bright pink nail polish.

He was so distracted just watching her and noticing things about her that he didn't realise that everyone had turned to look at him, including her.

She was giving him a look filled with curiosity, her almond-shaped, dark brown eyes sparkling in the overhead light. Ashar kicked him under the table and belied his aggression by politely asking him if he wanted to add anything to their order. His legs would be finished by the time they left at this rate.

He cleared his throat. 'The cookie dough, please. Thank you.'

There was a subtle change in her expression, as though she had been watching him just as closely as he had her a moment ago. She nodded and turned to walk away, giving him a spectacular view of her behind. Her ponytail swayed with her steps, brushing her shoulders every now and then and Ibrahim had the oddest urge to run his fingers through it.

He felt something hit the side of his head, looked down to see a balled-up napkin and then looked up at Harry, who was grinning like a monkey who'd just found a sack of nuts.

'You like Jiya!' He jabbed the air with his finger. 'Ibby likes Jiya, Ibby likes Jiya!' He was using his sing-song voice and Ibrahim tried to reach for the bastard across the table until Zafar pulled him back.

'Why won't you tell him to stop pissing me off?' he complained to his older brother.

'Stop reacting to him as though you're both back in primary school. The more you rise to his bait, the more he'll do it.' Harry nodded in agreement and then scowled as Ashar clipped him on the back of the head. 'Stop it, Princess. He's stressed out as it is. We're supposed to be helping him and you're not.'

'Haroon.' It was Zafar's tone of voice that did the trick because Harry's expression changed instantly and he sat up straighter.

They all loved and respected their eldest brother immensely, but Harry practically worshipped him. He would never do anything he thought Zafar might be unhappy about and when Zafar said stop, Harry stopped. Which came in handy when he was being an arse.

'So, if Selina's a no, then what are your options? Did Dad say anything about his friend's daughter? You never know, she might—'

'Don't even bother finishing that sentence, Zaf. I'm not doing it. Full stop. As for options, I don't have any in mind at the moment.'

'What about a fake girlfriend?' They all turned to look at Harry, who had both his hands up in surrender. 'Just hear me out before you shoot me down. I didn't even finish my earlier suggestion properly.

'Instead of asking Selina, get a friend who you know and trust, and who knows the score beforehand, and get her to pretend to be your girlfriend for the party. Then after a while you can tell everyone that it didn't work out. At least it'll give you some breathing space and time to think about a more long-term solution.'

Ibrahim sat back and thought about the suggestion. It actually wasn't that bad an idea and although he would never say it to the brat, Harry was right. It would definitely give him some time to think about what to do. His grandmother's birthday celebrations were in just over a month. He couldn't call his ex-girlfriend because that would be the equivalent of taking a loaded shotgun and firing it at his own foot. Both feet in fact.

So, this was the next best thing given the time frame he had. Except . . .

'Where am I going to find someone who fits the bill in such a short space of time?'

'Here we go. Two coffees, one milkshake and a cookie dough with vanilla ice cream. Enjoy.' Jiya placed the items on the table and after smiling at them all, turned and walked away.

Ibrahim watched her as she made her way back to the counter and started chatting to one of her colleagues. She had an easy way about her that he found refreshingly different, giving him 'girl next door' vibes, which he'd never thought were his thing.

He jerked his head back towards his brothers when he heard a snort. It was Harry. Obviously.

'What's happened to you?' Ashar spoke with his straw hanging out of his mouth.

'Don't say anything stupid, Harry. I won't be happy.' The fact that Zafar had to warn the shrimp was quite amusing.

'It's nothing, bhai, the coffee was just a bit hot.' Harry was hardly ever serious, always ready for a laugh, especially at another's expense. The only person he seldom did that with was Zafar. In fact, although he should address all of them as *bhai* for the simple fact that they were all older than him and it was a sign of respect, he only addressed Zafar that way. Ibrahim would worry if Harry ever referred to him as *bhai*.

Finishing off his own dessert, he ran his hand through his hair and let out an exhausted sigh. 'I'll just have to figure something out and take it from there. I'm done for this evening so shall we make a move?'

Being the eldest, Zafar had the honour of paying the bill and Harry went back to chat with Jiya, his charming smile back in place. Ibrahim made his way outside with Ashar, taking a deep breath of fresh air and feeling some of the tension leave him. Sure, he had to find a way to thwart his father's plans, but it wouldn't make a huge difference if he figured things out tomorrow instead of tonight.

CHAPTER TWO

Jiya

'Fine, let's catch up tomorrow. And you're buying lunch.' Jiya pointed her finger at Harry, who had come over to have a chat with her as his brothers were leaving The Lounge.

'I tell you what I can promise: *you* won't have to pay for lunch. Deal?' Harry waggled his eyebrows at her and Jiya giggled. He was a complete rascal but he was also one of her closest friends, so she let his mischief slide.

The first time she had met him had been on her first-ever waitressing shift the year before. He had been with a group of friends and had bantered with her outrageously as though they were good old friends and had always interacted that way. And then they *had* become good friends. The best of friends, in fact, much to her surprise.

Jiya had never been comfortable being friends with the opposite sex until recently. Her mother had always warned her that girls and boys couldn't be friends. 'If a boy says he wants friendship from you, it is probably a cover-up for something else.' She'd raised her eyebrows and widened her eyes as though that explained everything.

Jiya had followed her mother's thinking until she'd got to university, where she realised that boys came in all shapes and sizes. Some were exactly as her mother had predicted, often expecting more than she was willing to give and backing off – sometimes rudely – when it wasn't forthcoming. Others – like the Haroon Saeeds of the world – were happy to be friends and respected the boundaries she put in place.

Besides, she was totally focused on her ambition and had no time for anything beyond friendship. She was going to finish her MBA and get a job in a top ten firm and although she would love to do a short stint internationally, she had to be realistic. Her parents would never allow that, so she'd focus on doing the best she could where she was and no one and nothing was going to come between her and her ambition.

'Tomorrow then, at midday.' Harry turned to follow one of his brothers out, waving his fingers at her as he went. 'See ya.'

The next day Jiya met Harry outside the café they often caught up at. She sat down at the little table outside, enjoying the feeling of the summer sun hitting her face. Thankfully it wasn't too hot that she'd burn, and she wouldn't mind that slightly golden tone her skin took when she spent some time in the sun.

'So, what are the latest goings on in the life of Miss Jiya Ahmed?'

Harry slurped his drink out of the straw like a four-year-old.

'Eww.' She gave him the reaction he was after and giggled as he grinned at her. 'So, last week, I went home after an early shift and coincidence of all coincidences, Auntie Nadia was there with a boy I think was her nephew.'

'Ooh, an ambush.' He leaned forward on the table after rubbing his hands together like some dastardly villain. 'Let me guess – the nephew was single.'

'What gave it away?'

'Tut, tut. Sarcasm isn't desirable in a good bride, Jiya,' he said with mock severity.

'I wasn't sarcastic with them. I was perfectly polite and even smiled at Abdul when I was introduced to him.'

'But you're not interested in him.'

It wasn't a question, but she answered anyway. 'You know the score, Harry. I want to make something of myself beyond being a dutiful daughter or wife or daughter-in-law or mother or—'

'I get the picture, J. Look, you don't have to tell me, I know what you want. What I don't understand is why your family doesn't get it.'

She groaned into her palms as she covered her face. 'I don't know.'

'It's the same bloody drama everywhere. My brother was ambushed by our dad last night but at least he didn't have the potential bride in tow. That'll be the case on the day of the party. I'm glad I've got a few years to figure out how to avoid such a fate. There's three of them before it's my turn.'

Jiya saw his smug expression at not having to put up with unwanted matchmaking and wished she could wipe it off his face. Better still, she wished *she* could have the freedom of time, so she could at least make her dreams come true before agreeing to settle down with someone.

The barista brought their food out as she was sitting there contemplating when the most brilliant of ideas struck her. She leaned across the table, her sudden action surprising Harry into jerking his head away from her, his expression half worried, half horrified.

'Maybe I should take you home as my boyfriend. You're from a good family with great prospects and maybe they wouldn't stop me from seeing you. We could "go out" while I'm doing my MBA and then, once I've secured a job, I can dump you! It's the perfect plan.'

'Gee, thanks J. Way to boost a man's confidence.' She barely noticed his dry remark, instead watching in disgust as he opened his panini to load it with ketchup. He closed it again and, waggling his eyebrows at her, took a noisy bite. 'Yum!'

'This is the best plan ever!' she said with absolute conviction.

'This is the worst plan ever because that's not us. Besides, I don't want you cramping my style. I'm a man in much demand, Jiya – you dumping me wouldn't be believable in the least.'

She rolled her eyes. 'Fine. You can dump me – I don't mind. Happy?'

His phone bleeped twice, indicating a message alert and Jiya got busy eating while he checked his message. His loud chuckle had her looking up again.

'What is it? Another lewd joke?'

'Even better. My dad sent my brother a picture of the girl he thinks would be perfect for him and Ibrahim's forwarded it to us, whinging about it in the group chat.'

'Poor guy. He should get a temporary girlfriend, too.' She said it spontaneously and took another bite of her panini.

Harry slapped his hand on the table, making her jump and pointed a finger at her, his other hand still holding the phone. 'Yes! You two can help each other.'

'Uh, you what?'

'Yes.' He shook his head and let out a low chuckle in the way someone did when the penny finally dropped about something. 'Ah, Haroon Saeed, you bloody genius!' he congratulated himself.

'Hello? What on earth are you talking about?' Jiya looked at him closely, confused at the sudden change in both him and the conversation.

'I told Ibrahim the same thing yesterday, believe it or not, about having a girlfriend to take the pressure off. Look, you need a boyfriend to help stop your parents from bringing Abduls home to see you, and give you enough time to finish your MBA and get yourself a job. Yes?'

'What does that have to do with—'

'Just answer me with a yes or a no. Don't ruin my flow with your questions.'

She rolled her eyes at him again. 'Yes.'

'Good. And Ibrahim needs a girlfriend to stop my dad from matching him up to some friend's daughter. At least for long enough until he can find a different solution, because my dad is ready to make the introduction. I can introduce *you* to Ibrahim instead.'

'But I hardly know him. In fact, I don't even know which of your brothers you're referring to? Is he the one you came in with yesterday?'

'No, the one who came after we did and you can get to know him. You tell him about yourself, he tells you about himself, or of course I can dish the dirt on both of you, and you both help each other out in your year of need. Simples.' He winked at her as he said the last bit.

She chewed quietly for a moment, mulling over what he'd just said. It wasn't as outlandish an idea as it had first seemed. But . . .

'Question: why would your brother agree to this?'

'Because he wants to thwart the old man and his nefarious matchmaking.' He cackled theatrically, the drama queen.

'Ha. That's rich coming from you. You're playing match-maker right now.'

'But for the greater good, child. Look, let's say you both agree, your family will stop bombarding you with Abduls . . .'

'So, you've said.'

He flung a balled-up wrapper at her head. 'Let me finish. Your family stop harassing you because you'll be "with" a perfectly suitable boy from a great family with a genius younger brother,' he pointed at himself with both index fingers, 'and you can focus on completing your course, making your applications and sodding off to wherever you get a job.

'My old man will see Ibrahim with a gorgeous, bright girl like you with a genius best friend,' he pointed at himself again, the conceited joker, 'and think that he doesn't need to set him up, thus getting off his case. It's a win–win situation, sugar.'

She narrowed her eyes at him as her mind ran on at breakneck speed, trying to pick holes in his argument. But she couldn't see any.

He was watching her closely as he ate the last bite of his own sandwich, and after swallowing, he leaned forward and whispered conspiratorially, 'Ibrahim has contacts in the business world. Contacts across the globe even, if you get my drift. Maybe if he's feeling generous, he could help his "girlfriend" with some networking, maybe even in an office abroad.' He leaned back and shrugging his shoulder dismissively he added, 'Just a thought.'

He had a point, and judging by the supremely smug smile on his face, he knew it. She lobbed the balled-up wrapper back at his head, earning herself a laugh as he caught it cleanly.

As he'd promised, she didn't pay for lunch and, agreeing to call her soon to further his genius plan – his words – they each went their own way.

A week later, Jiya found herself pacing her little room, waiting to be summoned downstairs. An annoying woman – an old friend of her mother's actually, intent on destroying her life – was downstairs with another proposal of marriage and Jiya hadn't been given the chance to avoid today's meet-up.

Her mother had waited until late last night to tell her that 'Auntie Nadia is coming and she's bringing a boy and his family with her. I've ironed the light blue suit for you and make sure you don't have any absurd colour nail polish on, OK? All right, *shabba khair*.'

Good night? It had been a dreadful night after that. She had hardly slept.

She was supposed to be meeting Harry and his brother today, which she'd had to postpone and instead, here she was, being paraded in front of some random boy and his family. All in the hopes that he liked her and would marry her.

'No, thank you. Not if I have anything to do with it.'

'Talking to yourself again, sis? Carry on like that and no boy will have you.'

She turned and glared at her brother, who had stuck his head around the door and was circling his index finger by his temple.

Jameel Yunus Ahmed, her God-given tormentor on this earth, though he thought of himself more as a God-given gift, something her parents both agreed with wholeheartedly.

Jameel had arrived after a string of miscarriages and as a result, he was treated like treasure. Jiya could understand her parents' sentiments. After all those losses, the gift of a baby truly was precious but what she struggled to accept was the flagrant favouritism, the fact that Jameel got away with practically everything and that he did diddly squat for himself. In fact, earlier that day, he had woken up later than everyone else after getting to bed at the crack of dawn after a night of gaming, and instead of getting him to make his own breakfast, her mother had herded her into the kitchen to make it. To say she had been supremely cheesed off with him was an understatement and now he was standing in the doorway being his annoying self.

'I don't need any boy to *have me*, thank you very much. I just need them to clear off. I've got things to do, places to be.'

He shrugged, looking bored with the conversation already. 'Whatever. Ammi said to tell you to come down.'

'This is sooo awkward – I hate having to do it.'

Her brother scoffed. 'Yeah, rather you than me.' And with that, he preceded her out of the room. So much for brotherly support.

The following meeting went exactly as the previous ones had and was no less torturous for it. Her mother came to the door to receive her as though she couldn't make her way to the sofa unaided and would lose her way; Auntie Nadia started rattling off traits and qualities that Jiya was sure she didn't possess and her father . . . well, he didn't say anything. Just sat there making small talk with who she presumed was the potential suitor's father.

Said suitor was firmly ensconced between Auntie Nadia and his mother and seemed to have his eyes glued to the floor rug – which wasn't all that attractive in Jiya's opinion but her mother loved it. His mother's eyes, however, were glued to Jiya as she sat down on the sofa with her mother.

'Well, at least once she's married, all this extra studying and waitressing business you mentioned will stop.'

Yes, because intelligence and independence in a woman are such ugly traits, aren't they? She remembered Harry's crack about sarcasm and held back a smile.

'She'll get busy with her home, husband and children. No time for anything else then.' That particular gem was from Auntie Nadia.

Jiya really was amazed at the things she could come out with. She was a self-proclaimed matchmaker and so far, all she'd shown Jiya was that the one thing she couldn't do well was match. For starters, she was wearing a bright orange and yellow suit with splashes of green and brown on the print and her shoes were red. Second, and more importantly, all the so-called matches she'd found for Jiya so far had been no matches at all. There hadn't been a single thing she'd had in common with any of the guys and Jiya wasn't hopeful about today's candidate either. Not that her opinion would be sought just yet; Auntie Nadia was too busy enumerating her skill set to the boy's mother.

'She can even do sewing.' *Yes, if the one ugly blouse she'd made in her textiles module in school counted.*

'That's so handy and such a cost-saver. Clothes these days are so unnecessarily expensive. My Jameel here is very good at budgeting. No frivolous spending with him at all,' the boy's mother said.

OK, she was not marrying a man with the same name as her brother. Nuh uh, not happening. She turned to look at her mother and before she could make a face to show her feelings, her mother widened her eyes in warning and – as was her way when there was a pending crisis – she offered the visitors more tea.

This was unbelievable. She couldn't believe her parents were entertaining this farce of a meeting. They knew her thoughts on the whole set-up, but apparently this was the way it had always been done and had been working for decades. For them, Jiya getting married and proving herself as a good wife and mother was a measure of their success as parents.

They welcomed all her academic achievements and successes but it was a bonus as far as they were concerned. The real deal for them was her securing a suitable match. They would rather she focused on becoming better domesticated rather than further educated. She was constantly reminded that at the end of the day she was a girl, as though it were a weakness of some sort.

Thankfully, the cringeworthy meeting didn't last much longer and the visitors took their leave, promising to be in touch with their answer. As though Jiya were waiting with bated breath for them to say, 'Yes, we think Jiya is the perfect girl for our son.'

'That wasn't so bad, was it, Jiya?' Her father and brother had scarpered and her mother was righting the cushions.

'No, it wasn't bad at all, Ammi, it was awful.' She took off her stole, balled it up and threw it on the sofa. 'That boy didn't say a single word the whole time, leaving his mother and Auntie Nadia to do all the talking while he admired your rug. And his name's Jameel.'

'That's because he was being respectful, letting the adults do the talking. And how is his name his fault? He hardly chose it himself and it's a lovely name.'

Well, it was no shocker that her mother was partial to the name. But still, 'If he's not adult enough to do the talking, Ammi, then he's not adult enough to be my life partner. When Auntie Nadia phones you, you can tell her that Jiya said no.' And with that, she snagged a biscuit from the tea tray and walked out of the room.

CHAPTER THREE

Jiya

Harry had spoken to Jiya two days ago to tell her that he'd *briefed* – his word – Ibrahim and their plan was a *go* – again, his word. As though they were on some sort of secret mission, which she supposed they were to a certain extent.

She had asked him what his brother's reaction had been but all he'd said to her was, 'Trust me and I'll sort this out in such a way that everything will work out in the end.' She couldn't say his words filled her with confidence, but she didn't have much of an alternative.

'The last time I trusted you, I ended up with a full fringe and I looked awful.'

'*You* thought you looked awful, I thought you looked cute. Anyway, that happened so long ago, your fringe has grown out about a foot since then – get over it. I'll see you in two days; Mr Grumpy will be with me and I'll text you the address. Cheerio.'

She wished she didn't have to go ahead with a ridiculous plan like this. Why couldn't her parents support her decision to complete her course and give her the freedom to work? They happily supported all of Jameel's daft ideas but *her* dreams, which she'd been vocal about since at least the age of fifteen, were deemed unrealistic. Why? For the simple reason that she was a girl and she was supposed to be a homemaker rather than a decision maker. Those dreams were for other girls; i.e., any girl who wasn't the daughter of Yunus and Samina Ahmed.

Trying to shake off her thoughts, she focused on the present. She opted to go for smart casual, wearing a pair of dark jeans, a red silk blouse and her peep-toe wedges. She did her usual make-up routine, put her hair up in a ponytail and left home with enough time to get to the place Harry had sent her the address for.

Thankfully, she had the freedom to meet up with friends whenever she wanted without answering too many questions. Her parents were cool on that front.

She got there before they did and since it was a lovely summer's evening, she opted to wait outside for them. She had only been waiting for a few minutes when she saw the pair of them walking towards her.

Jiya felt her tummy swoop and instinctively placed her hand on it. *Just nerves.*

Both brothers were devastatingly good-looking. She had always acknowledged – only to herself, because Harry's ego was monumental enough – that Harry was an attractive man.

His older brother was no exception. Everything about him screamed style, sophistication and power.

He wore a dark grey suit which fitted him to perfection, his silk tie knotted perfectly against his perfect white shirt. His hair was styled perfectly too, falling in neatly cut layers. His jaw was smooth without any hint of stubble on his – you got it – perfect face and his sunglasses were polished enough for her to see her own reflection in them. If she had to describe him in one word it would have to be perfect. Just perfect.

Cheesy much? Perhaps.

The craziest thing was that this wasn't the first time she was seeing him. She'd seen him a few times at The Lounge and she'd even waited at his table but he'd never affected her in the way he was now, as he walked towards her, his gait confident and easy beside Harry's swagger. Maybe it was because she could now put a name to the face.

Well, whatever it was, what followed would definitely be interesting.

Ibrahim

'Why are you lurking outside like a weirdo?'

Ibrahim glared at his brother and gritted his teeth. 'What the hell, Harry?' He turned to glance at Jiya who seemed a bit stunned, taking turns to look at him and Harry as they approached her. 'Ignore this rude infant – thanks for agreeing to come.' He extended his hand towards her and she tentatively extended her own, giving him a shy smile.

'No problem.' Her voice was soft and slightly husky.

'Oh, for God's sake you two.' Harry tugged her ponytail and then threw his arm around her shoulders. Ibrahim rolled his eyes as he followed the two of them into the restaurant towards the table reserved for them, though he was grateful for his brother's easy way of cutting through the awkwardness.

He sat down opposite Jiya while Harry sat next to her, waggling his eyebrows at him suggestively. Ibrahim stuck two fingers up at his younger brother and turned back to look at Jiya, who was studying the menu in front of her intently and had missed the exchange. Her head was bowed as she browsed the selection, giving him a chance to observe her up close.

The day after he'd shared his concerns over dinner with his brothers, Harry had come to him saying he might have a solution to his problem, at least for the interim. He'd told him a little about Jiya and then suggested that if they met up, they could both decide if they wanted to help each other out and effectively kill two birds with one stone.

His father would get off his case and her parents would get off hers, although Ibrahim had some concerns about how acceptable this kind of a set-up would be to them *if* they happened to believe it but he'd have a chat with her about that.

She was an attractive girl with a relaxed and friendly mien. She wouldn't stand out in a crowd but once you noticed her, you wouldn't forget her. If his father had ever paid any attention to the women he had dated before – your typical city worker – he'd be able to tell from a mile off that Jiya was as different from them as could be. But Ibrahim didn't think that was something he needed to worry about for now.

The arrival of the waiter halted his train of thought and he quickly skimmed the menu and made his choice.

They kept the conversation superficial through most of their meal, talking about Jiya's MBA, her work and his work. They both turned to look at Harry, who shrugged as he said, 'I don't want to kill my creativity and free spirit. I need time and space to figure out where my talents will flourish.'

'You're a good problem-solver, maybe try something along those lines. You're helping us.'

'He's also good at causing problems. Trust me, I know, I live with him.'

She gave a tinkling laugh at his crack and he smiled in response, strangely pleased with himself at having made her laugh, even though it was at his brother's expense.

'There's just no appreciation for my genius among you peasants.' Harry gave a feigned look of disdain and loaded the last of his food onto his fork. 'But I do want to remind you that if it hadn't been for me, you two would still have your problems looming over your heads. You'd be introduced to Dad's idea of a perfect wife for you, and you, Missy, would have a line of Abduls to greet.'

Jiya gave Ibrahim a somewhat pained look. 'He is right, you know?'

'Of course, I'm right. This is the perfect solution to both your problems. You can help each other out. So, now that I've been fed, I'm going to love you and leave you both to sort this out among yourselves.' Harry leaned towards Jiya and kissed her on the cheek and nodded at Ibrahim as he walked away, leaving just the two of them at the table.

He'd had countless dinners and lunches with women, personally and professionally, but something about the set-up of this evening made him feel on edge for some inexplicable reason.

He wasn't the only one because Jiya had all her attention focused on the little cup in the centre of the table which held sugar sachets.

Needing a moment, Ibrahim got the waiter's attention and ordered a coffee. 'Would you like anything?'

She looked up at him, her lips pressed between her teeth. 'Um, yeah, I'll have a pot of tea please. Thank you.' She smiled up at the waiter as he nodded and left them again.

'You know, I'd never say this in front of him, but Harry's idea has some merit from what I can see, although I think there's plenty we need to go over.'

She smiled fondly. 'He's a bit of a joker but one of the nicest people I know. He goes out of his way to help those he cares about.'

She was right about that. He and his brothers lived by that ethos. They always went out of their way to help whoever they could, especially if it was a friend. And when it came to each other, there was never any question. 'Brothers before others' was a code they lived by.

'If you don't mind, can I ask you a question?' He looked up to find her looking at him closely.

Jiya

Having Harry here with them had made her feel somewhat comfortable being with his older brother but as soon as he had left, a strange nervousness had come over her and, afraid she would say or do something silly, she had focused on straightening the stupid sugar sachets that someone had stuffed into a teacup. Her inner waitress had been horrified. Some people had no sense of pride or presentation in their work.

Thankfully the awkward silence hadn't risen to unbearable levels because Ibrahim had started talking, though after that one sentence, he'd seemed to stall as well, but he'd given her an opening to keep talking. Well, sort of anyway.

He looked up and his open expression encouraged her to carry on. 'Harry told me that your eldest brother's wife was chosen by your father and that's the way it's always been in your family, so why are you reluctant for your father to introduce you to someone? She might be great.'

'The simple answer: I don't want to get married, at least not any time soon. And yes, my father did choose my sister-in-law and although I wouldn't go as far as saying she's a bad person, she's not the right wife for my brother. They hardly even got to know each other before they got married.'

'Yeah, but plenty of people have arranged marriages, especially in our culture and they're happy in them and make them work. Has your brother said he's unhappy?'

'He doesn't have to say the words, I know him. He'd never say anything openly that would oppose my father or his choices, but that doesn't make them right. I don't want to give him the chance to even attempt doing the same thing with me. If he's given half the chance, it'll be game, set and match before I know it.'

Jiya nodded, not entirely sure if she understood or agreed with everything he had said, but she had nothing more to add.

'So, what's going on with you? You're in the middle of doing an MBA.'

She had the same fizzing feeling within her as she always did when thinking about her ambition, just about stopping herself from bouncing in her seat. 'Yes, I'm doing a distance-learning MBA course and I'm hoping to be able to get a job in a city firm. It would actually be amazing if I could get a short-term contract to work abroad somewhere but I think that might be pushing my luck a bit too hard. Not that working in London would be shabby.'

She took in a deep breath, belatedly realising that she had just powered her way through her little speech.

'Sorry, I tend to get a bit carried away when I talk about it.' She started fiddling with the teacup in its saucer, but realising that she needed to show confidence in her choices and abilities rather than nervousness, she straightened up and looked at him directly.

Instead of looking horrified as many people did when she spoke like that, he smiled at her. 'Don't apologise. I think it's a great plan. And your passion for it is admirable.'

'Really?'

'Yes, really. I don't think you should be sorry about it or tone it down at all. If you want it badly enough, you need to make it happen.'

'Have you done an MBA?'

'God no. I'm afraid I'm just a boring old solicitor. But I may be able to help you with some networking if not the studying, or at least my older brother might.' He grinned and leaned back in his chair.

'Is that Zafar? Harry talks about him all the time.'

'Yeah. Zaf's the eldest, then it's Ash, or Ashar, then me, Rayyan and then baby Harry. Zaf is the best of brothers and Harry dotes on him.'

She couldn't help but smile at the warmth and affection in his voice as he spoke about his brothers.

'So, what's it going to be? You up for this?' He quirked an eyebrow as he leaned forward.

'Being in a fake relationship?'

He rested his arms on the table and she was hit with a wave of his aftershave. 'There's a party to celebrate my grandmother's eightieth birthday in roughly a month or so. My father wants to introduce me to a friend's daughter before then and he'd like to announce an engagement on the day of the party. I'd like to avoid such a fate so I need him to think that I'm already in a relationship, which is where you would come in if you agree. Harry told me your family are keen on you settling down rather than studying, so this would help you too, right?'

'It's a bit more than that.' Jiya screwed up her nose to emphasise her feelings. 'They know I'm doing an MBA but they think it's a bit like doing an evening or weekend course as a hobby rather than career building. They also know I want to get a job but my father thinks it's a whim and once I get engaged, it'll divert my attention onto more important things like a husband. They just want me to "settle down" now. There's this lady my mum knows who keeps turning up with *un*-suitable boys and presenting them to my family. It's the worst thing ever.' She scrunched her nose as she spoke. 'That day when I had to postpone meeting up with you and Harry, it was because she was there again with a prospective partner and it was so awkward. It wasn't so bad to start with about a year or so ago, but now it's happening more and more often and at times I'm finding it harder to say no and give a good enough reason as to why a particular chap is not the right guy for me.'

She paused and found he was looking at her intently. 'Do you not want to get married and have a family?'

Was he in agreement with what her parents were doing? Harry had said he needed similar help, so surely he would understand her predicament. Wouldn't he? Or was he one of those guys who had a different set of rules for themselves and a different set of rules for women? Allowing them to have dreams but not to pin their hopes on them actually coming true.

'Woah. That scowl could curdle milk!' He leaned back in his chair for emphasis. 'I was only asking out of curiosity, nothing else, though I guess the answer to my question is a no.'

She relaxed her features at his words and gave him a little grin to try and make up for the scowl. 'No. I mean I do want to get married at some point, just not yet. And definitely not with the frogs they keep putting before me. I have nothing in common with them.'

He chuckled and Jiya felt pleased at making him laugh and lightening the mood once again.

'Well Princess Tiana, it seems like we've both got problems and we both might be in a position to help each other.'

'Hold on a minute. Have you seen *The Princess and the Frog*? Do you watch Disney films?'

His face fell as though she'd questioned his manhood and she grinned at him. 'No, I don't usually sit there watching Disney films but I have seen bits of *The Princess and the Frog*. My brother's wife has them on sometimes when they're on TV and I remember catching parts of that one. I take it from your reaction that you watch them?'

'Uh, yeah, those films are life.'

He shook his head at that, making her grin.

They settled the bill and they made their way outside into the balmy evening, falling in step with each other.

'I have a question.' His hands were jammed into his pockets and he seemed completely relaxed but she picked up from his tone that the question wouldn't be.

She nodded, bracing herself for what he might ask.

'By the sounds of it, your parents seem to be somewhat traditional in their views, in that they want you to get married. So, how are they going to react when you say you have a boyfriend? Surely they'd object to something like that?'

'It's definitely not something they've ever encouraged but I can't think of what else to do. Besides, I'm hoping that with your credentials, they'll be impressed enough to at least give me a chance to introduce you to them and that in itself will give me some breathing space.' She grinned at him as she said that. 'To be honest, I can't think of what else to do.'

He wasn't far off the mark with his observation. Her parents would hardly welcome news of her having a boyfriend with balloons and party poppers, but with Ibrahim being what her mother would deem a 'splendid catch', she was hoping they would at least consider letting her have her choice. Her parents held traditional views, but they didn't hate her.

'What do they say when you tell them you want to finish studying and forge a career as a professional?'

'They think it's a pipe dream. My parents never went to university; in fact, my mother didn't study past the age of sixteen. She was raised with the ideology that a woman's place is in the home and she never fought that. She's spent her whole life living up to that ideal instead of fighting it.'

'Like you are?'

'Someone has to. Who says I can't do as well as any other woman in this city – or man for that matter?'

They had stopped outside a random clothes shop and faced each other, the lights from the window display slowly brightening up against the setting sun, casting a soft glow over the pavement.

'I can't say that's not essentially what I'm doing, fighting the ideal that my father knows better than me what *my* life partner should be like, just because his father chose his wife and he chose my brother's.'

He looked around him as though he were trying to capture every detail he could see. 'You know this whole thing could go pear-shaped?'

'You know this whole thing could go perfectly smoothly?'

A grin slowly broke out on his face, dimming the display lights into nothingness in comparison and Jiya felt a swooping sensation in her stomach. Probably all that caffeine she'd consumed today.

'So, what do you say? Are we doing this?' He held his hand out to her.

She regarded him, tapping her chin in obvious considera-tion. Being his fake girlfriend would be no hardship and, as she'd said, she was short on alternatives.

He quirked an eyebrow, something she felt he probably did to save himself from using any words and gave her a lop-sided smile.

An answering smile pushed her doubts about whether or not this would work to the back of her mind and she fluttered her eyelashes at him theatrically, extending her hand towards him and earning herself a full-out smile as he clasped it in his. 'I guess we are.'

CHAPTER FOUR

Ibrahim

Ibrahim walked into the office building a week later with a spring in his step. Nothing beat the feeling of closing on a deal that had looked impossible at the beginning. The combination of his legal background and Zafar's financial acumen gave them a combined expertise that was fast becoming unrivalled.

Not that their father often acknowledged or applauded the fact. But then they weren't doing it for him. Not anymore.

There was a time when he had always wanted his father's approval, doing whatever he could, knowing it would please the old man.

Nasir Saeed had been a proud and self-important young man, using the foundation his own father had built to become successful with some hard work of his own. Had it not been for their grandfather, his father would have messed things up as he almost had once and the family would have suffered severely as a result, although for some reason, he felt all the success they had achieved was down to him, the deluded man.

After his wife had given him five sons in succession, his ego had gone firmly through the roof and had sat on cloud nine ever since. Despite being in the twenty-first century, nothing pleased the mentality of some people more than the birth of a son. And five practically made you royalty.

Before Harry had been born, he, Zafar and Ashar – Rayyan being too young at the time – had spoken about how much they wanted a sister, but had got quite the lecture from their father when they'd asked him for one. They had cousins near and far but had wanted a sister of their own who would stay with them.

What shocked Ibrahim then, and even now, was how different his father was to his grandparents. He'd often heard the saying that the apple doesn't fall far from its tree but here, it seemed that this apple had rolled down the hill and moved to the other side of the orchard.

His father was nothing like his grandfather.

So, Ibrahim had decided that he was done with trying to please him, especially if the situation didn't align with his own thinking.

Zafar was and always would be the model child, even to his own detriment, but that was his choice. Ibrahim wasn't going to be the same.

But today wasn't about the old man, it was about savouring that sense of accomplishment with his older brother, after their hard work had paid off.

He walked into Zafar's office, saw he was on the phone, and went and stood by the floor to ceiling windows, staring out at the Thames. A sense of calm washed over him as he thought of his wins that week. The closure of this deal, which had been the most complex he'd come across, and Jiya agreeing to be in a 'relationship' with him.

That was a big win because if she hadn't agreed, he didn't know what he would have done to manage the situation. Sure, he could probably be blunt with his father, but that would have unleashed a whole host of other problems which he didn't need or want. The set-up with Jiya worked neatly and ticked boxes for both of them, and she had such a firecracker of a personality once you got to know her, that spending time with her was something he was actually looking forward to, strangely enough.

His brother's voice brought his attention back to the present.

'No, you don't need to, he's right here. Hold on a minute, let me put you on speaker. There, he can hear you now.'

'Ibs?' Ibrahim turned at the sound of his brother Rayyan's voice coming through the phone.

'Ray, what's up? Where you at these days, man?'

'I've been swamped. We're approaching the end of term, got the bloody end of year production to do, just had parents' evening and then one of the teachers walked out. Anyway, that's not why I wanted to talk to you. I got promoted to head of department.'

'What?! That's amazing, Ray.' He shared a look of sheer pride with Zafar, who looked just as pleased. 'About time you got some recognition for all the hard work you put in.'

'Yeah, thanks. Glad you two believe that. The folks weren't as impressed.'

Ibrahim shared a different look with Zafar this time. Being older than Rayyan, they were more than familiar with the way their folks thought and acted. Rayyan had disappointed them by not choosing the family business, but they had considered it a personal affront when he had declined choosing medicine and had instead decided to go into teaching. And their parents, or more so their father, reminded him of that at every opportunity.

He considered it a personal failure that his second- and fourth-born sons, Ashar and Rayyan, had both declined to join the family business.

'Well, you've certainly impressed us, Mr Head of Department. Have you told Daadi?' Their grandmother was bound to be over the moon. She was one of the few elders in their family who believed that the children should choose whatever path they wanted to, something Harry had certainly taken to heart, he thought with an internal eye roll.

'Yeah, she was pretty pleased. Then she started being her inappropriate self so I got off the phone. You wouldn't think she's about to turn eighty.' He could hear Rayyan's embarrassment loud and clear through the phone and had to suppress a laugh. Of all her grandchildren, Mumtaz Begum loved winding Rayyan up the most. There wasn't a single boundary she wasn't willing to cross, and rather than becoming more circumspect with age, she felt it was a licence to be as shocking as possible.

Only last weekend, Ibrahim had gone into the front room and had caught her hunched over a laptop which he and his brothers had shown her how to use.

'What are you looking at, Daadi?'

'I'm buying myself a car.'

'Huh. What's wrong with the one you've got?' He'd sat down next to her on the sofa.

'It's an old man's car. I want one like this, a red convertible with leather interior and a nice and loud set of speakers. Oh, and I want a driver. A strapping young fellow, preferably with arms like Dwayne Johnson.'

'What sort of criteria is that?' And how did she know who Dwayne Johnson was?

'My criteria.'

'"A strapping young fellow" might not be as careful on the road.'

She carried on scrolling down the page. 'None of these have a decent set of speakers, but I suppose I can get those fitted.'

'You don't want to go deaf and have everyone on the street turning to look at you as you go by, do you?'

'Exactly. What's the point if people aren't looking my way when I pass through the streets? With this car, everyone's eyes will be on me, as they should be. I might even find you a new grandfather.' She waggled her eyebrows at him and he'd had to stop himself from bursting out laughing.

'We'll see what your son has to say about that.'

'Ha, what does he know!'

Indeed.

'I hear congratulations are in order for you, too.' Rayyan's voice crackled through the speaker.

'Oh, you heard, huh? Yeah, all finalised just this morning and I couldn't be happier. This deal was doing my n—'

'I'm talking about your *girlfriend*, you dodo. Harry gave me the good news. He thinks of himself as something of a matchmaker now.'

Ibrahim scowled as both Zafar and Rayyan laughed. 'He does, does he?'

'Be nice. He helped you, didn't he?' Zafar reminded him.

'Yeah, and I'll never hear the end of it.'

'Right, I've got to go. I still need to give Ash and Harry a bell. I'll see you guys around.'

After ending the call, Zafar made his way to his coffee machine and set it to action.

'So, talking of which, how's it going with Jiya? Is she ready to take on your disapproving parents?'

'She's so not their type, it's hilarious. Dad's probably going to have a major fit. She's good though. Really easy to talk to and get along with. She's got a wicked sense of humour.'

'And you find her attractive.'

'I never said that. I mean yeah, she's attractive but . . . that's not what this is about.'

Zafar brought the two coffees to the sofa in his office and they both sat down.

God, he felt like an old man, sitting here with his brother having a mid-afternoon coffee.

'God, I feel old.' Ibrahim laughed at Zafar's words and shared his own thoughts, earning a chuckle from his older brother.

'She's so determined, Zaf – kind of reminds me of Safiya sometimes. She's heading for big things, that's for sure.'

His brother's expression darkened slightly at the mention of their estranged cousin-sister and he swiftly moved on. 'So, what's next with you two?'

Ibrahim shrugged. 'We're still just getting to know each other, so when the time comes, we can pull it off and come across as a "regular couple". Other than that, I've not seen much of her recently because of this deal. Which by the way,' he leaned forward and clinked his coffee cup with Zafar's, 'great job on those last-minute numbers. I reckon that's what cinched it for us.'

'That deal was always going to be ours, I didn't doubt it for a minute.' Ibrahim had always admired Zafar's business sense and confidence in the boardroom. He had never seen his brother struggle or falter and his keen sense of business was becoming legendary. He had already surpassed their father in terms of accumulating wealth and if he had his way, which Ibrahim was sure he would, they would make the transition into multi-million-pound deals in a very short space of time.

He drained his coffee cup and stood. 'Right, I'm going to shoot, I'm meeting Jiya.'

'All right for some.' His desk phone started ringing and shaking his head, Zafar made his way to his desk, calling out over his shoulder as Ibrahim left, 'Have fun.'

Jiya

Jiya looked at her watch, glad to have made it in time for her 'date' with Ibrahim. She had arranged today's date after they had decided to take it in turns. He had chosen a steakhouse in Central London, and she had been pleasantly surprised at how relaxed it had been given its posh location. They had chatted a bit on the phone since then but he had been quite busy with work.

These, what he called 'information gathering meetings', were for them to get to know each other on a deep enough level to pass off as a couple but she figured they could have some fun at the same time, which was why she had chosen today's location.

She knew he had finished with a particular matter today so she had asked him to duck out of work an hour earlier, if he could.

'What did you have in mind?'

'It's a surprise.'

'Since Harry's birth, I hate surprises. That's how my grandmother broke the news of his arrival to the rest of us. She said she had a surprise for us and naturally, as boys, we were hoping for a surprise of the furry and four-legged variety. She then presented us with what looked like an overboiled potato with two legs. I was not impressed.'

'That is so mean. My surprise is good, I promise. But it's timed, which is why you need to come earlier. Oh, and bring your trainers.'

'You've intrigued me, Miss Ahmed. I'll be there.'

And there he was, striding towards her in another one of his *perfect* outfits, this time a pair of jeans and a black T-shirt under a light jacket. His hair was swept back and his sunglasses were firmly in place. Her tummy did a funny twist and she felt her heartbeat do a little jump at the sight of him. No, it was probably because she'd had an early lunch. It couldn't be the sight of him making her feel like that, surely? Because that would be just plain crazy.

He was wearing trainers, as asked, and he looked as comfortable casually dressed as he had in his suit the last time she'd seen him. He probably hadn't thought much about what to wear, unlike her. Her usual MO of grabbing what was at the top of the pile had been rejected as she'd carefully chosen today's pair of skinny jeans, cute printed T-shirt, high-top trainers and her favourite football hoodie.

He came up to where she was standing and ducked his head to kiss her on the cheek. She was instantly enveloped by his scent and her throat went dry.

Oh my God. Wow.

'Hey you.' His voice had that slight huskiness to it, as if he'd not used it for a couple of hours, which she knew couldn't be true given the rate at which his phone rang.

'Hi. You came.' She could have kicked herself for saying the stupidest thing. Of course he was going to come. This whole charade was for his sake as much as hers.

He lowered his glasses down his nose and quirked an eyebrow.

'Obviously you were going to come. I asked you to. Shall we go in?' She really had to put a lid on her recently acquired tendency to babble around him. It was so unlike her and so embarrassing but she couldn't seem to help herself.

A corner of his mouth lifted up and he ushered her forward. 'After you.'

Feeling her cheeks go aflame, she set off briskly around the corner, towards the entrance to the building. He held the door open for her and she made her way to the counter to join the queue.

'Bowling?'

'Surprise!'

He was grinning at her fully and she knew her idea had been the right one.

'This is definitely better than seeing Harry when he was born.'

'You don't mean that.'

'No, I don't.' They grinned at each other as they were called up to the desk and then made their way to their allocated lane.

Whenever Jiya had come bowling before, it had always been in a bigger group of friends and she had always enjoyed being a part of the group. But bowling with Ibrahim was a different experience entirely. She couldn't put her finger on exactly how to describe it. All she knew was that it was something she'd never felt before. There was something intimate about it being just the two of them.

He took his sunglasses off and then his jacket, his movements methodical and efficient. Her eyes were drawn to his forearms. They were no different than any others she had seen before, but for some reason, the sight of them had her mesmerised. She chanced a glance at his face and was greeted by *the* quirked eyebrow.

'Prepare to be annihilated, Saeed.' She tried to cover up the fact that she had been staring at him by fiddling around with bowling balls on the stand, trying to pick out which one was the right size, when she knew very well which one was.

'We'll see about that, Miss Ahmed. Just because I hold doors open for you doesn't mean I'll let you walk all over me when the game is on. You forget, I've been raised on competition.'

What ensued was a combination of laughs, cheers, groans, fist pumps and some serious ogling. On her part at least.

He stuck to his word and didn't go easy on her at all. In fact, he played down right dirty, distracting her repeatedly, calling out her name just as she was about to bowl, and the worst, coming and standing close enough behind her that she could feel the heat radiating off his body.

Of course, when it was his own turn, he was as cool as a cucumber, not being waylaid by anything and hitting strike after strike.

The first game finished with her score in the region of pitiful and his resulting in triumph – obviously – and she was rewarded with a raised eyebrow and a smug grin.

Right. Game on, buster.

She removed her hairband and shook out her mass of hair, running her fingers through it before pulling it up into a messy knot. She took her hoodie off and threw it in the direction of his discarded jacket. She turned to see if he was ready for round two and saw that he was watching her intently, making her skin prickle in awareness.

She waited for his eyes to reach her own and quirked her own eyebrow at him when he didn't move, cracking her knuckles for impact.

'It's your turn first.'

He looked at the screen in a daze and blinked a couple of times before mumbling, 'Right,' and grabbing the first ball on the stand.

It went down the side and knocked just the one skittle at the end and it took Jiya a monumental amount of effort not to shriek out loud and punch the air. His next attempt was just as lousy.

He stepped back for her to come forward and she waited until he was behind her before she made her way to the stand, making a production of taking a ball and taking a few faux swings before launching her ball down the lane.

The rest of the game progressed in the same way and it ended with her emerging victorious and Ibrahim looking seriously bothered.

They both employed their own dirty tactics for the final game, which ended with him winning on the last ball, which happened to be his only strike.

As his name flashed on their screen, he looked at her.

'Don't you dare gloat, Ibrahim Saeed – you only just won. *Just*,' she emphasised.

'My grandmother has always said, a win is a win, whether it's by an inch or a mile. Just like a loss is a loss whether it's by a point or a thorough thumping.'

She playfully punched him on the shoulder, 'You did *not* thump me.'

He tutted. 'Nobody likes a sore loser, Jiya.'

CHAPTER FIVE

Ibrahim

Ibrahim watched as the colour drained from Jiya's face. She had been absolutely fine until then, ready to take him on and just as competitive as he was.

He had put his years of training in trying to best his siblings to good use in beating her in the first game and if he was being honest with himself, he had enjoyed every single minute of it. She had cottoned on fast and done her utmost to distract him as he'd been distracting her, but what had actually worked in getting his attention was what she'd been doing completely unintentionally.

He would bet she didn't even know that her little sashays up to the lane did incredible things for her hips and behind, and he'd been standing behind her with his chin resting on the floor.

He felt his own scalp tingle as she finger-combed her hair after loosening it and then tied it back up.

She'd shed her tomboy look and had become pure temptation in her fitted T-shirt and jeans. The clothes followed the lines of her lush curves, making his mouth go dry.

He felt like a complete lech. She wasn't doing anything intentionally to get such a reaction out of him but here he was, feeling an attraction towards her that was so much stronger than any he'd felt before.

It was actually kind of scary.

The second game had been all hers because he couldn't take his eyes off her for long enough to focus on getting the ball through those damned skittles.

He had seen that she was attractive that day at The Lounge but the effect she was having on him today was completely different. This was a side to her he couldn't have imagined.

There were no airs and graces or any kind of artifice with Jiya. She was just trying to win a game and happened to be distracting him at the same time.

He'd managed to win and she'd been right. Only just.

She'd been all right with that, he could see. She was right there with him, bantering as they had been after she had issued her challenge.

And then it was like a cloud had come over the sun, obliterating its rays and making everything grey. The playfulness in her eyes had vanished and been replaced by a look that was . . . almost haunted.

'Jiya? What's happened? Are you all right?'

She shook her head, as though just being jolted into awareness, and then just nodded at him, her eyes still looking a little lost and her cheeks still a little pale.

'Yes, I'm fine. I'm good. Yeah. Well done on winning. You're really good at this.' She was babbling again, but not as she usually did, and he knew she wasn't really all right. He'd obviously said something or done something to upset her but he couldn't think what it could be.

He'd grown up as one of five. During their childhood, playing games, being competitive, goading each other and then gloating had been par for the course, more so whenever they got together with their cousins. It was a case of survival of the fittest among a rabble of children, especially the boys. And even though they'd all grown up,

43

that competitive streak hadn't diminished, although there was a big question mark against Harry. If anything, it had become stronger and he'd been so relaxed with Jiya that he hadn't even realised that he could have upset her.

She had picked up her hoodie and was in the process of trying to zip it up but the zip wouldn't catch.

'Here, let me.' He lightly batted her hands away and slowly zipped her hoodie up. He didn't take it all the way to her chin, leaving it open a couple of inches and instead dropped his hands to grab a hold of hers.

'Look at me, Jiya.' She slowly lifted her eyes to his and he was sure he could see a sheen of moisture in them.

'What happened? I need you to tell me what I said to upset you.'

She blinked back the moisture in her eyes and gave him a forced smile. 'You didn't say anything. I'm fine, honestly. Let's go grab something to eat.'

Ibrahim gently manoeuvred her towards one of the benches off to one side and without letting go of her hands, he sat her down, sitting next to her. Her hands felt small and fragile in his own big ones, her bright turquoise nail polish visible through the gaps.

'I'm not sure where, but on some social media page I remember seeing a post that said that when a woman says "nothing" or "fine", she usually means the opposite. So, what do I have to do or say to get it out of you? Because I'll tell you one thing, we're not leaving here until you've told me what I said or did to upset you.'

Her head was bent down and she was looking at their joined hands. He didn't pay much attention to the fact that it felt so natural to have her hands in his own and was instead focused on wanting to know the answer, needing to know the answer to what had bothered her.

She spoke after a long moment of silence and when she did speak, her voice was soft. 'It must be nice, growing up with siblings who, despite all the fighting, bickering and playing, actually really care for one another.'

He'd never really thought about it in those terms but now that she'd said it, he could agree. 'Yeah, it is. I know that no matter what, I just have to say the word and they'll all be here in a heartbeat.'

'I suppose that's what happens when parents care about their children getting along and actually having a positive relationship.'

'I guess, sometimes. But not always. In our case, it was my grandmother who sat me, Ash and Zaf down and told us about the importance of unity between siblings. Zaf being Zaf thought it was his duty to ensure that no matter what, at our core, we were all always singing off the same hymn sheet. So really it's thanks to Zaf that we all stick together through thick and thin and help each other in any way we can.'

'I've got an older brother. But we've never been close like I wanted to be. He's always been everybody's favourite and got the lion's share of everything. It was only when he started using that to tease me when I was little, but old enough to understand, that I started fighting back and wanting what he had. Inevitably, I usually ended up getting into trouble while our parents would side with him. He's their pride and joy, born after years and years of trying and struggling.

'My mother suffered five miscarriages before my brother was born, so for her, he holds a very special place. He's my father's heir, so that's that as far as he's concerned. Sometimes I wish I had been born a boy. Maybe then I would have the chance to do what I want without it being such a struggle and I might even have had a relationship with my brother like you do with yours. The only thing expected of me as a girl is for me to marry a suitable boy.'

Ibrahim felt his insides lurch as she spoke. The sheer desolation in her voice was enough to give him pause. Although to a passer-by she would seem stoic, he could feel the depth of emotion in her voice all the way to the very core of his being.

She pulled her hands free from his and stood up, going towards the spare ball racks behind the benches and trying to furtively wipe away tears.

On instinct, he went and stood behind her, wanting to offer her some words of comfort, or hope. Something to try and ease the pain that was coming off her in waves and piercing his own sense of peace.

'When you said, "nobody likes a sore loser", it reminded me of . . . well, it reminded me of how I felt as a child, because it was often said to me whenever I complained about something my brother would do. And I wasn't. Complaining about you winning, that is. I just . . . I . . .'

Ibrahim could hold back no longer and put his hands on her shoulders and turned her around, swiping his thumb across her cheek to wipe away a teardrop.

She sniffled in the cutest way possible, her lips turned down at the corners and he gave in to the urge to pull her into his arms and just hold her, comfort her.

After a moment of standing there absolutely still, he felt her soften and she rested her head against his chest. Tightening his hold on her, he willed her pain away, feeling her silent tears slowly dampening his T-shirt.

Who would have thought that the woman who came across as so determined would have such deep-rooted insecurities. It was hard to imagine that this was the same person who had spoken so passionately about her dreams.

He held her for what only felt like a second but must have been a few moments, when he felt her hands slowly pull away from around his waist. Her silent sobs had stopped and she gave an endearing little hiccup. He looked down at her as she lifted her head from his chest and he felt it squeeze in protest at the loss.

Her eyes were a deep brown, a rich coffee colour, and he felt as though they were pulling him in deeper the longer he looked, something he felt compelled to do.

What on earth was happening to him?

In an effort to look anywhere except into her eyes, his gaze dropped to her lips.

Big mistake.

Her lips were slightly parted and she ran her tongue over her plump lower lip, making it glisten like a freshly washed cherry.

He wanted to kiss her. The thought slammed into him from nowhere and made him take a step back and stuff his hands into his pockets. There was no place for that kind of thinking in this set-up whatsoever and he'd do well to remember that. 'You OK?'

She hauled in a deep breath as she shuffled away from him; her cheeks tinged pink and tucking a lock of hair behind her ear, she gave him a decisive nod and a small crooked smile. 'I'm good.'

Jiγa

Her mini meltdown had caused some sort of power cut in her brain because bizarrely, she was feeling a keen sense of loss at not being held by Ibrahim anymore. She had felt warm, secure and cared for, all feelings she was attaching to the moment, when in reality all he had done was comfort her because she had been crying. What on earth had got into her?

He had moved back and thank God for that. She wouldn't have known what to do if she had given in to her moment of madness and held onto him. It would have ruined everything. *She* would have ruined everything for both of them.

He was trusting her to help him and was offering her the same in return. Turning this into anything else – whatever the hell that might be – was completely out of the question.

She moved away from him in a bid to restore some of her lost equilibrium after assuring him that she was fine now, grabbing her bag and putting the strap over her head to rest on her shoulder.

Ibrahim had put his jacket back on and they quietly left the bowling alley.

'So, where are we going?' he asked as he led her towards the exit.

'Umm . . .' She actually hadn't thought that far ahead. 'I don't know. What do you want to have?'

'Today's date was all you, Jiya. You were supposed to decide.' She was grateful that he was talking to her normally, as though the last twenty minutes had happened in another lifetime.

If only.

Her embarrassment was two-fold. Firstly, because of the fact that she'd started crying and got upset at what he'd said. The classic was that she'd heard a lot more and a lot worse, especially from Jameel, so why those simple words about being a 'sore loser' had affected her so deeply, she didn't know. And then he'd held her and comforted her and it felt like finally, after all these years, someone cared. Someone was actually interested in how she felt. And it made her cry even more.

The connection she had felt with Ibrahim while he'd held her had been something completely new for her. She'd never felt such a connection before and a part of it scared her a little. This was all supposed to be a means to an end. They were helping each other achieve something and then they would go their separate ways. She couldn't afford to start connecting with him on any other level. But in that moment, she had.

They were out on the street now and since her mind had gone completely blank on where they could go, she stopped at the street corner looking around in different directions, hoping for some inspiration.

'I tell you what,' Ibrahim's voice had her looking his way. 'There's a really great Italian place not too far from here, let's go there. I'm sure the little walk will do us both good.'

They made their way towards the restaurant, Ibrahim telling her about the deal he had recently completed as she pulled in some much-needed breaths of fresh air, tuning back into the sounds of traffic around them and the feel of the evening sun on her face. They were standing at the traffic lights, waiting to cross the road, and he looked down at her, giving her a smile that made her nerve endings tingle.

If she wasn't careful, she could be in serious trouble.

He lifted his hand and placed the pad of his index finger gently against her chin. 'What happened here?' His finger was against the little scar she had there and the contact made her feel a flutter in her tummy. 'I'm only asking because maybe it's something a boyfriend should know about his girlfriend?'

Seizing the excuse he'd provided with two hands, she nodded her head enthusiastically, breaking the contact and strange feelings it was eliciting as they crossed the road. 'I fell over when I was six years old in the school playground.

Soft tarmac wasn't a thing then, it was all about the concrete playgrounds and my chin wanted an introduction.'

They were standing outside the restaurant now and barely a foot separated them. Ibrahim rubbed his thumb across the scar and she was sure it was glowing because she could feel the tingles. She could feel the heat from the palm of his hand which wasn't quite cupping her cheek and she had the insane urge to move her face towards it.

'Poor Jiya.' His voice was little more than a murmur but the vibrations of it went all the way to her toes.

What on earth was up with her?

Before she could do something crazy or try and decipher the look on Ibrahim's face, the tinkling of a bell above the doorway broke whatever spell had come over her and she took a step back as a couple came out of the restaurant.

The couple lingered long enough – giving her a chance to shake off whatever had just come over her – and Ibrahim seemed to have moved on from that strange moment as well, before holding the door open for her to step inside the restaurant, his expression impassive.

The little Italian restaurant was a gorgeous place with divine food, which made her feel more like her normal self; less maudlin and less crazy, with the dynamic between them back to being closer to normal. *Thank God.* Their mains had been cleared away and she had a big bowl of chocolate-flavoured gelato in front of her but she was eyeing Ibrahim's bowl of hazelnut gelato.

'Don't even think about it – I can hear your nefarious thoughts across the table.' He pulled his bowl closer to himself as he took a mouthful.

'Just a taste, please?' She extended her spoon towards his bowl and he tapped it away with his own. 'Oh, come on. You can have some of mine.' She pushed her bowl a few inches towards him, the epitome of generosity in her humble opinion, but he shook his head.

'Nuh uh, Missy. If I wanted chocolate, I would have ordered it.' She extended her spoon again and before they knew it, they were spoon fighting, Ibrahim defending his bowl from her attack.

They were both grinning at each other as she tried to drag his bowl towards her when they were interrupted by a softly voiced, 'Ibrahim?'

They both looked up as a stylishly dressed woman came and stood a foot from their table. Jiya saw the warmth and humour leach from Ibrahim's face, replaced with an iciness that made her sit up straight in her seat, her head moving from Ibrahim to the mystery woman.

'I thought it was your voice I heard.' She turned to look at Jiya and, as was her MO, Jiya extended her hand out on autopilot.

'Hi, I'm Jiya.' The woman looked at Ibrahim, then at Jiya and then at Jiya's hand. Jiya was about to pull her hand back when it was clasped in a cool grip. The woman lifted a corner of her mouth but her eyes were on Ibrahim as he spoke.

'Jiya, sweetheart, this is Anushka Verma. We went to university together.'

Sweetheart? What was he—

Her thought was cut short as he reached across the table towards her hand and placed his fingers between hers, clasping and squeezing them as he gave her a slow smile which made her swallow hard. She looked between Ibrahim and the newcomer, unsure about exactly what was going on – and something *was* going on – but taking her cue from Ibrahim, she closed her fingers around his and squeezed back.

After a few seconds of tense silence, the woman spoke. 'I didn't know you were . . .' waving her hand in the air to encompass what she didn't want to name.

'In a relationship?' Ibrahim looked back at Jiya, his eyes and smile both warm. 'I am. With this gorgeous woman.'

Jiya bit the inside of her cheek to stop herself from giggling at his words. She also hoped she wasn't blushing because a teeny tiny part of her melted at those words. She clocked he was 'faking it' but his hold on her hand and words were strangely affecting her.

He broke eye contact and looked back up. 'How are you, Anushka? Doing well, I hope.'

Anushka flicked a lock of hair behind her shoulder, her other arm bent at the elbow where her oversized bag hung. 'I am, thanks. I'm here with my fiancé; we're celebrating a huge win for him.' Belatedly, Jiya noticed the mini-mountain on the woman's ring finger that she was waving around. 'You must have heard that he was working on the . . .'

'Actually, I've not been keeping up with news about anything, but good for him. J darling, you'd better take this before it all melts.' He loaded his spoon with the hazelnut ice cream and held the spoon out to a stunned Jiya.

J? Darling? It turned out that talking about faking it and actually faking it were two very different things. She felt supremely awkward with this Anushka lady watching them like a hawk and to add to the awkwardness, Ibrahim was now holding his spoon out to feed her himself.

Not wanting to flop at the first hurdle, she closed her hand around his as she took the spoon into her mouth, her lips closing around it as he held it in place. He pulled it back slowly, keeping his smouldering eyes on her as a corner of his mouth lifted. Were his nostrils flared or was it her imagination?

The flavour of the ice cream burst on her tongue – as delicious as she had expected – but it was the look on Ibrahim's face that had her attention. Her hand was still on his as he held the spoon in mid-air between them, their eyes not straying once from each other.

'Ahem. Well, I'll leave you two to . . . *enjoy* your dessert. Perhaps I'll see you around.'

Jiya gave a perfunctory smile to Anushka's departing back and turned to face Ibrahim. 'What was that all about?' She pulled her hand back and moved her hands up and down her thighs to see if they'd stop tingling.

He looked at her as though he were in a daze and then looked past her, presumably to where Anushka had gone. He looked back at her and she saw his face slowly morph back into its usual expression of cool confidence. He pulled a corner of his mouth up in a smile but she could see it was forced. 'Nothing. It was nothing important. Here,' he pushed his bowl of gelato towards her, 'you can have it.'

She shook her head and nodding once, he signalled to the waiter for their bill.

There was some story there with Anushka Verma, but it seemed that Ibrahim wasn't ready to share anything except his gelato with her just then.

CHAPTER SIX

Ibrahim

'Your head's not in it, mate. Focus.' Boxing gloves raised, Ashar bopped towards him and jabbed. Ibrahim side-stepped and went in with a cross of his own, catching his brother on the chin.

'How's that, Grandad?'

Ashar stretched his neck muscles each way and grinned at him before coming towards him full pelt, leaving Ibrahim no choice but to raise his own gloves in defence.

Both of them were panting hard as they took their gloves and wraps off. Ashar was like a machine but Ibrahim was pleased that he'd got some decent shots of his own in there too.

'Well?'

Ibrahim looked towards Ashar and quirked an eyebrow. 'Well what?'

Ashar shook his head after pouring water over it and then guzzled some down. 'Don't be long. What's on your mind? Even Zaf said something was off.'

He should have known better than to assume his brothers wouldn't know that he was distracted. Since seeing Anushka in the restaurant that day – on the back of his rollercoaster of thoughts and feelings after spending time with Jiya – he'd been more preoccupied than he liked or she deserved. Anushka, that was. His brothers knew what had happened with her so he didn't need to go over any details with them but that didn't mean that those details didn't go round his head again and again.

As he'd said to Jiya, he and Anushka had gone to university together but it was so much more than that and the feelings that came with it were something he'd happily avoid for the rest of his days.

'I was out with Jiya the other day, having dinner. Anushka was there.'

His brother's face hardened as he'd known it would. 'Avarice not killed the bitch yet, then?'

'I don't think it's a fatal condition as such.' They gathered their things and made their way out of the gym towards the changing rooms. 'I think curiosity got the better of her, which is why she came up to me. She's been happy to ignore me before, but she saw me with Jiya and came over to the table.'

Jiya's reaction had taken him by surprise. She was open and friendly with no artifice or pretence. She had casually stuck her hand out and introduced herself to Anushka, catching Anushka off guard and he couldn't have hoped for a better meeting with his ex if he had planned it.

And then he'd surprised Jiya – and himself if he was honest – with what had followed. He didn't care what Anushka thought about him but for some reason he had gone ahead and introduced Jiya as his girlfriend and thankfully she had cottoned on. He smiled as he remembered her widened eyes at his endearments and when he'd clasped hands with her; not that he'd been unaffected.

If he was honest, he'd been feeling rather affected for a while, especially during that wild moment outside the restaurant.

If he hadn't been distracted in that moment with Anushka and trying to communicate to Jiya without words about what he wanted, he could have zoned in on the feeling of her fingers tangling with his, or the way he had felt as she'd closed her lips over the spoon as he'd fed her, her hand covering his.

Remembering the moment had his skin prickling with awareness, which was completely unreal because the last thing he needed was complications between him and Jiya. Not only would he be letting her down, but he'd be moving away from his own goal, practically in the opposite direction.

'Please tell me you told her to fuck off.' Ashar was well versed when it came to betrayal and heartbreak and as a result he saw things in black and white, although Ibrahim wouldn't go so far as saying Anushka had broken his heart even if it had seemed that way at the time.

'Not in those words exactly, but she got the message when I didn't really respond to her and she left.' He hoped he wouldn't set eyes on her again and even if he happened to, hopefully he wouldn't have to talk to her.

In fact, now when he thought about it, seeing Anushka brought home his reasons for doing what he was and why he needed to stick to his guns.

Jiya

Jiya let herself in through the front door after a long week of classes and work at The Lounge. She had been covering shifts for a colleague and if it hadn't been for the extra wages and tips, she would have preferred the time to work on those pending assignments and her reading list.

She'd barely had much time to catch up with Ibrahim, except for a mini catch-up a couple of days ago and a quick lunch date earlier that day, which had been the highlight of the week for her. Although having some space from him after their bowling date wasn't a bad thing. Or so she kept trying to tell herself.

God, her mind was in such a funk lately.

She couldn't make up her mind where he was concerned.

She was beginning to look forward to his calls. She would find herself reading through their chat messages and smiling to herself and then guiltily putting her phone down when she realised what she was doing.

She was enjoying his company so much more than she had thought she would, not noticing where the time went when they were together. They were relaxed and managed to cover so many different topics when they got chatting, agreeing and disagreeing with each other in equal measure.

On the odd occasion, and in moments of clarity, she remembered her end goal and tried to recalibrate her thoughts away from him. She needed to focus on completing her course and getting a good job. A job which would prove to everyone that she was capable of big things which went beyond the mould her parents had tried to fit her into.

They were in a fake relationship and she needed to remember that fact above all others, and to that end, they'd gone through a question round with each other at her insistence. The meeting with Anushka had put them on the spot and they needed to make sure they knew each other as well as a real couple would.

It was the first time they'd had to pretend and it had felt to Jiya that they had their work cut out. She was thankful that the woman hadn't asked too many questions and Ibrahim had managed to fob her off but if she had, she might well have seen through their charade. Their parents would definitely not go so easy on them and she'd told Ibrahim as much the last time they'd met up.

'We need to know things about each other which only someone close to you would know, otherwise they'll know it's a sham.'

'What do you suggest we do? Fill out a questionnaire?'

'Very funny.' They had been walking in the park after work and she pulled him by the hand to sit on the grass. 'I'll say a word or phrase and you can respond with the first thing that comes to mind. Instinctive answers like that are often more telling than answers that have been thought through.'

'And which magazine did you read that in, Dr Jiya?'

She ignored his sarcasm and began. 'Favourite food?'

He rolled his eyes, but answered. 'Steak and chips.'

'Colour?'

'Blue.'

'Holiday destination?'

'Hmm . . . Italy. No, Spain. Actually, that's a tough one, France was pretty good too.'

'Let's go with Europe. Hobby?'

'Don't really have one.'

'Really? You don't have a hobby? So what do you do when you're not working?'

He shrugged. 'Different things. Go out with my brothers or mates, watch or play football, go to the gym, go out with my fake girlfriend.' He waggled his eyebrows.

She grinned. 'OK, tell me something about you that no one really knows. Ibrahim Saeed's top secret.'

He had looked at her for a moment, his expression inscrutable, before looking over the rest of the park, his face in profile.

He looked relaxed but she sensed an underlying tension. It wasn't obvious but something told her that there was a secret he held close and suddenly she felt she was being intrusive. More so than their sham relationship warranted.

He turned to look back at her and grinned. 'God, you don't have to look so serious, Jiya, it's nothing creepy or outlandish.' He looked slightly self-conscious as he admitted, 'I enjoy photography but it's something I don't really talk about or do much of.'

She stared at him wide-eyed. 'You're a photographer? That's awesome. Can I see the pictures you've taken? What sort of photography do you do? Did you do a course? How many cameras do you have?'

He had started laughing and then to shut her up, he'd covered her mouth with his hand, overreaching as she moved back and landing on the floor beside her, both of them laughing like schoolchildren.

She had never connected like this with any of the guys she had been introduced to on any level, able to talk about anything or mess around like this. She connected with Ibrahim in a way which seemed to be unique to him. They seemed to understand each other and even if they weren't of the same opinion about certain things, like the fact that he put ketchup on his eggs, which was just gross, it never seemed to be a sticking point between them.

And today he had officially invited her to his grand-mother's birthday celebration as his plus one when she'd met him for lunch. She'd already had an invite from Harry but Ibrahim said that his invitation superseded Harry's.

'I'm older and better-looking.'

'The first one I can accept, but how did you come to the conclusion that you're better-looking?'

He'd quirked his eyebrow. 'Are you saying Harry's better-looking than I am?'

She'd felt her cheeks burn as he looked at her keenly and had shrugged her shoulders. 'I'm not saying anything

– I'm simply asking how you decided which of you is better-looking.'

'I asked Daadi, she said I was and since she's the matriarch, I didn't refute what she said.'

'I'm going to take a wild guess here, Ibrahim, and guess that she probably says the same thing to each of you when the others aren't there. Have you asked her that question when all of you are there?'

He had sat back and refused to make eye contact with her and she had laughed out loud at him. 'You have! Well, we're not leaving here until you tell me what she said.'

'I have work to go back to and if I'm not wrong, you've got a shift as well.'

'You're not getting out of this, Saeed. Spill the beans – who does Daadi think is her best-looking grandson?'

He mumbled something and she moved closer towards him, pressing herself against the table. 'What was that?'

'She said it was Rayyan, but I don't think that should count because it was only the once and many, many years ago.'

'Really?' She had leaned back in her chair. 'I don't think I've ever seen him. Has he been to The Lounge with you lot?'

'Trust me, darling, if you'd seen him, you'd remember him.'

'Ah. He'll be there for your grandmother's birthday, won't he?'

'Yes, but don't forget that you're there with me. We're there "together", remember?'

He'd looked at her pointedly and she'd grinned at him. 'Are you worried I'll fall head over heels in love with Rayyan and leave you standing? Aww, poor Ibby.'

'It wouldn't be the first time,' he'd muttered, pulling a face, and she'd laughed. 'He gets a lot more attention than the rest of us.'

Remembering time spent with him always made her feel happy and today was no exception.

She walked towards the stairs when she heard her mum's voice calling out to her from the front room. She hoped this would be quick; she really was exhausted. Taking in a steadying breath, she went into the front room, where her father and Jameel were sitting on one sofa and her mother was sat on another one, beside none other than Auntie Nadia.

A rather sombre-looking Auntie Nadia.

'Salam everyone.' Jiya looked from one to the other of the room's occupants, trying to figure out what she was missing. While Auntie Nadia looked solemn, her mother looked like she'd sucked a lemon and there was something in her eyes which she was trying to blink out. Her brother's expression was indecipherable but it was the look on her father's face that made her swallow hard and her shoulders automatically drooped.

To an onlooker, he would look mildly irritated but Jiya knew there was nothing mild about the mood her father was in.

His arms were folded across his chest and she could see his nostrils flaring. Judging by the set of his jaw, he was probably grinding his teeth in an effort to hold back in front of Auntie Nadia.

Oh no.

Auntie Nadia stood up just as Jiya sat down on one of the several empty chairs in the front room and addressed her mother. 'I'll be off now, Samina, I'm already late. I hope you'll all be able to resolve this and it's not too late. It was my duty to bring this . . . *situation* to your attention and I've done that. I'll speak to you later.'

'No, Nadia. You can't—'

'Thank you, Nadia. We'll be in touch.' Her father's voice boomed across her mother's like a crash of thunder. Even Jameel flinched at the suddenness of it. 'Samina, see Nadia out please.'

The two women left the room as quickly as they could, leaving her sitting in front of her father and brother.

He didn't seem to be in any hurry to ease her nervousness and waited for her mother to rejoin them.

Jiya risked opening her mouth, albeit hesitantly. 'What's going on?' She hated that her croaky voice made her sound guilty even before they'd said anything.

'Where were you this afternoon?' Her mother was kind enough to kick-start things.

'This afternoon? I was at work, at The Lounge. Why?'

'Nadia says she saw you this afternoon. With a boy.'

Oh shit.

'Do you have anything to say to what your mother has just said?'

Her father had never laid a finger on her but his low menacing growl still had her jumping in her seat.

'I . . . I was . . .' She cleared her throat. Stuttering like this was only going to make her look like she had something to be guilty about, when she didn't really.

'I had lunch with a friend today, and yes, it was a guy.'

'And he's just a friend? Only Nadia seemed to think there was more to it, given the way you were both sitting across the table from each other.' Her father's eyes were focused on her, his jaw set.

Jiya sat there stunned into silence for a minute. She had been nowhere near home when she'd met Ibrahim for lunch. In fact, they'd been closer to his office than anywhere else because his meeting had overrun. How on earth had she been seen there?

Whatever it was, now was the time to put her plan into action. Now was when she was supposed to tell her family that Ibrahim was her boyfriend and they could tell Auntie Nadia that they weren't going to pursue any of the proposals she had.

Except her tongue seemed glued to the roof of her mouth and she couldn't get the words out under the scrutiny of her parents.

'Jiya, how many times have I told you about close friend-ships with boys like that? And look at what's happened. Nadia's come straight here and in not so many words questioned how we've raised you because you're freely associating with boys like that. Shame on you.' Her mother didn't sound like her usual dramatic self. Instead, she sounded distraught, as though Jiya had committed some heinous crime.

'It's not like that, Ammi. I didn't do anything to be ashamed of. I was in a restaurant having lunch.' Taking a deep breath, Jiya took the plunge. 'And I like him.'

Her mother's gasp and her father's growl said it all.

'In comparison to some of our relatives and acquaint-ances, I've given you a lot of freedom.' Her father spoke in even tones. 'I've allowed you to study whatever you've wanted to and I've even allowed you to work at a restaur-ant, despite the fact that I don't like the late-night finishes. You're allowed to come and go as you please, meeting up with friends and what not, and this is what I get in return? You dishonouring me like that?' His voice had risen significantly through his speech.

Some of what he said was right. She'd been allowed to do things some other girls of her acquaintance weren't allowed to do. Like being able to work, go to university and then study further. But why were these things offered to her as a luxury?

As far as she was concerned, studying was a fair choice. If someone wanted to do it, then why shouldn't they? There certainly wasn't any harm in it. And working made her independent. She couldn't remember the last time she'd asked her parents for money.

The thoughts swirling around in her mind helped firm her resolve a little.

'I didn't dishonour you, Abba. I did nothing to be ashamed of or to embarrass you, believe me. Yes, I had lunch with a guy and after getting to know him, we've decided that we like each other and—'

'Get her out of my sight, Samina.' He got up from the sofa and turned his back on Jiya.

Jiya felt her heart plummet to the ground.

This was not what was supposed to happen. How had things spiralled so dreadfully out of control?

Her mother looked between her and her father and then stood up, taking Jiya by the wrist and pulling her towards the door while Jameel looked shocked, as though unable to believe what had just happened.

To be fair she was in shock herself. She had never expected things to be taken out of her hands like that and she had never thought her father would react so badly to things and practically kick her out of the room.

Her mother took her into the kitchen and closed the door behind them, making her way to the sink.

Tea. Her mother's answer to practically everything. She always said that even if it doesn't solve your problem, it certainly makes you feel better enough to try and solve it yourself.

Hopefully that would do the trick now.

'Jiya . . .'

'Ammi, before you say anything, please let me explain.' Her mother's lips were pressed in a line and she gave a single nod and got on with making the tea and taking it to the kitchen table.

'I don't know what Auntie Nadia has told you or what spin she's put on things but I promise, I've done nothing wrong. The guy I had lunch with today is a friend's brother and I met him some time ago at The Lounge.' All true so far.

She cupped her hands around the mug of tea and noticed her mother had done the same, sitting opposite her quietly, allowing her to speak.

'We hit it off and I've met up with him a couple of times. We . . . we're interested in each other.'

Her mother was silent for several minutes and, just as Jiya felt compelled to break it, she spoke. 'What's his name?'

'Ibrahim Saeed. He's a lawyer and he works with his older brother for the family business.'

A smidgeon of guilt made its presence felt as she was laying the foundation for her lie, but what choice did she have now?

If she said there was nothing between her and Ibrahim, her parents would worry that she'd go off the rails and up the search for a husband for her and she couldn't let that happen no matter what. She just had to go through with this and hope for the best.

'Your father is furious, Jiya. I've not seen him this angry in years.'

Jiya gulped down a hot mouthful of tea, the scalding liquid making her eyes water. 'I know, Ammi, but I don't know what Auntie Nadia said or what angle she came from.'

'That's just it, Jiya. How do we know Nadia won't go and open her mouth to other people about what she saw and add on a few more details? What's to stop her, especially if we reject her nephew's proposal which she brought? It's not just your reputation that'll be in tatters, our upbringing of you will be questioned and no one will want to have you for a daughter-in-law and no one will want their daughter to marry Jameel. Do you understand the seriousness of all this?'

That smidgeon of guilt gave a little nudge from within but she ignored it. She had to brazen this out and hopefully, with Ibrahim's support, they'd be able to weather this storm and come out on the other side, both with what they wanted.

'I do, but why won't you believe me when I say that I've done nothing wrong, nothing to bring this family's reputation into question. I never would. Why do you believe Auntie Nadia more than you believe me?'

In a completely unexpected move, her mother extended her hand and took Jiya's hand in her own. 'That's not true. I do believe you and I trust you. Let your father cool down and I'll have a chat with him. Maybe we can meet this boy, and then take things from there.'

Jiya nodded as she prayed that this whole thing would work out as her and Ibrahim had planned. The alternative was too frightening to think about.

CHAPTER SEVEN

Ibrahim

Ibrahim had just settled back against the headboard with Netflix's latest offering when his phone rang. He hoped to God it wasn't his father. He'd done a damn good job of avoiding the old codger all week, something he was supremely pleased about, but on the downside, that meant that at some point this weekend seeing him was imminent.

A quick glance at the screen brought a huge grin to his face and he answered the phone as he muted the television.

'Jiya, Jiya, Jiya. How's my favourite MBA student doing?'

'Not good. And I'm the only MBA student you know. Aren't I?'

'Why, what's happened?'

'Do you know any other MBA students?'

'Jealous?' He couldn't hold back the smile from his voice.

'Pfft, puh—lease. I was only asking so I could see how that person might be getting on with that reading list which is like a mile long.'

'Yeah, whatever, Jiya darling. Admit it, you're becoming possessive about me. And your MBA reading list has nothing on my legal career reading list, so stop whinging. What's up?'

He heard her sigh loud and clear and settled back against his pillows. Her words had him sitting straight back up within seconds.

'My parents found out about us and would like to meet you.'

'What?'

'I said my parents—'

'I heard you the first time, that was just a reactionary "what". How did this happen? I mean, I know we weren't exactly keeping this a secret and would have met up with each other's families at some point, but how the hell did they find out?'

'Do you remember I told you about Auntie Nadia and those proposals she brings? She's the one who saw us this afternoon when we were together. Now that I think of it, we were at a window table so she must have seen us as she was walking past and we didn't even realise we'd been seen.'

'So, what did your parents say?'

'Ha.' She gave a dry laugh but it was completely lacking in humour and Ibrahim picked up on a tone in her voice that made him clench his fists. 'My dad was furious. He didn't even want to see me. I've never seen him that angry before, Ibrahim, and definitely not with me.'

He could hear the emotion in her voice and really wished he could be there to comfort her in that moment. Despite all her protests, she deeply loved her parents and wanted their approval. Angering them would be the last thing she'd want.

'Ammi wasn't as angry, although she was upset to begin with. In fact, she spoke to me about you and said that she thinks it would be good if you came over to meet her and Abba. It's all that nosy Auntie Nadia's fault. If she hadn't come and opened her big mouth and spewed out God knows what truths and untruths, none of this would have happened.'

'What exactly did this Auntie Nadia say to your mum?' Ibrahim's head was reeling with everything Jiya was saying. He was just about managing to keep up.

'I have no idea and my mum didn't say exactly what, but as a result, my dad is super annoyed and not talking to me, Jameel's being nice to me, which is really weird, and my mum said she'll talk to my dad once he's cooled down but they want to meet you, sooner rather than later.'

He heard a little sniffle.

'Jiya?'

'I'm fine, just really tired.'

Ibrahim threw himself against the pillows again. What a palaver! And he'd not even added his own family into the mix yet. His brothers knew what was going on, but that was it.

'Take it easy, we'll figure something out. This is kind of what we wanted, isn't it?'

'It is, but I didn't expect to be caught completely off guard like that or for my dad to get so angry. It also doesn't help that I've now got the potential of a dirty rumour looming over my head. I really should have thought about all of this before deciding to go ahead with a fake relationship plan.'

'Hey, stop letting your mind go into overdrive. If your parents want to meet me, I'm fine with that, honestly. It'll ease their minds and hopefully make them more open to listening to what you actually want. Where did you leave things with them?'

'I told Ammi that I'd have a chat with you and we'd arrange something at some point. But I want this done soon, Ibrahim. I don't want my parents to have to deal with any kind of social fallout because of me.'

'When we meet up on Sunday, we'll sort something out. Try not to let it bother you, OK? You still planning on studying all day tomorrow?'

For the next few minutes, Ibrahim managed to distract Jiya from freaking out and ended the call after confirming their meet-up for the day after tomorrow.

He had been feeling pretty good about the set-up he had arranged with Jiya, but a niggle of doubt had crept in as she had shared her concerns just now. This was what they had wanted, wasn't it? So, then why had her call left him feeling unsettled and uneasy about the whole thing?

This is what they'd been leading up to. In fact, their charade hadn't even kicked off properly. He was supposed to meet her family so they would stop pressurising her to settle down and she could focus on her career. He needed to introduce her to his family so he wouldn't be forced down the same path as Zafar had been and could do what *he* wanted, *when* he wanted.

Once they'd been convincing enough and the timing was right, they would be calling the whole thing off as well. That was something else that would need to be considered properly, otherwise the fallout from that had the potential of being catastrophic, especially given Jiya's parents' reaction today.

With all these thoughts churning around in his mind, Ibrahim knew he would never be able to concentrate on the film. Switching everything off, he went to the Juliette balcony doors and opened them up, watching the night sky. Living just on the outskirts of London meant that the sky was clear enough on a cloudless night for him to see the stars bright and clear. The later sunset meant that tonight the sky was filled with the most beautiful shades of blues, purples and some pink too. His inner photographer itched to capture the colours, a thought that brought him up short.

He hadn't thought about his photography for so many years he'd lost count, but lately, he'd been thinking about it, eyeing the camera in its cover sitting on top of the bookcase.

Feeling irritable at practically everything after Jiya's phone call, he decided to just go to bed. Tomorrow was soon enough to try and figure all these stupid problems out.

The next morning, the sweet smell of something fried and sugary drew Ibrahim towards the dining room. Zafar's wife Reshma was in there loading French toasts onto a plate.

'Smells good.'

She turned to him with her usual sunny smile.

'There's plenty more coming. Why don't you sit down and have these? I'll make another batch for Harry when he comes down. He specifically asked for these.'

'Princess Harriet won't be down any time soon; she needs her beauty sleep,' Reshma smiled, shaking her head at him and left the room.

She was actually a lovely girl. She didn't have a single bad bone in her body but she just wasn't the right person for his brother. Since marrying her, his brother hadn't been the same and Ibrahim couldn't understand why Zafar hadn't put his foot down with their father and refused to marry her when he'd been told to.

Seeing how Zafar and Reshma's relationship was made Ibrahim even more determined not to toe the line where his father and marriage was concerned. He'd either find a partner of his own when he was good and ready or not get married at all and at the moment, the latter seemed more likely and preferable.

'There you are. Finally!' His father's voice boomed in the empty dining room and Ibrahim could have kicked himself. So much for avoiding him. It's almost as though he'd conjured him up with his thoughts.

He was a sitting duck here in the dining room. A duck with a plateful of French toast and a mug of coffee in front of it. He wasn't waddling off anywhere anytime soon and his dad would know it. Even if his appetite *had* just vanished.

Ibrahim greeted his father and lowered his head, shovelling his breakfast into his mouth to try and limit the duration of the coming inquisition.

'Even your mother didn't seem to know your whereabouts these last couple of weeks. What have you been up to?'

Well, this was different. It certainly wasn't the approach he was expecting. He'd anticipated a barrage of edicts about what was expected of him and what it was his *duty* to do, followed by questions with no time to answer them.

'Well?'

'Sorry, I was chewing.' *Buying time, actually.* 'I've been busy at work, Dad. The deal that went through a couple of weeks ago had some bits and pieces I needed to go over and then we've recently done a reshuffle—'

'Yes, yes, I'm aware of all of that. Zafar's been filling me in on the goings on in the office during our weekly catch-ups. The ones you're also supposed to attend by the way, but coincidentally, you always happen to have a double booking.'

Ibrahim avoided making eye contact and focused on his breakfast.

'Make sure you're home tomorrow after five. I've asked Hatim and his family to come over for dinner tomorrow. His daughter will be there as well and I want you to be here.'

Ibrahim stopped eating and looked up at his father. He wasn't even looking at Ibrahim but was instead busy flicking his fingers across his tablet as he drank his tea. He wasn't waiting for an answer; he simply expected him to accept what he'd said and show up on the day. Much like Zafar had.

His mother and grandmother chose that moment to come into the dining room and take their places.

If he waited for the right time to say anything to his father, he would end up waiting a long time. He needed to speak now and if his mother and grandmother were present, then so be it. Perhaps it was better that they were there too.

'I can't be there tomorrow, Dad, I've already got plans.'

His father looked up from his tablet slowly – for greater impact, of course – his reading glasses perched at the end of his nose.

'And those plans can't be postponed or cancelled for you to be somewhere your father asks you to be?'

Asks or tells?

His mother looked up at his father while preparing her tea, her expression one of alertness.

'The thing is, Dad, I'm happy to be there to meet your friend and his family, but I'm not going to meet his daughter for any purpose other than as a social meeting because our fathers happen to be good friends and they're coming here for dinner.'

His father looked at him for a few seconds before switching his tablet off, carefully taking his glasses off and putting them to the side and sitting back in his chair, his elbows on the armrests and his fingers steepled beneath his chin.

An errant part of Ibrahim's brain concluded that his father had seen *The Godfather* too many times, with the whole 'make them wait and squirm' routine honed to perfection.

His mother and grandmother were more focused on what was happening rather than their own breakfast, then he saw Reshma walk in and, sensing the tense atmosphere in the room, she sat on a chair nearest to the door to have her own breakfast. *Smart girl.*

Time to grab the bull by the horns. Jiya had yesterday with her parents so it was only fair that he spoke to his family. And there was no time like the present.

'The thing is . . .' he cleared his throat. 'The thing is, I've already got a girlfriend and it wouldn't be right or fair to either of them if I met your friend's daughter tomorrow with the intention you have in mind.'

The only reaction he got was a slight widening of the eyes.

There was absolute silence in the room.

And then his father laughed. Long and loud, as though Ibrahim had come out with the joke of the week.

'Is that it? That's your concern? Don't worry about it, son. I'd expect my boys to go out and have a good time.'

Ibrahim felt heat flush through his body and he ground his teeth.

Was he serious?

They were sitting there, with his grandmother, mother and sister-in-law in the room, and his father was talking like some archaic lord from medieval times.

This would probably go down as one of the most embarrassing moments of his life. Not to mention the frustration and annoyance he was feeling at what his father had said, but he reined it in.

'No, Dad, I'm serious about Jiya. I'm not going to lead her or any other woman on. That's not me. In fact, that's not any of us.'

'Is that right? I seem to remember something similar with Zafar. Now look at him. He's happily married with the right sort of woman.'

Ibrahim saw Reshma's cheeks glow scarlet but she stayed where she was, not saying a word.

Come to think of it, why *didn't* she say anything? Why

did she put up with rubbish and being told what to do if she didn't agree with it?

He turned as his mother spoke. 'Is he, Nasir? I think we should give Ibrahim and the girl he's chosen a chance. I'd rather we didn't do the same thing with the other boys as you did with Zafar. I won't have another of my sons in a marriage of *your* choice.'

Before his father could say anything, she turned to Ibrahim, 'Her name's Jiya? That's a lovely name. Where did you meet her?'

He watched Reshma pick up her empty plate and excusing herself, she quietly left the room. His mother tapped Ibrahim's hand to get his attention, ignoring the fact that she might have just upset her daughter-in-law with her acidic words. Again. As she had done since Reshma had joined the family. She never lashed out at Zafar for marrying Reshma but punished Reshma for it verbally any chance she got.

'She works at a restaurant I often go to, that's where I met her.'

'Ha! A waitress. Our son wants to bring home a bloody waitress. No regard for the Saeed family name and our prestige.' His father scoffed.

'I don't think I raised you to look down your nose at someone who's hardworking, no matter what work they do, Nasir.' It wasn't often Ibrahim heard his grandmother go all authoritarian but when she did, everyone listened. Including her son.

'My point is, Amma, she's not the right partner for Ibrahim.'

'That's not what you said. If that's what you mean then those are the words you need to use.'

Ibrahim wasn't sure what to make of that. Was his grandmother agreeing with his father but telling him off

75

on a technicality or did she disagree with everything he was saying?

'We won't know if she's the right girl for Ibrahim unless we meet her, Nasir,' his mother placated.

How could Ibrahim, in all conscience, bring a woman into his family and expose her to this kind of toxicity? His father's out-of-date and sexist thinking, his mother's extreme emotions of love or hate with no middle ground.

Be it Jiya or anyone else, how could he bring a woman into such an environment and expect her or their relationship to thrive? Was Zafar and Reshma's example not enough to show him what would happen?

Ibrahim ran a hand through his hair and pushing his plate away, he stood up, his mind in too much of a turmoil to eat any more.

'If you'll all excuse me, I'm going for a run.' Ignoring his father's sarcastic rejoinder about literally running away, Ibrahim left the dining room before he said something his father would deserve but he himself might later regret.

CHAPTER EIGHT

Jiya

Jiya looked out over the water as the sunlight rippled on its surface. A few boats were making their way along the Thames with people enjoying an afternoon out. People waved at those on the bridges and banks and they waved back in return. It was too good a day to be indoors and after yesterday's intense study day, today she would make the most out of being outdoors and soaking in some much-needed sunshine. Watching everybody around her having a good time made her feel relaxed and helped slow her mind down a little.

She'd left the house earlier than the time she had arranged to see Ibrahim, just to be able to get out. Apart from the fact that she was getting bored of being indoors just studying, her father's mood had her feeling uneasy.

He was still not talking to her properly and despite her mother's reassurance that she'd have a chat with him, she was yet to hear anything happening on that front. Jameel had taken to being nice to her but avoided the subject of Ibrahim. Yesterday he told her to carry on doing what she was, when her mother called for her, and said that he would do the dishes. She'd done a double take but he'd just shrugged.

Her mother had kept herself preoccupied with house-work, leaving Jiya with few chores to do so she'd spent that time catching up on her coursework.

This morning, when Jiya had said that she was going out later, her mother had asked her plenty of questions about where she was going, who was going to be there and when would she be back home.

'This goes against a lot of my thinking, Jiya, but I'm letting you go. If, when I meet this boy, I think he's no good or if your father or brother refuse, then that'll be that.'

With her mother's words tumbling around in her head like clothes on a spin cycle, Jiya made her way over Westminster Bridge and down a set of steps, making her way past the attractions on the parade along the South Bank.

Being outdoors, especially in the sunshine, was the cure for everything. It made everything feel and look great. The warmth hitting her face, the laughter of children as they queued up with their families for the giant Ferris wheel that was the London Eye, people having a good time, the distant but ever-present sound of traffic. Everything.

Feeling calmer than she had in quite a while, Jiya went and sat on an empty patch of grass facing the river, leaning on her hands behind her and watching the world go by. Having a busy job that kept her on her feet and in a rush most of the time, and being at her desk the rest of the time, made her treasure these moments of having absolutely nothing to do and being able to people-watch.

Her thoughts drifted like clouds in the sky, moving from one thing onto another and then, inevitably, onto Ibrahim.

If she was honest, she was confused about her feelings towards him. She liked him and got along really well with him, but that didn't seem to sum up her feelings entirely. Her thoughts about him were conflicted and she had no idea how to unravel them or her feelings enough to make sense of them.

What she should be concentrating on was her end goal. The entire reason why she had embarked on this crazy idea in the first place.

The reaction of her family had seriously jolted her and now she also had the worry of what their reaction would be when they found out that she and Ibrahim had been faking their relationship the whole time.

If only she could come clean to her parents without them jumping at the next potential husband for her and focus on her course and getting a job without any distractions. Except the biggest and most attractive distraction in her life was of her own doing.

She needed to focus on the plan. That's it. The key was not to think too far ahead. She just needed to concentrate on a few things and let future problems take care of themselves.

For now, she had to think about her next assignment and arranging for Ibrahim to meet her family. He could easily manage a meeting with her family and he'd know what to say and do to make sure their plan stayed on track. He was a big boy and knew how to take care of things.

She had never thought she'd be attracted to the hotshot, corporate, city guy type of man but it seemed like she was. Or maybe it was just him.

And just like that, her thoughts circled back to him.

There was so much about him that she found fascinating and if she didn't control herself strictly, she could easily get lost in just watching him while he did the most mundane of tasks.

Closing her eyes, she allowed her mind thirty seconds of freedom. She thought about how she could watch him for hours as he took his sunglasses off, folded them carefully before putting them away either in his jacket pocket or placing them on the table if they were sitting at one. Or when he absently ran his fingers through his hair and it fell back in its soft layers, making her want to run her fingers through it as well.

Jiya let out a deep sigh, enjoying the feelings within and the feeling of the sunshine on her face, which a moment later was blocked by a shadow.

'Your cheeks are completely flushed. How long have you been sitting out here in the sun?'

She opened her eyes and took in the sight of the object of her thoughts from seconds earlier.

Dear God but he was gorgeous.

Ibrahim stood in front of her, casually dressed in trainers, jeans and a T-shirt with the Batman logo on it. His signature sunglasses were firmly in place and he looked so good that Jiya had to swallow twice to moisten her mouth enough to speak. She was grateful that she could explain her flushed cheeks as a result of sitting in the sun rather than her wayward thoughts.

'How did you find me?' She sat up and looked at her watch, partly to see how long she had been sitting there and mostly to have something else to look at so she could get her errant reaction under control.

He dropped himself down on the grass beside her and leaned back on his elbows. 'I got here a bit earlier and decided to take a walk along the South Bank to clear my head. I was about to call you when I just happened to see you by chance. Imagine finding you among all these people – crazy right? It must be like a one in a thousand chance kind of thing.'

'Tell me about it. I did the same too – came earlier, that is, just to sit here and do nothing; empty my mind of everything.'

He lowered his sunglasses down his nose but not all the way as she turned her head over her shoulder to look at him. His eyes twinkled in the sunlight, turning their colour to a burnished gold.

'Did it work?' His voice was low and husky, the depth of it making her feel like her hair was standing on its end. She turned her gaze away from his and looked at the people lining up in front of the ice-cream van.

Focus, Jiya.

'Did what work?'

'Sitting here to clear your head. I have to say, I've not come here in a while but it felt good to get out today and stretch my legs. I wouldn't say it's blown away all the cobwebs but it's certainly helped.'

'That's good. Same for me too I guess, especially after yesterday's work on my assignment. But we're not going to talk about assignments or reading lists today.'

'OK then. What do you say we join those tourists and go on the wheel?'

Jiya scrunched her face up in disappointment. 'We probably can't. We need to get tickets and the chances are they'll be sold out given that it's a Sunday and we have such gorgeous weather.'

Pushing his sunglasses back up his nose, he put his hand to his back pocket and pulled out his phone, turning it to show her the screen after a few seconds. Jiya let out an audible gasp. 'You didn't?'

He gave her a smug smile. 'I most certainly did. I took a chance and went in to see if they had any. Spur of the moment kind of thing. What do you say?'

Ibrahim stood up in one fluid movement while Jiya stayed where she was. 'You need to help me up. I've got pins and needles in my legs.'

She couldn't be sure, but judging by the movement on his forehead, she thought he might have quirked his eyebrow behind his sunglasses. He bent down onto his haunches and giving her a devilish grin, he lightly smacked her legs one at a time, causing the sensation of the pins and needles to intensify.

Jiya pulled her legs back instinctively, groaning at that horrible feeling one got when you moved your legs while they felt like lead weights.

'Ibrahim!' she cried, pouting up at him. He shrugged unrepentantly.

'There is no way I could have passed up such an opportunity, Miss Ahmed. It was way too good and you handed it to me on a platter. You should know better than to tell someone within two feet of you that you've got pins and needles. My brothers and I would rather die than let each other know. Once, when we were younger, Harry made the mistake of telling me and Ash that he had pins and needles. He acted like he'd been paralysed after we were done smacking his legs. Zaf had to carry him out of the room. Ash and I laughed so much and we still remind him of that day, much to his embarrassment.'

Jiya always found it bittersweet when Ibrahim told her stories about him and his brothers. A part of her wanted to hear every single story and she loved the way his eyes lit up when he spoke about them. But then a part of her didn't want to hear anything along those lines because – and she wasn't proud of feeling this way – it made her feel jealous. Jealous at the fact that she hardly shared that kind of a relationship with her own brother, although he had been different since their dad had been giving her the silent treatment.

'Come on then, let's get you up, Grandma.' Grabbing one of her hands and placing his other hand at her elbow, he easily pulled her up to her feet but instead of letting her go, he held onto her hand. 'Is the feeling back in your legs yet?'

They were standing a lot closer than she had realised. The citrusy scent of his aftershave enveloped her and all she wanted to do was run her hands across the broad expanse of his chest and up those muscular shoulders.

His hand that wasn't clasped around her own came to rest on her hip and Jiya felt the heat of it permeate through her T-shirt, branding her skin underneath and sending shockwaves through her body.

Unable to stop herself, she rested her free hand on his chest, feeling the steady pulse of his heartbeat.

Ibrahim

He wondered if she could hear how hard his heart was pounding. He thought it might actually burst through his chest the way it was going. He was glad that he wasn't the only one affected by their close proximity. Jiya's cheeks were streaked red and it wasn't just because of the heat of the sun – her breathing was visibly fast, making her breasts move with each breath in a way that had his mouth feel as dry as the desert.

If they didn't move within the next few seconds, he would claim her mouth and to hell with the fact that they were surrounded on all four sides by people who didn't need them to do the whole fake thing.

Ibrahim groaned internally at the track his thoughts were taking and Jiya must have felt the change in him because clearing her throat, she took a step back, gently pushing against his chest.

'Last one to the queue buys the food.' She raced off towards the wheel, leaving Ibrahim standing there for a second as his brain tried to catch up with the different thoughts and feelings clamouring for attention.

He jogged after her and reached the queue just a couple of seconds after her. She seemed to have recovered swiftly after the moment they'd just shared, and excitement about the ride was taking over everything else. If only it were that easy for him.

Even in her exuberance, he found her attractive, when normally he would find such displays of excitement childish.

Jiya was making him question so many of his previously held beliefs. Things he'd never thought or felt before were slowly beginning to creep into his mind and the scary thing was, he wasn't running for the hills. This was something that was happening more and more as he spent time with Jiya.

She was beginning to consume his thoughts in a way nothing ever had before and at some point, he was going to have to figure out exactly what he was going to do about it.

Blowing out an audible breath, Ibrahim ran his fingers through his hair. If he wasn't careful, this little stick of dynamite would blow his plan to smithereens and the way things were going, he'd be sitting back happily, popcorn bowl in hand, watching her do it.

They reached the front of the line and got into the moving capsule, the stunning vista of London on a sunny afternoon gradually emerging as they went higher up. Jiya's enthusiasm was infectious and he found himself just as awed as her as they soaked in the sights.

She was bouncing from one end of the capsule to the other, asking him which buildings she wasn't sure about – not that he knew that much more – and it felt good. The clear skies meant they had a spectacular view of the city they were proud to call home and it filled him with both a sense of peace and a sense of wonder.

They came out of the capsule and Jiya decided that before they did anything else, they should make a stop at the ice-cream van. He was glad to see that the tension that had been so clear in her voice over the last couple of days seemed to have taken a back seat.

'Which one?'

'Is that even a question? Flake 99 obviously.' She gave him a big grin and turned back to the vendor and got two cones with mini mountains of vanilla ice cream in them and a flaky chocolate stick in each.

They sat on a low wall next to each other under the shade of a small tree, people watching as they ate. The sense of peace and quiet he was feeling was such a novelty for him he didn't want to move after he'd consumed his ice-cream at express speed.

Jiya finished eating her ice cream and then turned to face him, crossing her legs under her on the wide wall.

'Thank you. That was amazing. Just what I needed after the last few days.'

'I'm glad. I don't think I've enjoyed doing such a touristy thing in a long time.' As though it had a mind of its own, his hand lifted and he ran the backs of his fingers down her soft cheek, tucking loose strands of hair behind her ear.

He had edged closer towards her, enough that he could smell her sweet perfume and see her pupils dilate as her breath stuttered.

He had the urge to lower his head and claim her lips in a sweet kiss he'd been craving for a lot longer than he cared to admit. Her big soulful eyes were fixed on his face and it took an enormous amount of effort to keep within the boundaries they should keep.

How had he never realised how expressive her eyes were? They weren't a unique colour or shape but there was an attraction he couldn't quite fathom, compelling him to look into them and not look away.

He didn't move an inch, watching as her eyes lowered to his lips and then lifted to his own eyes.

Unable to hold back a moment more, he lowered his head gradually, giving her time to change her mind but she met him halfway, her soft lips closing under his own.

The contact only lasted a few seconds, and while it felt like it was over in a heartbeat, he could recount every millisecond of the kiss. Her lips were soft and pillowy, and he could taste the chocolate, the ice cream, the wafer from the cone and the unique flavour he knew was simply her.

As his brain computed what they were doing, he pulled back, Jiya's expression showing shock but no outrage, thankfully. He stood up and jammed his hands in his pockets. She stood up as well and rubbed her palms down her thighs, both of them speaking at the same time.

'I'm sorry—'

'I shouldn't have—'

They both went quiet and stared at each other for a second before smiling nervously. She was the first to break the tension, reaching up and pulling his sunglasses off his face and placing them on top of her head. 'Let's walk for a bit.'

He fell in step with her and they were both quiet as they walked past the gardens along the river. Ibrahim was feeling relaxed after what felt like a long time – despite the awkwardness of acting on his urge, but it seemed to be mutual – and he wanted to savour the moment of peace and connection he'd just felt with Jiya, and that's exactly what he did.

Until his phone rang.

CHAPTER NINE

Jiya

Jiya stood by the barriers looking across the river while Ibrahim answered his phone.

The sights from the London Eye had been as breathtaking as she'd expected them to be and it had made her feel a myriad of emotions being in that capsule.

She'd felt as though hundreds of years of history was unfolding before her eyes with new buildings vying with the old for space on London's iconic skyline. She felt proud to be in a city that had such a rich history but she felt very relieved that she was here in the twenty-first century; she loved her modern-day comforts far too much.

Watching the mini waves hitting the wall below where she stood, Jiya felt more relaxed than she had in as long as she could remember, making her realise that she needed to do this more often. Just unplug for a couple of hours and take a break.

She wasn't naïve enough to believe that it was the sunshine, being outdoors and away from her family, although they were certainly contributing factors. The fact that she was with Ibrahim had a lot to do with it.

He had this aura about him that made her feel . . . comfortable. Happy and relaxed. Wanted. Important.

When exactly this had happened, Jiya couldn't say. But she was feeling mellow enough to accept and acknowledge that those were the feelings she had when she was around

Ibrahim Saeed. It was as though all her worries and problems took a back seat for a while.

And then there was that kiss.

Sigh.

It had been over before it had even begun, but it had been potent enough to make her feel unsteady on her feet. Jiya could still feel the imprint of Ibrahim's lips on hers and the banked heat from his body coming off in waves against her own. Her nerve endings had tingled and a low, simmering heat had unfurled in her tummy, but before she could identify what it might be, he had lifted his mouth from hers and she had moved back herself.

She had felt satisfied, but at the same time it had made her feel like she wanted something that was just out of reach. What was that feeling?

It was never a part of their plan to be intimate with each other. But it was just a kiss, right? A moment out of time. Something they could just pretend hadn't happened, but she didn't have to erase it from her mind altogether.

It didn't mean that they were desperately in love with each other. It just hinted at a mutual attraction. An attraction she thought she had glimpsed in his eyes a few times now and which she acknowledged she had most certainly felt for him, and they had simply acted on it. Yes, definitely a moment out of time.

'He's got to be the world's most blinkered man. The only thing he can see is what he wants and to hell with everyone else and their desires.'

Ibrahim growled an expletive and a passing couple looked at him as though he had lost his mind.

He immediately apologised to them and running his fingers through his hair agitatedly, he came and stood beside her, resting his arms on the barrier and looking across the expanse of water before them.

Jiya gave him a minute before speaking, feeling the tension come off of him in waves. So much for blowing away the cobwebs.

'What was that all about?'

'My father being his usual dictatorial self, that's what.' He hung his head and Jiya had the urge to hold him. He was angry, she could tell, but she also sensed a degree of hurt in his voice. Disappointment.

She settled for placing her hand on his shoulder. 'Do you want to talk about it? What did he say?'

He lifted his head and looked towards the other side of the river, though he wasn't taking in the sight. After a moment, he straightened up. He carefully took his sunglasses from her, which had been on her head the whole time and put them on. 'Let's walk.'

She wondered if she'd overstepped a boundary by asking him about the phone call. Even if he'd been complaining about his father, it didn't really give her the right to ask intrusive questions and expect him to tell her everything.

One kiss didn't mean having to share everything about their lives with each other.

They began walking and Jiya was surprised when Ibrahim took her hand in his and began talking. 'Yesterday morning, my dad told me that he'd invited his friend over for dinner with his family. They'll be coming to our place this evening and he wanted me to be there.'

Jiya stopped walking and gave him what she hoped was a reassuring smile. 'That's it? That's all right, you can go. We can always catch up another day. I hope you didn't refuse to go just because we had decided to meet up. We could have rearranged our plans.'

Judging by the tightening of his mouth, she guessed he was scowling down at her behind his sunglasses.

'You know, Saeed, if you want to glare and frown at me, you should take those sunglasses off. It'll have more of an impact.'

He lowered them down his nose instead and narrowed his eyes at her. 'If you had let me finish, before magnanimously giving up my company, you would have found out that there's more to it.'

She gave him a sheepish look and taking his hand again she gave it a squeeze. 'Sorry, my bad. Please, continue.'

He mumbled something under his breath like a grumpy old man and carried on walking, making her smile.

'You'd spoken to me the evening before, telling me that your family had found out about us, so I thought it would be a good time for me to tell my dad. Mum and Daadi were there as well, so I thought it was the perfect time to drop the bombshell. Especially since the friend he'd invited for dinner was bringing his daughter with him and that's who Dad wanted to introduce me to.'

The penny dropped with Jiya. 'Ohhh, one of *those* meetings. Eww, I hate those kinds of meetings. But why were they coming to your house? Normally a guy goes to the girl's house.'

'I don't know and frankly, I don't care. I want no part of this bollo— Anyway, I used that moment to tell my parents and grandmother that I'm already in a relationship and so I won't be meeting any potential brides. I told him that I'm meeting you today, so I wouldn't be there.

'I figured that had been the end of it, but obviously I was wrong. He just phoned me to ask where I was, what time I was getting home and if I remembered that we had visitors coming today. Can you believe it?'

She could absolutely believe it. Her mother wasn't all that different when she got a bee in her bonnet about something. Recently, she had become relentless in her pursuit of finding a potential husband for Jiya and it had got so bad that she had started dreading going home some days, not knowing who would be sitting in the front room clutching a cup and saucer in their hands, waiting to be introduced to her.

'The sad thing is, Jiya, he thinks it's perfectly acceptable for me to have a girlfriend and "go out and have fun" but when he's ready, I'm supposed to settle down with a girl of his choice. Just like Zaf did.'

'Let me guess: you told him that you're not willing to do what Zafar did.'

'If there was any confusion yesterday, there certainly wasn't just now. I told him that I'm out with you and I'll be coming home when we're good and ready to call it a day and not a minute before that. I also told him that he doesn't need to introduce me to any potential brides because I don't need him to find me a wife.'

'I bet that went down well.'

'Well enough that my mum came onto the phone and said not to worry about not joining them today and to have fun.'

Jiya gave his hand another squeeze. 'Then that's what we'll do.' She turned him around and started walking back in the direction they had just come from.

Ibrahim

Ibrahim was certain there was steam coming off the top of his head. His father was driving him absolutely nuts lately and it seemed as though there was no way of getting through to him. If Ibrahim decided on a whim to actually marry Jiya and take her home, it was probable his father still wouldn't believe that Ibrahim wasn't going to do what he wanted him to.

The cogwheels of his brain screeched to a halt at the thought of marrying Jiya.

That was not the plan. That was *sooo* not the plan.

Then why had the thought popped up in his head? And why wasn't he running in the opposite direction rather than letting her drag him back the way they had come?

They were helping each other. That was it. Nothing more, nothing less. He had no plans to settle down anytime soon and she certainly had no such plans. She wanted to study and then focus on building her career.

It was all his dad's fault. All this talk about potential brides, marriage, settling down and repeatedly shoving Zafar's example under his nose. He wasn't going to do it. Full stop.

'You know if you keep frowning like that, you'll get permanent frown lines on your forehead.' He turned and saw Jiya watching him closely.

He cleared his expression. 'Where are we going?'

'We're going to see if we can get into the London Dungeon.'

'What? No, I don't want to go there.'

She let out a theatrical gasp. 'Don't tell me you're scared.'

He scoffed. 'Of course, I'm not scared. I'd just prefer not to go to attractions aimed at kids. Besides, I'm really not in the mood right now, J.'

'Aww, Ibby. You have nuffing to be afwaid of, I'll hold your hand the whole way, I pwomise.'

'You really believe I'm scared?' He held off grinning at her Tweety Pie impersonation.

'Why else would you not want to go?'

'Fine, let's go. I bet you I'm not the one who's going to feel afraid.'

'Ha, whatever.'

'In fact, let's bet on it. Winner gets to choose the prize and the loser has to pay up. No questions, ifs or buts.'

'And what are we betting on?'

'The first person to jump or scream or yell, or anything that gives away the fact that they're scared, loses. Deal?' He extended his hand to shake on it.

'You're on.' She placed her hand in his and he tugged her towards him.

'Remember, you wanted this.'

They went in and managed to get into the next round of entrants. It seemed like the good weather had people choosing outdoor activities rather than underground ones, unlike the lunatic he was with.

The dark and eerie set-up was enough to give the hardest and bravest of people a shiver down the spine. The lighting was deliberately terrible so you couldn't see all that far ahead and the ambient noises were enough to make one repeatedly look over one's shoulder, which of course, Ibrahim was not doing.

He manoeuvred Jiya to walk slightly in front of him to the right along the narrow corridor. She was holding his hand like she said she would, and as she was looking at the walls on either side of the tunnel they were walking through, he lightly ran his left index finger down her spine.

She turned her head back so fast, her ponytail swished in protest. She glared at him, unamused. 'Nice try. But think very carefully before you start playing dirty.' He just grinned in response.

As the pair of them progressed through the various stages and scenes, Jiya tried all sorts of ways of trying to scare him or getting him to jump. It was actually really amusing because none of them worked. For his part, Ibrahim didn't try to scare her even once.

They went through different sections depicting the plague, the gunpowder plot, some other more gruesome stages and then the rather grotesque Mrs Lovett's Pie Shop and a Sweeney Todd set as well.

They went into a chamber that told the story of Jack the Ripper, the infamous serial killer from the late nineteenth century. This particular chamber sent a shiver down Ibrahim's spine but thankfully, Jiya didn't see it. He, however, saw her squirm at what she saw.

They had a few more chambers to go before they reached the end and Ibrahim was determined to win the bet. He just needed to figure out how to go about it.

He dropped back a bit without her noticing because they had let go of each other's hands to go through a narrow corridor earlier. While she was looking the other way, he went around her towards the door leading to the next set and, spotting a little alcove which was shadowed, he went and stood in it. He could see her but hopefully, she wouldn't be able to see him.

The crowd moved on to the next chamber and he could see Jiya looking for him but moving ahead at the same time.

'Ibrahim?' She looked around but as the chamber emptied of people, she obviously didn't want to be the only one left behind. She moved towards the opening of the next chamber, behind a small group of people, and as luck would have it, she was standing just in front of him.

Ibrahim didn't wait long and grabbing her from behind he whispered in her ear, 'Gotcha.'

Jiya froze for a split second, her body going as stiff as a board in his arms and then she let out a yelp. His arms were around her waist and he had lifted her a couple of inches off the ground. She clawed at his hands until she realised it was him and then she gave them a cracking slap which stung like hell.

'Ouch.' He let go of her and she spun around and glared at him furiously.

'Just you wait. I'm going to get you back so badly your ancestors are going to feel it.'

'I'm pretty sure you just did with that smack.' He rubbed the back of each hand in turn and followed her and the rest of the crowd into the next chamber.

They went through a few more sets and then came to a vertical drop ride. The kind where you wait and wait and wait for the drop to come and just when you least expect it, but think you're totally prepared for it, it falls.

That's exactly what happened and it had both him and Jiya yelling like schoolkids when the bench dropped. They turned and looked at each other when the safety bar lifted and grinned.

Feeling the rush of having done something exhilarating, they made their way outside, squinting in the early evening sunlight after being in the darkness of the dungeon.

Jiya put her hands around his arm and giving it a squeeze, she looked up at him. 'Feeling better?'

He gave her a puzzled look and she, in turn, looked very pleased with herself, as she spoke rather smugly. 'I can see you are, so I'm happy.'

'What are you talking about?'

'You were so stressed after speaking to your dad and I didn't want you to be thinking about that and feeling rubbish, so I thought we should do something that would distract you. It worked.'

Ibrahim looked down at her, her face upturned towards his, her expression open and happy.

Here was a woman who had plenty of stress of her own and she'd gone out of her way to try and make him feel better. Ibrahim felt touched by her thoughtfulness.

'Now,' her ponytail swished as she moved. 'We're going to go and get dinner and then I'm going home. I'm absolutely knackered.'

He grinned down at her as he spoke in a low voice. 'Easy sunshine, I still need to collect on my bet before you can go home.'

CHAPTER TEN

Ibrahim

'Ah, Mr Ibrahim Saeed. So nice of you to finally make an appearance. I hope your day out with your *girlfriend* was worth defying your father for.'

Ibrahim didn't like the way his father emphasised the word girlfriend. As though it was something dirty and he should be ashamed of it.

It was also a typical move of his, to use emotion as a way of getting what he wanted; using his sons' sense of duty or responsibility towards their parents or each other to get them to do as he pleased. He really was a master manipulator.

Well, Ibrahim was done with his antics. After what had been the best of days, he didn't want it to end with a blistering row with his old man, but it seemed like his father had other ideas.

He had just let himself in through the front door and into the hall when his father spoke to him through the open glass doors that led to an informal sitting room. A few members of the family were gathered: Zafar, Rayyan, his mother and grandmother. He didn't respond to his father straight away but instead he acknowledged his brothers, kissed his mother and grandmother on their cheeks and then turned to face him.

'Is there a question in there, Dad?'

His father was sitting in the armchair reserved solely for him. No one else ever sat in that chair and it seemed to give his father the false impression that he was sat on a throne and the rest of the family were his loyal subjects.

Ibrahim made a point of sitting down himself, rather than stand in front of his father like a child standing before a headteacher to be reprimanded.

His father raised an eyebrow and spoke over his steepled fingers. 'I distinctly remember telling you that you were to be here today because Hatim was coming with his family. Yet, you were absent. Would you care to explain why that happened?'

'Nasir, we've had this conversation. Please drop it.'

'I'm talking to my son, Farida. Don't interfere.' Ibrahim gritted his teeth at the way his father spoke to his mother. He was sure his brothers were equally annoyed but quiet for now and his grandmother would only let so much go before putting her foot down. Sure, his mother could be trying at times, but no woman deserved to be treated that way, no matter what.

'It's all right Mum. I don't mind telling Dad what today's plan was. Again.' He knew he was skating on thin ice but he'd really had enough of his father's despotic attitude and his ridiculous expectation that everyone should bow and scrape as soon as he so much as entered a room.

It was his phone call earlier that had cemented Ibrahim's resolve that he would no longer put up with the bullying, whether it was subtle or in your face. Like right now.

He could tell his answer had annoyed his father by the subtle tightening of his jaw.

'I was out with Jiya today. We had made plans for today last week and I told you this when you told me about today's dinner over breakfast yesterday. I told you that I wouldn't be here and I also told you that I'm not interested in meeting any potential brides.'

'You *told* me? I do the telling in this house, boy, not you. It is your job to listen and do as you are told. Not the other way around. You'd do well to learn from your older brother. There's an example of a good son.' Ibrahim gritted his teeth while his father addressed Zafar. 'You need to teach your brother, Zafar, what it means to respect his elders. To respect those who know better and to respect the decisions they make.'

It was a good thing that as brothers, they all shared a strong relationship on which thankfully, their father had no influence because if it was up to him, they would all resent and hate each other immensely, given how he played them off against one another. Constantly comparing one's successes with another's failures. Well, what *he* deemed failures.

His father turned to face him again, not giving anyone a chance to speak.

'What kind of example are you setting for your younger brothers, Ibrahim? They're watching you and seeing your behaviour and they're going to think it's perfectly acceptable to go against their father and his decisions. They're going to think it's perfectly acceptable to disrespect me, to just do as they please and to hell with the consequences. Rayyan's already said he has no interest in the business or family. He's even moved out of the family home.'

'I never once said I wasn't interested in my family,' Rayyan responded. 'That's always been something you've said, Dad. I moved out because I needed to be nearer to the school, no other reason. And we're not discussing my life choices here.' Working with children and sometimes their difficult parents had put Rayyan in good stead when it came to dealing with their own father. Ibrahim was pleased that his brother kept his cool and followed suit.

'Look, Dad, what I've chosen to do today has nothing to do with how good a son Zaf is, how bad a son I am, what Ray's life choices are or what Ash and Harry choose to do. We should have the freedom to do what we want to do. Just because I choose to do something, it doesn't mean I'm disrespecting you or my family. It just means I'm choosing to do something for myself, as an individual.

'I like someone and I want to give our relationship a chance. That's it. It's got nothing to do with anything else.'

'Don't treat me like I'm the fool, boy. And don't patronise me.' Jesus, the man really knew which buttons to push to piss his sons off.

'I'm not patronising you – I'm trying not to lose my temper.'

'And you say you're not disrespecting me? What do you call this then?' He turned to face his wife. 'Is this how you've raised my sons? To talk back to me like this?'

Ibrahim didn't wait for his mother to respond to his father. 'What the hell does that have to do with any of this? Right now, the only thing that is happening, and has been happening for a while, is that you're just not listening. You don't really care what we might want to do or hope for. You just want all of us to do your bidding unquestioningly. That's it.'

'I'm your father, Ibrahim, and you will do as I tell you. Hatim is coming over again with his family and you *will* be here to meet his daughter. And, if you decide not to show up again, then you can meet her at your Daadi's party when I announce your engagement to her.'

Ibrahim felt his control over his temper snap and despite Rayyan placing his hand on his knee to stop him, he saw red as Zafar intervened.

'Dad, I think we should just call it a night and discuss things rationally another time. There's no sense in discussing anything when you're both close to losing your temper. Nothing will be resolved.'

'No, Zaf. We're not going to discuss anything at any other time. I want this concluded now.' Ibrahim got up and with his back towards the glass doors, he faced his father. 'You've just gone and proved my point, Dad. You've not listened to a thing I've said up until now and you can do the same with what I'm about to say next, but then don't say I didn't tell you or expect any explanation afterwards.

'I've found someone who genuinely makes me happy and I do the same for her. We like each other and see ourselves spending the rest of our lives together and I'm going to ask her to marry me.'

The only sound in the room was the ticking of the clock. Everyone in the room was absolutely silent. His brothers looked at each other with a look of concern on their faces. His mother and grandmother looked shocked and his father looked the same. His usual, indifferent expression was back on his face as he stared back at Ibrahim. The only telltale sign that he was supremely pissed off was the clenched jaw and slightly narrowed eyes.

'Now you listen to me, boy—'

'That's enough.' Ibrahim turned to look at his grandmother. She looked small in the big wingback chair but her voice carried enough authority that no one said another word while she spoke.

'I'm still the head of this family after your father died, Nasir, even though you seem to think I've relinquished the role to you and at times, I'll accept, I have let you assume the position.

'I will not have you all arguing like that again. Do I make myself clear? I've not raised you to just sit there and expect the children to do your bidding as though what they think, feel or say is of no importance. And you, Ibrahim, you were certainly not raised to take that tone of voice with your father no matter what.

'Now, Nasir, you will stop trying to force Ibrahim into an engagement he quite clearly doesn't want. There's no sense in pursuing something that will just cause misery for everyone involved. Ibrahim, how serious are you about Jiya?'

He felt everyone's eyes on him. He was still feeling pretty vexed with his dad but his brain wasn't frazzled to the point that he couldn't appreciate the fact that things had spiralled a bit out of control.

Understatement!

They had spiralled a lot out of control.

Tempers hadn't been close to being lost; they'd blown a hole in the ceiling. He'd raised his voice at his father and he'd said things that perhaps if he'd been thinking rationally, he might not have.

Like the fact that he was planning on marrying Jiya. Had he really said that just to get at his dad? And now what was he going to do?

He could hardly go back on his word within five minutes. But he could hardly go through with such a life-changing action.

And what about Jiya? This wasn't what she wanted at all.

What the hell had he got himself into?

'Ibrahim? Honey, I asked you a question. How serious is your relationship with Jiya? I hope you're not messing the girl around for the sake of it.' He heard the steel in his grandmother's voice and shook his head.

'No, Daadi, I'm not messing her around at all. We are serious.' He looked in the direction of his brothers. Rayyan's expression was intense and Zafar's looked just as grim. Giving them the slightest nod, he turned to face their grandmother. 'I'm very serious about her and I do want to pursue a relationship with her. I just don't think we're quite ready to actually get married yet. We're still finding our feet with each other.'

Hopefully that would placate the family and give him some time to figure out just how to get out of the mess which in all fairness, he had created all by himself. With some help from his old man of course.

But really it was his crap and he had to wrap it up.

'That is what engagements are for, sweetheart. For a couple to find their feet with each other before the main event. I tell you what, bring her round one of these days to come and see us, preferably before the party. Completely informal, of course, but it'll be nice for us to meet her and I'm sure she'd like to see your family at some point.'

There wasn't really a question there and with his energy shot to pieces after this evening, he wasn't going to get into another discussion just then.

'I'll have a chat with her, Daadi, and let you know when she can come.' First, he had to tell Jiya that there was a slight glitch in their plan.

Giving him a nod, Daadi got up and left the room with his mother and after giving Ibrahim a death glare, his father got up and walked out too, leaving Ibrahim with his two brothers.

Zafar shook his head and leaned back against the sofa while Rayyan looked at him seriously. 'What the hell was that, Ibs?'

Ibrahim flopped down on a sofa himself, his head resting back on the cushions, his eyes on the ceiling. He gave a deep sigh. 'I have no idea, mate. No fucking clue.'

'Look, Ibrahim, I know now's not an ideal time after what's just happened but you're going to need to figure this out fast. You mentioned proposing to her, for God's sake.' Ibrahim could hear a combination of concern and frustration in Zafar's tone.

He knew his brothers had his back, but that didn't mean they wouldn't call him out on his shit.

'You need to think very carefully about how you're going to move this thing forward. You told me yesterday that Jiya's parents know about you both and want to meet you and now Daadi's told you to bring her round. I'm getting the feeling that this thing is moving faster than either of you anticipated.'

Ibrahim rubbed the back of his neck and sighing heavily, he moved forward to rest his arms on his thighs. His train of thoughts was running too fast for him to be able to keep up with it, but his brother was right – he needed to pull his finger out and figure this shit out before it really hit the fan.

'Did you talk to her today about what you're both going to do?' Ibrahim looked up at Rayyan's question and shook his head in answer.

'We didn't. We were supposed to, but then we decided to play tourist and went on the London Eye and then to the Dungeon.' Thinking about his day had him smiling. 'We spent dinner talking about both and then I dropped her home and that's it. We didn't talk about what we're going to do or where our relationship is headed.' It sounded suspiciously close to a real date.

Rayyan spoke so softly that if there hadn't been absolute silence in the house, Ibrahim might have missed his question. '*Are* you in a relationship?'

'No.' Even he knew that he'd answered way too quickly and emphatically to have even processed the question properly.

The three of them sat in silence for a few minutes and then Zafar stood up. 'I think you've got a lot of thinking to do, mate. You know where to find us if you need us.' Rayyan stood up as well and after giving Ibrahim's shoulder a squeeze, he left the room after Zafar.

After sitting there in silence for a few minutes, Ibrahim heaved himself off the sofa and made his way to his own room, making his way straight to the balcony doors. The night sky was cloudless, allowing him to see a few stars twinkling here and there.

Being a practical sort and having worked in the legal sector for many years now, it was second nature to Ibrahim to take a problem, deconstruct it and then solve each aspect in a way that gave him exactly what he wanted. Surely he could apply the same principle to his current situation.

It wasn't even overly complicated. He just had to satisfy his family and Jiya's family that they were committed to each other for the foreseeable future and then when they were both in a position to move on, they would each go their separate ways. Anything that cropped up later could be dealt with then; he wouldn't worry about that now.

And if in the meantime, he and Jiya got along and enjoyed spending time with each other, then that was a bonus he would happily accept.

CHAPTER ELEVEN

Jiya

Putting the order book and pen beside the till at the lounge, Jiya made her way towards the staffroom to grab her bag. She wasn't in a great mood, thanks to a group of obnoxious patrons who made it their mission in life to complain about every item brought to their table. She had been more than happy to see the back of them and even more glad that her shift had ended.

There were days she really enjoyed working at The Lounge but there were days like today when she was extremely glad it was home time.

Her supervisor Felix was in the staffroom as Jiya entered and waved her across.

'Jiya, Millie's taken the afternoon off because she's not feeling well. Any chance you can do another couple of hours? Have a break first, of course.'

Her heart and feet were desperate for her to say no, she couldn't do it, but her head was reminding her that another couple of hours would help her put more money aside for herself. And this was Felix. The nicest of the supervisors.

'Just a couple of hours? Two, to be exact?'

Felix gave her a lopsided smile. 'Take a half hour break and then just two hours.'

Agreeing to the additional hours, Jiya was about to leave when Felix called out to her, 'Jiya, good job with the dick table. I know how difficult they were being but you were fantastic. As always.' He gave her a thumbs-up and Jiya felt some of her tiredness ebb away. It was times like this when she felt that all the hard work she put in was worth it.

With things being difficult at home, confidence boosts like that were good for her morale and although Felix was really good at getting people to do what he wanted by saying all the right things to them, he was appreciative of her work and never failed to say so. Also, he didn't act like a pillock just because he was a supervisor and that in itself was priceless.

She went to the kitchen and ordered a sandwich and coffee and took it back to the staffroom for half an hour of peace and quiet.

She pulled out her phone to check out what was happening in the world of social media and saw a couple of missed calls and messages from Ibrahim and Harry.

She called Ibrahim but it went to voicemail, so she called Harry.

'You rang?'

'No, you rang.'

'Argh, you doughnut! I'm talking about the missed calls and messages you left to call you. What's up?'

'If it wasn't important, we'd be having a conversation about your tone of voice, young lady.' Jiya rolled her eyes but obviously the impact was lost on Harry. 'Apparently, Ibrahim had quite the bust up with our old man last night because he wasn't there for that dinner.'

'I thought it was an emergency. Have you phoned me at work like this to gossip, Haroon Saeed?'

'You know, you have this ridiculous habit of cutting people off while they're speaking and then sticking your tiny size three and a half foot in it. And I wouldn't be so uncouth that I'd gossip with you about my brother having a falling out with our dad.'

'Yes, you totally would.'

'You're right, I probably would, but that's not what I called to do today. The thing is – where are you?'

Jiya spoke with a mouthful of sandwich, 'The Lounge. Why?'

'Marvellous. I'm coming. Bye.'

'Wait—' Before she could respond properly, he'd already put the phone down. 'Such a drama queen.'

She finished off her sandwich and then tried Ibrahim once more, just to see if he was all right. It went to voicemail again so she dropped him a quick message and made her way back to start her two-hour stint.

Harry walked into The Lounge when Jiya had twenty minutes left to the end of her shift. Felix had managed to get cover and so he told her that she was free to clock off when she was ready.

She grabbed her bag as fast as she could and pulling Harry by the arm, she took him back out onto the street.

'That's a wonderful way to treat paying customers. Drag them back out by the arm.'

'Puh-lease, as if I could drag your sorry carcass anywhere without you moving it yourself. You weigh a ton.'

'Keep going, sweetheart. You're on a roll today. Really know how to make a guy feel special. How does Ibs put up with you?'

She looked up at him and gave his arm a squeeze. 'I'm sorry hun, I'm just super tired and wanted to get out of there pronto.'

Harry pulled his arm out of her hold and slinging it over her shoulders, he pulled her in for a hug. 'Let's get you off your feet then.'

They walked to where he'd parked his car and getting into the soft leather seats, Jiya groaned in relief. Why did one never realise how bone-tired they were until they sat down?

Harry got in and cut to the chase. 'My dad was pretty pissed off at the fact that Ibs had chosen not to come home for dinner yesterday and decided to stay out with you. Apparently when he got home after dropping you off, my dad let loose on him and they ended up having quite the argument until my grandmother told them both to pack it in.'

'Where were you?'

'Why is that relevant?'

Jiya shrugged her shoulders. 'Just curious. Anyway, please continue.'

He rolled his eyes. 'After dinner, I had gone over to a mate's place for some quality Xbox time. Anyway, when I got home, Ibrahim told me what had happened. He told me he'd talk to you today but he couldn't seem to get hold of you so asked if I could. He'll be finishing work himself shortly, so we're going to pick him up so he can give you the lowdown. So, make sure you act suitably shocked.'

'You mean you weren't supposed to tell me any of this?'

'Well, he never expressly said that I shouldn't say anything. He'll spill the beans and talk to you about it in depth when he sees you. I get to play driver.'

Harry filled the drive to Ibrahim's office with his mindless chatter and Jiya was grateful for it but at the back of her mind, she was wondering how bad Ibrahim's argument with his father might have been. She would hate to be the cause of any discord in the family.

They pulled up at the back of a tall building in Central London which housed the headquarters of the Saeed business and just in time too. Ibrahim was coming out of the doors behind his older brother, both of them looking devastatingly handsome in their workwear.

She got out of the car as Ibrahim approached it. On closer inspection, she could see the lines of tension bracketing Ibrahim's mouth and the fact that his eyes looked tired.

'Hey you.' She gave him a bright smile as he walked towards her. He bent his head and kissed her softly on her cheek, warming her up from within instantly, while her airways took their fill of his aftershave.

'Hey.' He gave her a smile that had an impact all the way to her toes and she was pretty certain they would have stayed standing there staring at each other if Ibrahim's older brother hadn't cleared his throat and Harry hadn't tugged at her ponytail from behind, as he often did when he wanted her attention.

'Let me introduce you properly to my eldest brother. Bhai, this is Jiya Ahmed and this, Jiya, is my eldest brother, Zafar Saeed the second.' The pride in Harry's voice was clear to anyone listening.

Jiya gave him a puzzled look and he smiled.

'I was named after my grandfather, but currently I'm the only Zafar in the family, so you don't have to number me.' He quirked an eyebrow at Harry – this whole eyebrow quirking seemed to be a family trait – and smiling at her, he extended his right hand. 'It's a pleasure to finally meet you properly, Jiya.'

'I've heard so much about you and before you ask, it's all been good stuff, I promise.'

'That's because there are only good things to hear about me.' He winked at her and she could see how the man could weaken a woman's knees. 'My brothers know better than to bad-mouth me. I control all the bank accounts.'

He leaned towards her conspiratorially, 'And I also know all their embarrassing stories since childhood. So really, it's in their best interest to be nice to me and about me.'

He shared a sardonic look with his brothers and ruffled Harry's hair, who grumbled good-naturedly in response.

Jiya felt that familiar pang of envy but ruthlessly suppressed it. When was she going to get over the fact that her relationship with Jameel was nothing like this? Though to be fair to him, he'd been less troublesome to her lately.

'You all right?' Ibrahim had his hand at the small of her back and looked at her closely. 'Long shift?'

She nodded at him distractedly, and he turned back to his brothers.

'If you take the infant home, Zaf, I'll take this car.'

'Sounds good.'

'I'm right here, you know. And this "infant" actually stopped what he was doing to bring Jiya here for you.'

'You're right, you did. Buy him an ice cream on the way home, Zaf, he's earned it.'

Jiya laughed at their ridiculous banter and a couple of minutes later found herself back in the car she had come in, only this time the driver was different.

'How was work?' Ibrahim manoeuvred the car through the evening traffic, mindful of the parade of cyclists on his left.

'It was all right apart from the fact that I had to work an extra two hours today to cover for Millie and before that I had a table of arsy customers who weren't happy with anything. Yours?'

'I've had a splitting headache for most of the day. I've downed about four paracetamols and it's just about taken the edge off. I had a blistering row with my father last night, to the point where my grandmother intervened.'

'Yeah, Harry mentioned that he wasn't pleased about you skipping the dinner yesterday.'

'That's the 12A version. Let's find a place where we can sit down, grab something to eat and I can tell you about it.'

Ibrahim

Ibrahim let out a sigh of relief as the waiter placed two coffees before him and Jiya after having taken their plates away. Today had felt like a forty-eight-hour day that was dying a slow death. He would be a very happy man when the clock struck twelve tonight.

He hadn't exaggerated the intensity of the headache he'd had since waking up. He could feel a dreadful tightness in his neck and shoulders and it was making its way up the back of his skull in a claw-like grip. Not nice.

'Maybe you should have gone home with your brothers and rested. I don't mean to be rude but you really do look terrible.'

He gave Jiya a half-smile and she beamed back at him. It was like sitting opposite your personal ray of sunshine.

He'd told her almost everything that had happened last night between him and his father and she had quietly listened, showing the understanding only the troubled child of a demanding parent could show. Of course, she understood.

From what Jiya had said, her mother could be as difficult at times as his father was. Although Ibrahim felt more inclined to show Jiya's mother a tinge of understanding given her history of losses.

What excuse did his father have for acting the way he did? He had lived a privileged life since his own childhood because it was Ibrahim's grandfather who had put in the hard work to get the Saeed family in a comfortable financial position.

'I know you said there was something else you wanted to talk to me about, but I think we should call it a night, Ibrahim. You're super tired and to be honest, so am I. You still need to drop me off and then drive—'

'I also told my father yesterday that I'm planning to propose to you. Daadi wants to meet you before you come to the party.'

Jiya stared at him, her face a picture of astonishment. Her eyes were focused on him in a dead stare, her lips slightly parted and her coffee cup was suspended in mid-air. If he hadn't been feeling like crap, he would have laughed at her and taken a picture because she looked seriously cute.

Ever so slowly, she closed her mouth, placed her cup back down without taking a sip and leaned forward slightly. 'You're going to propose to me? At the party?'

'What? No. I told my dad that I'm not going to entertain any prospective brides he sends my way because I'm going to be proposing to you.'

Her voice was barely audible when she spoke again, her eyes not quite meeting his. 'I thought we were just going to be in a fake relationship. I don't . . . we can't . . . this . . .'

'Jiya sweetheart, look at me. Look at me, please.'

She slowly lifted her eyes and looked at him. He could see the confusion in them clearly, which he could understand given that he had just blurted it out instead of phrasing it to her more tactfully. It was the slight look of distrust on her face that cut him to the quick.

'Just hear me out, OK? We're not going to do anything you're not comfortable with, all right? No matter what. Do you understand?'

She didn't answer him straight away and he felt his stomach plummet and his pulse accelerate.

She gave a jerky nod but her expression didn't change much. He still felt a hollow pit behind his sternum but he had to push aside his own anxious feelings and reassure her right now.

'I was feeling cornered by my father. He was refusing to understand my point of view on anything I said and was trying to force me into agreeing to what he wanted. He's exceptionally good at browbeating and manipulating people and will go above and beyond in trying to get what he wants.

'I figured the best way to get him off my case was to make our own situation a bit more official, but I did tell my grandmother that we're not there yet. I told her that we'd like a bit more time to get to know each other.'

Jiya's face was still pale and she looked conflicted. Ibrahim didn't want to say or do anything that would cause her to be upset or hurt in any way. Just the thought of it made him curl his fingers into his palms.

He forcibly relaxed his hands and then covered one of hers with his own.

'You don't have to say or do anything right now. Just hear me out, have a think about what I've said and am about to say, and then, when you're ready, let me know what you think. How does that sound? Good?'

She gave him another silent nod and with the hand he wasn't holding, she picked up her coffee cup.

He was somewhat reassured that she hadn't pulled her hand away from his and giving her hand a squeeze and pulling in a steadying breath, Ibrahim picked up his own cup for a sip of fortification.

'Here's what I'm thinking. Daadi would like to meet you before her party. So, I'll take you round and introduce you as my girlfriend. You don't have to say or do anything, just be yourself. I'll handle any awkward questions about our relationship. Maybe before the party, I could also come and see your family? What do you think?'

After a moment of thought, she spoke. 'Yeah, we can do that, I guess.'

'OK, good. Those can be our first steps. Actually, no. I think our first step needs to be me having a conversation with my family and making sure that they understand that even though I said I'd propose to you, I'll do it when I'm good and ready.'

She narrowed her eyes at him. 'When *you're* good and ready?'

He gave her a sheepish grin. 'When *we're* good and ready, which of course, we won't be, but they don't need to know that.'

He drained his coffee and signalled for the waiter to bring their bill. 'So, once I've told them that, we can meet each other's families. What do you think? Oh, and then there'll be Daadi's party, but we'll deal with that later.'

The waiter came to their table with the bill before Jiya could respond to him. He glanced her way as the waiter dealt with the card machine and she looked deep in thought, her face still showing the same confusion and doubt.

Ibrahim finished paying and thanking the waiter, and followed Jiya outside into the warm summer evening. They walked back to the car in silence, which wasn't awkward, but he wouldn't necessarily label it as companiable. They weren't even holding hands because hers were stuffed into the pockets of her unzipped hoodie.

Ibrahim desperately wanted her to speak but knew that if he pushed her right now, he might spook her. He had no idea what was going through her mind. Sure, what he'd blurted out to his dad hadn't been their plan but it wasn't the end of the world. Was it?

His headache from earlier was making its presence felt again and Ibrahim knew that the best thing to do now was to drop her home and then go straight home himself and hit the sack. This situation would still very much be there in the morning.

CHAPTER TWELVE

Jiya

Feeling decidedly off-kilter, Jiya was very glad that she didn't have a shift at The Lounge and since she didn't have any imminent deadlines, she had decided to stay holed up in her bedroom and read instead. For pleasure.

She had pulled out a well-thumbed copy of an old historical romance she absolutely loved and sitting back against the cold radiator in her room, with the bright summer sunshine beaming in through the window, she had spent the last hour lost in its pages.

She lifted her head and instinctively put her finger between the pages to mark her spot when her mother put her head around the door.

'No homework today?'

Jiya shook her head. 'No. I've got some bits and pieces to do but I'm feeling a bit tired so I thought I'd just take it easy. Was there something you wanted me to do?'

'Yes. Finish your page and come down.' With that, her mother left.

Typical really. She had just said she was tired but obviously her mother hadn't heard her. She probably had a dozen chores waiting for Jiya downstairs.

Feeling somewhat rebellious, Jiya took her time and went down after finishing the scene she had been reading, only to find her mother sitting at the dining table with the tea cosy-covered teapot in front of her beside a mountain of her absolute favourite onion pakoras and a bowl of mint chutney; instantly making her feel a bit guilty.

'You made pakoras?' she practically shrieked as she came to a standstill by the table. 'Thank you, you're a star.'

'Hmm. Now come and sit down.' Jiya sat opposite her mother as she poured a cup of steaming *desi*-style tea. Her mother only put the kettle on if she was seriously short of time. Her preference was always tea made in a saucepan, adding water, milk, sugar and teabags all at the same time – some whole spices if she was feeling decadent – and then simmering it. It tasted a lot richer than tea made using a kettle, but there were times when it hit the spot perfectly. Especially when paired with pakoras.

She loaded a plate up with the savoury fritters and coating the top of one with the minty sauce, she slowly took a bite. This had been exactly what she needed; she just hadn't known it. They were the ultimate comfort food as far as Jiya was concerned.

She had practically inhaled about four of them before her mother spoke. 'Slow down, otherwise you'll start hiccupping in no time. How's Ibrahim? Did you have a chat with him about coming over?'

Jiya did hiccup – it wasn't because she had eaten too fast – and her mother gave her an *I-told-you-so* look. Taking a gulp of the hot, sweet tea and not really savouring it, she looked across at her mother, who for all the world looked like she had asked something perfectly innocuous. They both knew that wasn't the case.

'He's fine.' She jammed another pakora into her mouth. Partly because she hadn't quite assuaged the need for more comfort food – had anyone ever? – and mostly so she didn't have to talk.

'You saw him yesterday?' Her mother poured the sauce over a pakora unhurriedly, and Jiya got the feeling that she was about to be interrogated quite thoroughly.

Her mother's timing was never ideal, but on the back of last night and given how . . . raw she was feeling after Ibrahim's bolt from the blue, Jiya really didn't want this. It was best to have her fill of the snack, nab another cup of tea and dart back upstairs. Until then, she would stick to the facts. She nodded at her mother as she reached for the teapot.

'Leave it, I'll do it. Did he say when he can come and see us?'

'He said he'd let me know this week sometime. He's quite busy at work.'

Her mother poured the tea and then broke a pakora into two, looking at it closely. 'Your father's not very happy about this, but I've managed to talk him round to meeting Ibrahim when he comes and not scaring him off with a stick.'

Her father was still miffed with her but he wasn't ignoring her as completely as he had been. It made her wish all the more that she could come clean and have them understand her point of view for a change and support it.

'Why do I always have to fight for what I want, Ammi? I bet if Jameel had said he wants to study something further, you and Abba would have been over the moon. If he brought home a girl he liked, you and Abba would welcome her with open arms. I know I'm not yours or Abba's favourite but is this all just because I'm a girl?'

Her mother gave her a small smile tinged with sadness.

'Jiya, if I didn't want you to study, you wouldn't be studying. And if I didn't care, you would have been married off to the first boy we found and we would have washed our hands of you.

119

'It's all so different with your generation; the opportunities, the relationships.' She shook her head as she spoke. 'Unfortunately, there was no guide book to tell me what, when, why and how to navigate motherhood when I was finally blessed with it.'

Jiya pushed away her empty plate, surprised at the tiny insight her mother had just given her into her own thoughts and insecurities.

'I'll admit I was very surprised when you said you'd found someone of your own choice, especially when I've always told you to stay away from boys.'

Jiya sensed no censure in her voice, she just sounded matter of fact. She had cupped her hands around the mug, just as Jiya had, and spoke softly.

'You see, Jiya, that's how I was raised. That's usually the way it works; we tend to raise our children similarly to how we've been raised unless there's something obviously wrong and doesn't appeal to your thinking. Like me choosing not to smack you even though I got my fair share of them from your grandmother and you really pushed me at times.'

She grinned at her and Jiya acknowledged that there were plenty of things her mother had been different about now that she mentioned it.

She had been so consumed by what she thought was unfair towards her that she hadn't glanced beyond it or looked at things from her mother's perspective.

'In my case, I was always happy to go along with what my parents told me to do; I didn't fight it and I didn't think I'd turned out too badly. So, I did the same things with you and Jameel. Some things were right, others maybe not,' she shrugged, 'but a lot of it falls somewhere between the two.'

This was the first time in . . . well, forever, that her mother had opened up to her in such a way. It was like speaking to someone completely different.

'Why haven't you ever said any of this stuff before, Ammi?'

She smiled at her, gathering the used plates together. 'I suppose the opportunity has never arisen. Conversations like these are usually triggered by something else so maybe that's what we were waiting for. Help me clear these things away.'

Her mother began putting things away as Jiya started loading the dishwasher.

'So did you have no say in your own marriage?'

'I did to the extent that I was asked if I had any objections. I didn't so . . .' She shrugged again. 'Although I don't think I did too badly in the husband stakes.'

She gave Jiya a conspiratorial smile and she grinned in response.

Putting the last of the Tupperware in the fridge, her mother came and stood beside the sink.

'You bringing a boy home was a surprise that might take your father some time getting used to, but if he's a decent boy and you'll be happy, then I certainly don't have any objections and I don't think he will either. We only want what's best for you and Jameel.

'And as for him being my favourite . . . I'll accept I pamper him a lot but I love you no less. I don't tell you often enough how proud I am of the woman you've become, Jiya, and that's all on me. I come from a generation that doesn't talk about feelings or openly say "I love you" to their children. It's just considered a given that you do.'

Her mother held her chin and kissed her on the temple as Jiya swallowed a pakora-sized lump in her throat, unable to move because her hands were covered in suds.

'Now, finish up in here and then take out the suitcase of your *desi* clothes. I don't want you in jeans when he comes.'

Back to business.

Her mother grabbed the two bunches of coriander lying on the worktop and started taking the leaves off the stalks.

Jiya made her way upstairs, her thoughts careening around her brain like a pinball machine. A myriad of feelings was making its presence felt, the uppermost being confusion and guilt.

She was confused at how different her mother had been with her just now.

Gone was the harassed mum with hundreds of things on her to-do list and just wanting things to be perfect for her son and husband, roping her only daughter in to help make that happen.

Her mother had been relaxed and open, blowing Jiya's idea of what her mother was like clean out of the water.

She didn't feel like picking the book up again so she just lay on her bed, staring at the ceiling.

Though she would describe her exchange with her mother as positive, it strangely left her feeling drained of energy.

She felt guilty about not being more understanding towards her mother and why she was the way she was. Her mother hadn't been open about her own thoughts and struggles, but Jiya wasn't completely oblivious to them. She had just chosen to overlook them.

This then led her to question whether she was really making an effort to be a good enough daughter. Could she do better?

Turning over, she closed her eyes and willed all the frustration she was feeling to disappear, along with the tears she couldn't hold back.

She wasn't a crier by nature, but the feelings inside her were too many to contain.

Her conversation with her mother, her pent-up emotions, her feelings towards Ibrahim, which were getting more and more confusing as time went on, and then there was the bombshell he had dropped on her last night.

And there you had it – the biggest culprit of the turmoil she was feeling, but was just too afraid to admit it.

Jiya sat up in bed and scrubbed her hands across her face. What on earth was she doing? She was supposed to be brave, a go-getter who didn't let obstacles of any kind get in her way. She was supposed to be honest, most of all with herself. Since when did she curl up in bed and cry rather than boldly face what was in front of her?

She was going to complete her MBA and get a damn good job.

Being with Ibrahim was supposed to be a mutually beneficial arrangement. She had no intention of changing her plans for anyone or anything. And he needed to accept that, whether he liked it or not.

But then, he *had* reassured her last night that he *did* understand and that they wouldn't do anything she wasn't comfortable doing.

He was talking about having a fake engagement – if they absolutely had to – so that they could both pursue their plans. It wasn't all that different to being in a fake relationship. And then they could call an end to it when they were both ready.

Plenty of people got engaged and then decided not to be together – it was no big deal. She had merely panicked at the mention of the word 'propose' and she probably had nothing to worry about.

★

Jiya looked at herself in the full-length mirror on her wardrobe door, turning one way, then the other. She hardly ever wore a traditional *salwar kameez* but her mother had insisted that tonight she should.

'It's our culture, Jiya, so if once in a while you have to wear it, it's no big deal. And look how beautiful the print is on this *kameez*.' Her mother had held up the tunic-style *kameez* for her to see and she was right. The paisley print really was beautiful and the colour combination of coral and white was perfect for the summer. The matching trouser-style *salwar* was plain white and looking in the mirror now, Jiya could see that it looked pretty good.

Tightening her ponytail, she left her room to join her family downstairs. They were all in the sitting room, her brother and father on the sofa, Jameel's eyes half on the TV and the other half on his phone, and her mother at the window, peering through the side of the prehistoric net curtains she refused to get rid of.

'Jiya, go and turn the hob off under the korma.'

Shaking her head at her mother's back and earning a slight glare from her father, who had typically looked up just then, she made her way to the kitchen and did as she'd been instructed.

She could see her mother had gone all out this evening. The kitchen table was laden from end to end with an array of food: three different types of curries, pilau rice, buttered naans, samosas, pakoras, sweetmeats and desserts were loaded on the table.

One would think they were expecting a half dozen people for dinner rather than just one Ibrahim Saeed.

Jiya hadn't seen him since the 'proposal bombshell' but she'd had enough time to give what he'd said considerable thought and while what he had suggested deviated from their original plan, it didn't really affect their end goal.

She'd had a few lengthy phone conversations with him and they'd agreed that they'd put off 'getting engaged' for as long as they could but if it helped their cause, then they would consider having a fake engagement.

So, they'd moved onto the next phase of their plan. Ibrahim was coming over to meet her family this evening and her mother had gone to town in preparation and was now firmly ensconced at the window awaiting his arrival.

There was nothing to be nervous about, given that this was all just for show, but she couldn't help feeling a keen sense of anticipation about the evening.

What would her family think of her choice? What would Ibrahim think when he met her family? Would they all get on or would there be awkward silences and moments of painful embarrassment?

All these questions were going round and round in her mind, like a spinning top and the butterflies in her tummy were making her feel jittery and on edge.

'Boo!' Jiya let out a yelp as her brother came behind her and yelled in her ear.

She spun around and slapped him on the arm. 'Don't do that.'

He gave her a cocky grin. 'Are you nervous?'

'No. Why would I be nervous?'

'In case your choice of Mr doesn't make the cut. We might not like him and he'll be out on his ear.'

'Or he might not like *you* and decide to marry me anyway.' She was strangely pleased to have her brother teasing her just then, breaking the tension and showing her attention in his own playful way.

The ringing of the doorbell stopped Jameel from saying anything silly just to rile her up and thankfully, it stopped her from pondering what she'd just said, even if it was just to shut him up.

Jiya went into the hallway and after giving her brother a death stare and shooing him into the sitting room, she opened the door to Ibrahim.

Whenever she thought she might be prepared for the impact he could have on one's senses, she was proved wrong. She would be better off accepting that whenever she clapped eyes on him, he would take her breath away.

Ibrahim was wearing a button-down shirt tucked into jeans and he looked absolutely delicious. His sunglasses were very much in place and if she wasn't mistaken, he'd had his hair trimmed. He took a step forward and a wave of his aftershave hit her senses.

He gave her a smile and taking his glasses off, he pocketed them and then gave her the smaller of the two bunches of flowers he was holding.

'Hi.'

The gesture caught Jiya completely off guard. No one had ever given her flowers and getting them like this, when she least expected it, made her feel all warm and fuzzy inside. She smiled at Ibrahim and moved to the side to let him in.

'They're beautiful.'

'I'm glad you like them. I mean, as your boyfriend I really should know which flowers you like, but since I didn't, I chanced it with these pink ones. By the way, you look incredible. The traditional look suits you.'

Her breath hitched in her chest and she had to look away from his intense gaze. 'Thank you. You don't look all that shabby yourself. And you're here to impress my family, not me.'

She said it more in a bid to bring herself back to earth rather than him, but it didn't work all that effectively. The fact that he'd bought her flowers touched her in a way she didn't want to analyse too closely.

Coward.

'I can't help but be impressive, sweetheart. By the end of this evening, your family will be well and truly signed up to my fan club with a lifetime membership, I promise.'

Shaking her head at his confidence and smiling at the same time, Jiya led him into the sitting room. 'It's show time.'

CHAPTER THIRTEEN

Ibrahim

As far as Ibrahim was aware – and he accepted his experience was somewhat limited in the area – all fathers were predisposed to be suspicious of their daughter's boyfriend. They automatically assumed he was worthless and not good enough for their daughter and spent most of their initial meeting, at least, giving them a stare that could burn a hole in said boyfriend.

Yunus Ahmed was no exception.

He had barely said a word, after a grunted greeting and a handshake that could have juiced a bloody pineapple when Ibrahim had first walked in.

Not that Ibrahim hadn't displayed a bit of strength himself, obviously he had, but Jiya's father had seemed to be out for his blood. And he was totally doing the whole unnerving stare thing. A couple of times, Ibrahim had thought he could try and outstare him.

Nope. Not happening.

The man had an iron grip on his eyelids and he was focused on Ibrahim in a way that made him feel as though all his past sins were signposted in little clouds around his head for the man to see. It made him feel as though he had something to feel guilty about.

Which he did really, given that this was all a big fat lie. Although, having said that, it wasn't as though his daughter wasn't getting anything out of it.

He and Jiya had a mutually beneficial arrangement which was set to work beautifully for both of them. The only thing not working right now – or working too well, depending on your point of view – was the attraction he was feeling towards her.

Not the fake boyfriend kind of attraction. The real kind of attraction a man felt for a woman. The kind of attraction that made him aware of his own heartbeat. That made his body ache to be close to her. The kind of attraction that had his eyes following her each and every move.

She must have felt his eyes on her because she turned to look at him and smiled reassuringly as she came over and sat down at the dining table next to him. Even her smile made him feel things he'd never felt before and he'd been at the receiving end of plenty of smiles.

Pulling his attention away from Jiya and her disapproving father, Ibrahim focused on the positive: Jiya's mother.

She had fallen hook, line and sinker after he had presented her with a rather large selection of flowers and a box of traditional sweets – thanks to his grandmother and her bright ideas – and was in the process of killing him with kindness, presenting one dish after another.

'Jiya told me you like tandoori chicken but you've hardly touched it, my dear.'

Giving her his most charming smile, Ibrahim took a bite of the chicken. Jiya's mother had really gone all out with the food this evening and all of it was delicious.

It was an unwritten rule never to compare someone's cooking to your own mother's, but Jiya's mother really had knocked this one out of the park.

His own mother was reluctant in the kitchen at the best of times and more recently, his sister–in–law had taken over making the family meals.

Was Jiya as good a cook as her mother? He'd never actually asked her that before but now found himself interested in knowing the answer. In fact, he found himself wanting to know so much more about her than he had about anyone before.

Except once. Many moons ago when he actually believed in fidelity and marriage.

More than perturbed at the thought that had come from nowhere, he focused his mind on the moment.

He felt like he'd been stuffed like the proverbial turkey as they carried the desserts and drinks into the sitting room, where thankfully, he wasn't in Jiya's father's line of sight. Ibrahim didn't want him souring what he knew would be the best part of tonight's meal, although his position wasn't all that great given that he was sandwiched between Jiya's mother and a huge table lamp on a table beside the sofa.

'Jiya, serve the dessert. Do you like *kheer*, Ibrahim? Today's the first time Jiya's tried making it, following my mother's recipe for an authentic *desi* rice pudding.'

Ibrahim raised his eyebrow at Jiya, who in turn narrowed her eyes at him. 'Really? I have to try some then.'

She smiled faux sweetly as she handed him a bowl filled with the creamy dessert.

At her mother's request, Jiya went to make tea and Ibrahim was certain that he would likely explode before the evening was over.

'So, what is it you do exactly? Jiya said you work for the family business?'

The question he had expected Jiya's father to ask was being asked by her brother Jameel, while said father ignored him, though Ibrahim was sure his ears were very much tuned into the conversation.

'Yeah, I'm a solicitor and work in that capacity for the business.' He gave the usual spiel when asked about his role at the family business.

Many people assumed that because he and Zafar worked for the family business, they didn't really have serious jobs and were simply figureheads.

Oh, how wrong they all were.

If anyone was a figurehead of the business, it was the old man Saeed Senior himself. But these folks didn't need to know that.

Ibrahim discovered that Jameel wasn't as empty-headed as Jiya had made out, talking about various topics with good all-round knowledge, though he seemed most knowledgeable about cars and related mechanics.

'My brother Ashar likes tinkering with motorbikes but he's pretty knowledgeable about cars too.'

'You're not talking about cars again are you, Jameel? You know, Ibrahim, I've told him several times that being a mechanic in a garage won't be as rewarding as an office job, but this boy doesn't listen. The mechanic we know,' she was moving her hands about just like her daughter and Ibrahim suppressed a smile, 'both his knees need surgery now because of his work. It's not a good job to have.'

Ibrahim looked at Jameel, who rolled his eyes.

'Actually, Auntie, things have changed. What Jameel is interested in is actually engineering and it's a pretty well-respected and well-paying profession.'

He turned back to Jiya's brother. 'You should definitely do something in engineering if it makes you happy. In fact, if you like I can introduce you to Ash – you can pick his brain. You've got a clear passion for it and I think it's important to do what makes *you* happy.'

He'd done what he had thought would make his father happy and while he enjoyed what he did, it had never been his passion as such.

'It's easy to say that when fathers are there to pay the bills. That's why your generation has the liberty of choice and focusing on what makes you "happy".'

'Yunus!' Jiya's mother looked at her husband in horror. It was the most he'd spoken the whole evening but the bitterness in his voice was clear to everyone.

Just then Jiya came in with tea and her mother diverted the conversation deftly to more casual topics and, apart from her old man, they were all relaxed and happy.

He just looked supremely bored and Ibrahim had the oddest urge to needle a reaction out of him but held back. He felt sorry for the guy who in the future would actually want to come and get Yunus Ahmed's approval to be with Jiya.

The feeling of anxiousness that crept in at that thought pulled him up short.

Why did such a thought make him feel restless?

Feeling like he needed fresh air and that he had been there long enough, Ibrahim thanked Jiya's parents for their hospitality and promising her mother that yes, he would come over again soon, he made his way towards the front door.

'Jiya, go and see Ibrahim out.'

She did as her mother asked and walked out into the balmy night with him towards his car.

Ibrahim thought of himself as a grounded man who was in touch with reality, but seeing the set-up of Jiya's home, the family dynamic and their struggles made him rethink how privileged he actually was.

There were no signs of the ostentation he often found in his own place when they were hosting guests and the simplicity of their home made him more comfortable than some of the rooms in his own, which had been decorated by indifferent interior designers at his mother's insistence. In fact, Jiya's house charmed him with vibes of a *home*.

And then there was the element of work. Sure, he worked hard but he'd never wondered about whether or not he'd get a job or how he might fund his further education or how much he'd have to prove himself in order to succeed. He'd actually taken most of that for granted.

But here he could see that Jiya was waitressing to fund her MBA, her brother was struggling to find a job that was meaningful to him and their mother was actively trying to better her children's future and he was fairly sure that as far as she was concerned, finding a husband for her daughter was her way of doing right by her daughter, even though her daughter balked at the idea.

'Thank God that's over. Such a drag.' Jiya gave a beleaguered sigh for emphasis and Ibrahim turned to face her, resting his arm against the side of the car.

'It wasn't bad at all. Your mum's such a gem and your brother's cool. But your dad was definitely the star of the show. I've never heard a man talk so much or be so bowled over by my presence before, I'm truly touched.'

She smacked his arm while giggling at the same time. 'Stop it. He's just a bit shy when he meets people for the first time.'

'Is that what you call it?'

'OK, so he was a tad unreceptive but he'll warm up over time.'

'Hmm. Well, it's your turn next under my crew's spotlight so let me know what day's good for you. Preferably before the party.'

She didn't say anything but he could tell she was deep in thought. 'Spit it out, J, what's on your mind?'

She was averting her eyes, staring at her feet and her mouth was downturned. Ibrahim lifted her chin, forcing her to look at him.

'What is it?'

'I felt guilty tonight. I'm basically lying to them outright and I felt so rubbish.' Her shoulders slumped and she heaved a sigh.

He knew exactly how she felt because he had felt the same way when her mother had been speaking to him this evening. But then he had reminded himself of the alternative.

'I know exactly what you mean. I felt the same thing too but we really had no choice, remember? Your family weren't listening to you and were looking for you to settle down with someone; something you weren't up for. And my father was going down a similar track, albeit with a different approach. This way we're getting a chance to think about what *we* want and pursuing our own goals. That can't be a bad thing, can it?'

She shook her head but he could see that she wasn't all that convinced and still felt uncomfortable about what they were doing.

'OK, what's our alternative? If you don't want to lie to your family and pretend to be my girlfriend, what are you going to do? Because I'll be honest with you, right now, I have no other solution that would be just as effective.'

'I don't know.'

He couldn't quite put his finger on why, but her answer irritated him.

'Fine. When you come up with something or decide what you want to do next, let me know.'

She looked up at him and her pensive expression slowly morphed into a full-out scowl, pout and all.

'You don't have to sound so put-out, you know. I was just telling you how I felt.' Pulling herself up, she gave him one last withering look and walked back towards the front door, leaving him standing beside his car. She was being oversensitive with him about something she had no answer to herself.

Ibrahim got into his car and firing it up, he made his way home the long way, hoping that the drive would calm him down before he got home and praying that he wouldn't come across his father.

Jiya

'I liked him.'

'Hmm?' Jiya picked up another bowl out of the draining rack and began drying it.

'I said I liked him, he's a very decent boy and handsome too. He even offered to speak to his brother about Jameel.'

Her mother was tidying up the kitchen after Ibrahim had left and Jiya was helping her put things away while the men of the house were typically vegetating in front of the TV.

'He genuinely is a good boy, the kind of boy your father and I would be happy to see you with.'

If only you knew that it's all a big fat lie.

'He was polite and courteous despite your father being glum with him, which I'll talk to him about. Allah knows what got into him.'

He probably smelled a rat, that's what!

'You haven't met anyone from his family yet, have you?'

'Only his brothers, but he wants me to someday next week.'

'Well, once you've done that, perhaps we can invite them over and—'

'Woah, what's the rush, Ammi? You've only just met Ibrahim.'

Her mother looked at her in alarm. 'There's no rush, I was just thinking ahead. Is that a crime? And what's happened to you all of a sudden? I thought you'd be happy after this evening.'

Jiya hung the dish cloth back on its hook and dried her own hands. 'I was happy. I mean, I am happy. I just don't want to rush anything. Let's just see how things work out. Besides, I've still got my MBA to complete.'

That's it, Jiya, keep your eye on the target.

'I'm tired so I'm going up. Can we finish up in here tomorrow?'

Her mother looked at her in puzzlement before nodding.

As she reached the door, she turned back and walked towards her mother.

'Thank you for today, Ammi.' She kissed her on the cheek. 'You were brilliant.'

Her mother smiled and patted her cheek. 'Hmm. Go and get some sleep. *Shabba khair.*'

'Good night.'

Jiya's mind was in utter chaos, the commotion of thoughts in her mind giving her a headache, while the churning of feelings she was experiencing made her insides feel tight, almost as though she was going to be sick.

The two questions that kept coming up in her mind were the ones Ibrahim had asked her.

What's our alternative? What are you going to do?

If only she knew. If she had a solution, she would have implemented it by now; surely he knew that?

But the annoying thing was that he was right.

They didn't really have much of a choice. Either she gave in to what her parents wanted and settled down with a husband of their choice and kissed her dreams goodbye or she could pretend to be with Ibrahim until she was done with her MBA.

She could cross any other bridges when she got to them. She didn't really want to think that far ahead anyway.

She got ready for bed and snuggling into the duvet, Jiya stared at the ceiling. In her heart she knew what she was going to do, but the guilt about lying to her family was real. It hadn't really hit her until she had seen the look of approval on her mother's face when she had first seen Ibrahim. It had cut her straight to her core.

And with her mother's recent softening towards her, the guilt of betraying her was beginning to intensify.

CHAPTER FOURTEEN

Jiya

Jiya wiped her hands down her *kameez* and then grimaced. It was another printed *salwar kameez*, floral this time, in pastel shades. She'd had the day off and since her mother had known she was going to Ibrahim's house this evening to meet his family, she had helped her decide what to bring and what she should wear. She had even given Jiya a pair of her own earrings which matched.

Guilt level in that moment: unbearable.

Ibrahim had picked her up since she didn't drive and she didn't want to use public transport while lugging all the things she had with her.

They had both been quiet in the car after a stilted 'hello' to each other and Jiya was determined not to be the one who caved.

She lasted all of five minutes before she couldn't handle the awkward silence in the car and the droning of the radio began to annoy her.

'Only because we've got to spend the rest of the evening together and I don't want there to be any awkwardness in front of your family, I suggest we call a truce. But just for the record, I'm still annoyed with you.' They had stopped at traffic lights and as he turned to look at her with that ridiculous arching eyebrow move, Jiya stuck her tongue out at him.

'What are we like, six years old again?'

'Well, you've certainly got the understanding of a six-year-old boy.'

'Huh, is that right? Because from what I remember, you were the one having trouble sticking to the script, not me.'

Jiya narrowed her eyes at him and carried on looking in his direction until he chanced a glance her way.

'Jesus, you look like your dad when you do that.' And then he laughed.

If he hadn't been driving, she would have probably gone straight for his jugular with her bare hands but she wanted to live more than she wanted to pulverise him. She couldn't chance him crashing the car.

She would get him though. When he least expected it, she would launch an attack of epic proportions. Maybe then this feeling of guilt, restlessness and . . . and . . . weirdness, yes, weirdness would go away. A feeling that had only intensified when, despite being annoyed with him, her heart had skipped a beat at the sight of him when he'd come to pick her up.

He'd been a complete angel with her mother, as though butter wouldn't melt in his mouth. The fiend.

Hello Auntie, yes Auntie, no Auntie, three bags full Auntie.

Aaargh. It had driven her mad.

'A particularly sage old woman once told me that if you frown like that, you'll get permanent frown lines on your forehead. So, if I were you, Miss Ahmed, I'd stop.' He grinned at her and she let out a fake laugh.

'Ha, ha, ha, you're so funny, Ibrahim. A big round of applause for you.' And she clapped him on his thigh a few times. Hard.

The third time she clapped her hand on his thigh, he trapped it under his own and held it there firmly. She could feel the strength of the muscle under her hand and realised belatedly how intimately placed her hand was. He wasn't squeezing her hand hard or hurting her at all but she could feel the heat from his hand permeating through her own and coursing up her arm. They were stopped at a red light again and he turned to look at her.

His eyes were intense and she felt as though he were looking deep into her soul. As though he could see all her thoughts and feelings and knew exactly what was going through her mind at that precise moment in time.

The fact that she wanted to move her hand upwards and feel the tensing and relaxing of the muscle. That she wanted to take her hand down towards his knee and then back up again and see how far he would let her go. She curled her fingers slightly and felt an answering squeeze of his own hand.

She swept her tongue across her bottom lip to moisten it and swallowed to alleviate the sudden dryness in her mouth. His eyes followed the movement and she felt him squeeze her hand again and pull it slightly closer towards himself. Upwards.

Someone pressed their horn behind them loud and clear and they were both shaken out of the moment. Ibrahim pressed the accelerator and the car glided forward as he gradually loosened the grip on her hand and placed his own on the gear stick between them, clearing his throat.

Jiya pulled her hand back and grasped it with the other, looking out of the window on her side and trying to regain some of the equilibrium she'd just blown in a moment of madness.

She wasn't going to even try to figure out what had just happened.

They drove for another ten minutes, and then they were pulling up outside what he had called his *humble abode*.

The only thing humble at that moment had been Ibrahim's *fake girlfriend*.

Jiya got out of the car and lifted her head to take in the sight, her fingers gripping the open car door tightly. Before her was what she would probably call a mansion. It was absolutely huge. She knew nothing of architectural terms and definitions, but she knew that it was bloody big and unless she had a map, she'd get lost in there.

She should have known it was this big when Ibrahim had stopped in front of a set of electric gates and driven into a mini car park in front of the house. Who knew properties like this could be found so close to London?

All the feelings that moment of madness had elicited were replaced by a sense of sheer nervousness and terror at the thought of going inside and she rubbed her hands down her *kameez* again.

Before she could turn tail and flee, the front door opened and Harry sauntered towards her.

'You look cute, Shortcake. I don't think I've ever seen you in traditional clothes before. I approve.'

'Your house is huge. Is it even considered a house?'

'How am I supposed to know? Maybe you can use that as a conversation starter with Dad.'

'She'll be avoiding Dad.' Ibrahim had come around and was standing just behind her. She turned in his direction and saw the little group of cars parked in front of the garage doors behind him.

'If all those cars are in front of the garage doors, what's inside the garage? No, don't answer that. It's ridiculously intrusive of me to ask. Sorry.'

Ibrahim looked over her head at Harry and they both laughed.

He pulled her close to him, his hands on her waist and her own hands landing on his chest.

'Relax, you have nothing to be nervous about, I promise. You're an absolute treasure and everyone will know it, so just take it easy, all right? Besides, no one inside there is as scary as your Abba, trust me.'

She smiled at the mention of her father and felt some of the tension leave her.

Of course, when she said some of the tension, it was only a very small percentage. In single figures. She was still feeling terrified about going into such a big and expensive-looking house and meeting a family that lived in a place like this.

'You do realise that we're from the family that live in a place like this?' Ibrahim looked at her with a half-smile and a quirked eyebrow, pointing between himself and Harry.

Jiya clapped a hand across her mouth. 'Did I say that out loud?'

'Yes, you did.' Harry grinned at her. 'You're babbling, which means you're nervous, Shortcake. Don't be. Everyone inside has been watered and fed and is under strict instructions not to bite you. Unless you start babbling, of course.'

'Will you shut up? You're not helping her.' Ibrahim glared at Harry, who shrugged unrepentantly and made his way towards the front door. 'Ignore him. You'll be fine, I promise, but as soon as you feel you need a time-out, you just say the word, all right? We'll get out of there before you can say Bob's your uncle.'

She let out a little giggle. 'I've got a distant uncle called Bob, though that's his nickname, of course.'

He grinned at her. 'Of course you have. Now, shall we?'

'We just need to grab the things I brought.'

Ibrahim

Ibrahim stared at his father, dumbstruck.

The man was smiling.

He was actually smiling as he spoke to Jiya.

Spoke *to* Jiya. Not *at* Jiya.

He couldn't believe what he was seeing. His father was talking to her as though he'd known her for a lot longer than an hour and they were getting along like the best of friends.

'What the hell?' He muttered under his breath.

'What do you mean?' He turned to look at Harry, who was standing beside him eating probably his sixth biscuit.

'What?'

'You said "what the hell" so I asked what you meant.' He popped the rest of the biscuit in his mouth, the glutton.

Ibrahim shook his head at his brother. 'I don't get it. How are they getting along so well? That's not what I expected.'

He had expected his father to act cold and condescending towards Jiya because she was the reason – as far as his father was concerned – why Ibrahim wasn't doing as he wanted.

The fact that they were getting along so well was causing him to wonder what his father was playing at.

'Oh, that. That's because of me.'

He turned to look at his kid brother and raised his eyebrows in question.

Rolling his eyes as he snagged another custard cream, Harry explained. 'Like you, I expected the old man to look down his nose at her and then ask all sorts of inane questions and make her feel uncomfortable. Deliberately. So, just before you both arrived, I told him that she's doing an MBA and she's really interested in business and the fact that he was so successful with ours, and that's it. The man felt ten feet tall and has been going out of his way to further impress her and show her how important and great a man he is.'

143

He clapped Ibrahim on the shoulder. 'You've got to learn to play the game, mate.'

'You manipulative bastard. That's brilliant!'

'Mind your mouth, there are ladies in the room.' His grandmother came up behind them and poked him in the leg with her walking stick.

'Where?' This earned Harry a poke but she ruined the moment by grinning at him.

'Rogue. I'm going to go and rescue that girl because none of you are brave enough to. The poor thing has been enduring your father's speech for fifty-nine minutes longer than she should have.' She waddled across to where Jiya was sitting across from his father.

'Nasir, stop monopolising the girl and let the rest of us have a chance to talk to her. Jiya, come dear, let me show you around a little.'

Linking arms with her, his grandmother steered her towards the door, where he was standing with Harry. 'You coming?'

Ibrahim followed along, leaving his brother behind.

'Tell me, Jiya, what sort of desserts do you have where you work?'

'Don't tell her, she's got diabetes.'

'I'm mildly diabetic, sweetheart, not dead, but these tyrants won't let a girl enjoy the life she has left.'

She pulled her arm free of Jiya's outside in the hallway. 'Right, you both owe me one. Now go and explore. And Ibrahim,' she pointed her walking stick at him, almost hitting him on his chest as he moved out of the way, 'behave yourself. You tell me if he's anything less than a gentleman, Jiya.' With that, she toddled off towards the kitchen.

Shaking his head at his grandmother and her unique style, he caught Jiya looking at him with a peculiar expression.

'What?'

'Don't you feel it at all?'

'Feel what?'

'The guilt. It's killing me, Ibrahim. These people are so lovely and we're lying to them. I'm so going to hell for this. In fact, I'm going to be fast-tracked. *Do not pass go, do not collect two hundred.*'

'Don't start this again, please. Let's just enjoy the evening and then we'll see where to go from here – agreed?'

She nodded reluctantly. Ibrahim knew what she meant, even though he wasn't verbally agreeing with her. Seeing the look of approval from all members of the family had made him feel like a traitor but what choice did he have?

'So, do I get a tour of this palace?'

Pushing away the feelings that Jiya and his conscience were generating, he took hold of her hand and took her into the family sitting room she hadn't yet seen.

Seeing the awe and delight on her face definitely helped do away with some of those niggling doubts he was feeling and she seemed to be happier too. She seemed to find each space worthy of a 'wow', but when he took her to the place which he thought was most deserving of such a description, she was quiet.

'So, what do you think?' He stood on the terrace that overlooked the garden and parklands beyond. It was a serene and peaceful vista and never failed to take his breath away. Jiya stepped forward towards the railings surrounding the terrace.

'Is that a church in the distance?'

'Yeah. Sometimes you can hear the bells toll all the way here. Beautiful, isn't it?'

She nodded and turned to look at him. 'This is probably my favourite part of the whole place. It's so calm and peaceful, like we're the only people here.'

Her eyes were bright and all her pent-up tension seemed to fall away in that moment. The light evening breeze moved tendrils of her hair onto her face and he instinctively lifted his hand to push them back, stroking her cheek at the same time.

Ibrahim had always found romantic comparisons cheesy, but at that moment, the only way he could describe the feeling was by comparing it to touching the petals of a rose. Soft, silky and delicate. Her cheek was warm and he felt compelled to keep touching it. He ran his fingers down from her temple and cupped her cheek.

She moved her face towards his hand and as she did, he placed his other hand at her hip. Her own hands had moved to his waist as she looked up at him with those deep, coffee-coloured eyes.

He hadn't said anything to her but when he'd seen her come out to meet him, he'd been struck anew by how gorgeous she was and it had been a true test of patience keeping his hands to himself.

When she'd put her hand on his thigh in the car, he had been surprised that the car hadn't careened off the road or gone up in flames because of the reaction it had invoked in him.

What was it about this woman that had his thoughts short-circuiting? His insides were in knots and his feelings were completely conflicted. He knew he shouldn't be getting this close to her but he couldn't help himself.

An invisible force was compelling him to lower his head and claim her lips in a kiss he knew he would feel the impact of right to his core, and since the teaser he'd had that day on the South Bank, he couldn't bring himself to hold back.

She sighed into his mouth and Ibrahim pressed forward, closing the gap between them by pulling her even closer to himself. She moved her hands up from his waist to his chest, further inflaming his desire for her, which was building up at warp speed.

He tentatively pressed his tongue against the seam of her lips and she opened up with her next breath, allowing him entry into the silky cavern of her mouth. She was doing some exploring of her own with both her tongue and her hands.

Her fingers were running through his hair, making his skull and spine tingle as sensations snaked their way down. She pressed herself even closer and as he felt her breasts brush against his chest, he thought he was going to combust on the spot.

He moved his hands from her hips to her waist, up to her face and back down to her waist before moving them round to cup her behind.

Jiya broke away on a soft gasp, pressing her forehead against his shoulder. Her hands were in fists against his chest and her breathing was as laboured as his own.

'What is happening with us?' Her voice was low and hoarse and it stoked his lust further.

'I don't know, but I'm struggling to fight it.'

She stepped away after a few moments and looked out at the garden, giving him a chance to get his own reaction under control.

'I hated how the evening ended yesterday, Jiya. It left me feeling so shit.'

'Me too. I . . .'

A discreet throat-clearing by the door pulled his attention and he found his sister-in-law Reshma standing there, a smile on her face.

Great.

'Dinner's ready.'

Turning away from the railing, Jiya smiled at Reshma nervously, tucking tendrils of hair behind her ear. 'I'll come down with you.'

Giving him a half-smile, she went down with Reshma, leaving him standing on the terrace wondering how he was going to get through the rest of the evening without reaching for his *fake girlfriend* again. Even though he knew kissing her had been a mistake, he couldn't seem to muster up any regret.

But he couldn't risk doing it again.

CHAPTER FIFTEEN

Jiya

'Thanks for an amazing evening. I had a great time.'

Ibrahim's family had been nothing but warm and welcoming. Jiya had been prepared to be interrogated by his father quite ruthlessly and found out for the imposter that she was, but nothing of the sort had happened. All the nervousness she'd been feeling before her visit had melted away under their affection.

The only awkwardness was what had settled between her and Ibrahim after . . . the moment she wouldn't name. They had both been quiet during the drive back to her house, Jiya only speaking to thank him. She pulled the lever to open the car door but it didn't open. 'Umm, you need to unlock the doors, Ibrahim.'

Smiling, he shook his head and kept his hands on the steering wheel. The street lights shone on half of his face, casting the other half in shadow, making him look mysterious. His cheekbones and jawline were highlighted and his eyes shone in the light, making her want to just sit there and keep looking at him.

God, he was gorgeous.

And there was her problem. Of course, she had acknowledged right at the beginning that he was an attractive man and her being a red-blooded female attracted to the opposite sex . . . well, she found him very pleasing on the eye. But at some point, finding him pleasing on the eye had turned into actually wanting him.

There, she'd acknowledged it.

Jiya wanted Ibrahim.

She wanted him in a way she had never wanted another man before. In fact, she had never really felt this way about any other man before. She'd had plenty of crushes on celebs – hello Chris Hemsworth! – but she'd never had a boyfriend. Her experience with Ibrahim was completely novel.

The thing with acknowledging that she wanted him was that it also gave rise to the conflict she was feeling about him being in her life. More specifically, the reason he was *currently* a part of her life.

'Stop. Don't do it.' His deep voice cut through her thoughts with precision.

'Don't do what?'

'You're overthinking something, I can tell. Don't.'

She gave him what she hoped was a smile but might have come across as a grimace.

'Thoughts are going around in my head and I need to try and make sense of them, otherwise I feel as though they'll consume me. I know you don't want to hear it but I do feel guilty about lying to everyone. You know your dad invited me and my family to your grandmother's birthday? He said he'd like to meet my family.'

Those weren't specifically the thoughts going around in her head at that moment but she wasn't ready to tell him what she was really thinking about, not when she barely understood it herself.

'He did?' Ibrahim sounded as shocked as she'd been when his father had extended the invitation. 'He said nothing to me about it. What are you going to do?'

'I don't know.'

'There's no harm in them meeting each other. In fact, it works in our favour.'

'How so?'

'They'll all realise that they don't need to be setting us up with anyone else because they'll see how happy we are with each other.'

'And what about when we're no longer with each other? I still want to finish my MBA and work, Ibrahim.'

'That's not happening before the party is it, so we'll cross that bridge when we get to it. Just focus on what's happening right now. Today. Like what happened on the terrace.'

She turned her head towards him so fast her hair whipped her on her face. Her cheeks bloomed with heat and the look on his face told her he'd seen it.

The one thing she'd been avoiding thinking about since it had happened.

The kiss.

An experience like no other.

An avalanche of sensations and feelings, enough to consume her whole if she let it. And that was what scared her. Her feelings were coalescing in a way she was beginning to fear she would have no control over.

'We need to talk about it, Jiya. We're attracted to each other, Jiya, and the kisses we've shared are testament to that.'

She tried to gauge what was going on in his mind from his expression, but failed. The lighting was bad enough but his face gave nothing of his feelings away.

She had only just acknowledged to herself that she wanted him, and to have him say that he was attracted to her too, put her in uncharted territory.

Jiya's mind was in a complete tizzy. It felt like they had both agreed to be in a fake relationship a long time ago and so much had happened since then but at the same time, it felt like they'd only just met and started to get to know each other.

How could they be attracted to each other like this? That's not what was supposed to happen. And what about their original agreement?

'So, what about it?'

She turned towards him as best as she could and saw that he too had turned in his seat to face her more fully with his right arm resting on the steering wheel.

His eyes glittered under the street light and Jiya's mind went back to the look she had seen in them just before he had lowered his head and kissed her just a few hours ago but felt like a lot longer.

An errant part of her wanted to experience all those sensations again and that left her feeling confused. What was happening to her?

Ibrahim leaned towards her slightly, getting her attention, and as her eyes locked with his, all thoughts fled her mind. If she could, Jiya would spend the rest of the night sitting exactly where she was quite happily, basking in the warmth of Ibrahim's presence.

He lifted his hand and rested his finger against her temple before slowly dragging it down, leaving a path of electric shocks in its wake. She swallowed down the dryness in her throat but it didn't work. The air in the car felt charged with . . . something she couldn't name and she was finding it hard to pull in a deep enough breath to help her brain function in that moment.

He was smiling as he looked into her eyes and she could swear she saw the same, numerous thoughts swirling in their depths, making her feel as though he understood perfectly what she was going through.

'Don't turn and look, but your brother is coming towards the car and he's watching us. Now would be a good time to show him what we want him to see.'

Her soaring thoughts jerked to a stop as his words penetrated the thick fog that was beginning to cloud her brain. *Huh?!*

He was pretending because her brother was watching. He was in complete control of their situation; it was her who was having trouble keeping the fake separate from reality.

She was beginning to want something that she had sworn she didn't at the start of this whole charade and something which wasn't even on offer. That's not what Ibrahim wanted from their arrangement and she needed to keep her eyes on her end goal, except his roaming fingers were distracting her to the point where thinking coherently was becoming seriously difficult.

Ibrahim's voice was a husky whisper as he spoke. 'At least now, he'll have seen us together and he'll be able to tell your parents that we're serious about each other. You need to look less like you're headed for the dentist's chair though, sweetheart.'

She gave him what she hoped was a confident smile but felt tremulous. The going was getting tough and she couldn't afford to crumble or fall just as things were getting serious.

Ibrahim

Jiya had been quiet for most of the ride, a strange awkwardness settling between them after they'd left his place.

During dinner, she'd been kept busy with one family member or another and he'd had some time to think about where he was at with Jiya.

If he went with his gut feeling, he'd say he wanted to explore the attraction between them.

Jiya Ahmed was clever, attractive, spontaneous and had a cracking sense of humour. What was there not to like?

Being with someone like that was a no-brainer as far as Ibrahim was concerned but Jiya wasn't just anyone.

Jiya was also the girl who was trying to forge a path for herself in a setting where the odds were stacking against her. Her family was lovely, but by her own admission, they didn't understand her desire for something different from what they wanted for her. They didn't back her dreams with the kind of fire she had for them and Ibrahim couldn't complicate things further for her by letting his attraction for her take centre stage and start calling the shots.

The whole point of their arrangement was to help them – both of them – get out of unwanted situations, not plunge them back into a situation of his making that was just as complicated.

And he was just about to come clean with her about his thoughts when he had spotted her brother making his way towards where he had parked.

Jiya still looked like a rabbit caught in headlights and it made Ibrahim want to laugh. She was seriously the cutest mix of sugar and spice. She could be as sharp as a tack at times and at other times, well, less so. But strangely, he found it to be an endearing habit, adding to her appeal.

The soft wispy hairs beside her temple felt like the softest down as he brushed them away from her face but kept his fingers against them, savouring the softness and the warmth. Her eyes were as wide as saucers and as she bit her lower lip, he curled the fingers of his free hand into a fist.

I'm trying to do the right thing here, Jiya. Help a guy out!

Before either of them moved, Jameel interrupted them by knocking on the window beside Jiya, grinning at her as she jumped.

Her expression morphed into a scowl as Ibrahim unlocked the doors and stepped out of the car at the same time as Jiya.

'Fancy seeing you two here. Tell me, Ibrahim, did my sister scare off your family?' Jameel tugged on Jiya's ponytail and she tried to elbow him. 'You know she's got this dodgy habit of talking to herself? I'm giving you fair warning mate, jet while you can.'

'Have you finished?' Jiya huffed at her brother and Ibrahim made his way round the car towards the pair, extending his hand to shake Jameel's.

'As expected, my family loved her and can't wait to meet the rest of you. Have you been out for the evening?'

'Nah, nothing so exciting. My mum had a package she wanted delivered to a friend's place, so I just went to do that. Anyway, hopefully see you around. And you,' he turned to face his sister, 'don't be too long. Mum's standing at the window watching. I saw her precious nets moving.'

Ibrahim laughed at the face Jiya pulled at her brother as he sauntered off before she turned to face him.

'I should go.'

He didn't want her to go. He wanted to cup her sweet face in his hands and kiss her again. He wanted to run his lips across hers and move up her cheeks and then back down, inhaling the scent of her perfume on her neck.

But his *wants* weren't what was important then. It was respecting the boundaries he knew he shouldn't cross and which he knew if he did, he would always regret it.

Running a slightly unsteady hand through his hair, he gave her a single nod. 'Yeah.'

He watched her close the front door after waving to him, not wanting to risk a hug or even a peck on the cheek with her mum's eyes trained on them, and then he made his way back, giving both the engine and the speakers a good workout as he made his way home.

Although his mind was at odds with itself just then, he knew he had made the right decision. He couldn't risk what they were working towards and hurting Jiya in the process, just to satisfy what he knew wouldn't be a long-term thing with her. He had been there, done that and wasn't keen to experience that toxic cocktail of emotions that came as a side when becoming entangled in something that had the label of 'forever' attached to it. *No siree!*

The lights were still on when he pulled up in the driveway but the hallway was quiet as he stepped through it.

'You've certainly got a spring in your step, son.' Ibrahim just about stopped himself from visibly flinching at his father's voice from behind as he made his way towards the kitchen.

What was with the guy? Ambushing people when they least wanted to speak to him, which was usually most of the time. He turned to face him.

'I must say, I'm impressed with your choice. Jiya's quite a lovely girl.'

He theatrically looked behind him to see who his father was addressing, his hand on his chest for effect. 'You're impressed by *my* choice? Wow, Dad.'

'No need to be facetious. She truly is a good choice. She's focused and has the right ideas for her future. Remind me again, how long have you known her?'

'*Daaad*, there you are! Mum's looking for you, wondering where you are.' Harry came down the hallway and Ibrahim breathed a sigh of relief.

Thank God for little brothers. Sometimes.

'What for?' His father was unimpressed as Harry shrugged his shoulders.

Ibrahim took advantage of his father's distraction at being summoned by his wife and made his escape, followed by Harry.

'Thanks for that.'

'Hmm. Seems like you've got a lot to be thanking me for lately, brother. God only knows how you'll ever repay the favour.'

He looked at Harry suspiciously. 'What do you want?'

'I'm glad you asked. Ash will be down any minute now demanding my head on a platter because he thinks I've cleaned out the tank of his motorbike and you will be my knight in shining armour.' He batted his eyelashes and Ibrahim quelled the urge to barf in his face.

'And *have* you cleaned out the tank in his bike?'

'Yes.' He grinned unrepentantly. 'I'm a busy man, Ibs. Got places to go, people to see and I needed transportation. His bike and key were both at home, so . . . *mi casa es su casa* and all.' He shrugged again.

'Just so I can pencil it into my diary, when are you planning on growing up and not being a royal pain in the arse?'

'That tone of voice doesn't sound very grateful all of a sudden.'

'HAROON!' They heard Ashar bellow from upstairs.

'Don't forget how much you and Jiya owe me.'

'I'll leave her to pay her own debts.'

'Where is he?' Ashar stalked into the room and spotted Harry standing behind a three-seater sofa. 'You!' He jabbed his finger in the air in Harry's direction. 'You are such a . . .'

Using every ounce of his power of negotiation, Ibrahim just about managed to placate Ashar, promising to report Harry's behaviour to Zafar and have him pay to refuel his bike for the next two tankfuls.

Obviously, Ibrahim would be paying out of his own pocket because he 'owed' the junior master manipulator. He was clearly learning well from their father.

Once he was sure Harry wouldn't end the evening with a broken nose, the three of them settled down to watch the highlights from the football matches they had missed earlier that day but as much as he loved it, he couldn't focus on the game.

His mind kept going back to Jiya. Spending time with her, talking to her, holding her and kissing her were fast becoming things he wanted to be doing a lot more of, even though the rational part of his brain promptly reminded him that it wasn't a good idea.

He wouldn't go as far as saying he had gone out with half the women in the city but he had enough experience of dating to know that what he felt for Jiya seemed to be a feeling exclusive to her. And he would love to explore that further, but he wasn't willing to pay the price for it.

If he told Jiya what he was beginning to want, things which were going pretty smoothly till now would either come to a screeching halt or take a detour down some hideously bumpy road and neither prospect filled Ibrahim with confidence.

She might reciprocate his feelings and want to act on their attraction, which he knew was mutual, but Jiya wasn't a girl out for a fling. She had told him categorically that she'd never had a boyfriend before. If they decided to pursue anything, she might expect promises of forever from him, a thought which made his heart sink.

Alternatively, she might get supremely pissed off with him for going rogue on their plan and decide to pull the plug on it, leaving him open to his father's machinations, another thought which made his heart sink further.

The sofa dipped beside him and he turned to find Zafar next to him. Reshma came in moments later and handed her husband a steaming mug and he silently took it from her. She caught Ibrahim looking at her and, giving him a small smile, she walked back out.

If he didn't come up with a permanent way to stop his father from arranging his life, that scene he'd just witnessed could well become his own future. An unknown face would walk into the room and hand him his coffee with a smile but derail his life in a way that could bring a man to his knees. Ibrahim suppressed a shudder at the thought, not wanting the nightmare to linger any further.

It was all well and good to leave future problems in the future to be dealt with later, and to focus on his present and what he was doing with Jiya, but the threat of Zafar's life becoming his own was very real.

Once Jiya had completed her MBA and was working, what would he do?

His father was nothing if not tenacious. He would mount another attack in no time, before Ibrahim had a chance to think of a way forward.

He was always just a phone call away from a potential bride and he'd waste no time in presenting him with a suitable candidate as soon as Jiya walked through the revolving doors of some glossy city firm.

He needed to come up with a solid, long-term plan for himself sooner rather than later.

CHAPTER SIXTEEN

Ibrahim

The week before the party saw Ibrahim personally going to Jiya's house to invite her family to his grandmother's party.

He'd seen her a couple of times since she had come to his place to meet his family but those meetings hadn't been long enough for him to be satisfied. Hopefully, after he'd spoken to her parents about coming to the party, he'd get a chance to have a moment or two with her.

'I speak on behalf of my whole family in saying that we'd be really pleased if you'd join us.' Jiya's father looked at him with the same disdain he had the day he'd first met Ibrahim and refused to move forward enough to take the proffered invitation card. Thankfully Jiya's mother had no such issues.

'That's so kind of you, sweetheart. Isn't it, Yunus?' Jiya's father simply narrowed his eyes at Ibrahim, but didn't say anything. 'We'd be delighted to come and celebrate your grandmother's birthday. It's so important to have elder members of the family with us for support and guidance.'

If only they knew the truth about Mumtaz Begum.

When asked what she wanted for her big day from her grandchildren, she'd asked if they'd take her to a nightclub.

'And we're not having this conversation with you, thank you very much' That had been a red-cheeked and very vocal Rayyan putting a stop to their grandmother's request.

'Oh, come on. At least hear her out.' This from Harry, the eternal shit stirrer.

'I'm not entertaining this. There's no way we're taking her to a club; she's our grandmother for God's sake.' Rayyan could barely contain his embarrassment.

'*She* is sitting right here, so stop talking about me as though I'm not in the room.' Ibrahim had just about stopped himself from laughing as his grandmother had pouted at Rayyan. 'Why can't I go—'

'I know, how about some new cardigans, the ones from Marks and Spencer? You like those, don't you? Or some jewellery?'

Their grandmother had smiled at Rayyan sweetly. 'Will you be a dear and get me some new slippers too? And maybe while you're there you can see if they will give you a sense of humour? I'd love that above all else.'

They had all burst out laughing – except Rayyan of course – who just buried his face in his hands, shaking his head in despair.

Support and guidance indeed! The woman was a menace.

'Jiya, have you asked Ibrahim if he'd like some tea? In fact, why don't you stay for dinner, sweetheart.' It wasn't a question since she reeled off half a dozen instructions for Jiya while Jiya's father gave Ibrahim a death stare. Again.

If it pleases you so much, Mr Ahmed, then I'll definitely stay.

'Ah, I'd love to, Auntie, thank you. I'm just going to go with Jiya and get a drink if you don't mind.'

'No, no, not at all, sweetheart, think of it as your own home.' Her mother really was a gem. What had she seen in Yunus Ahmed, Ibrahim wondered.

He followed Jiya into the kitchen and she busied herself getting a glass down from the cupboard. 'What drink would you like? There's a carton of mango juice here, there's—'

'How about a nice tall glass of Jiya?' He grabbed her waist and spun her to face him, her back against the worktop.

'What are you doing? My mum or dad might walk in.' Her hands were placed on his shoulders and he could feel the heat of them through the cotton of his T-shirt.

'It's more fun when there's a risk of getting caught like this, you know.' He was no more than a scant few inches away from her cheek, inhaling in her sweet scent.

She smelt like strawberries and Ibrahim was sure he could get intoxicated on the scent. Since when had the smell of strawberries been an aphrodisiac?

Feeling an overwhelming urge to give her a quick peck on the cheek – it was better than nothing – he lowered his head a fraction, only to freeze at her shocked gasp.

'Abba!'

Ibrahim pushed away from her so hard he was sure he had pulled a muscle. He whipped his head in the direction of the door, only to find it empty.

He turned to look at Jiya, who burst out laughing. 'You should have seen your face. Priceless.'

'Very funny.'

'Well, you asked for a glass of Jiya. It's not all sweetness, you know.'

'Really? Very clever, Miss Ahmed, very clever indeed. I'll have the other kind of drink now if you don't mind.'

Still smiling, she filled two glasses with the tropical fruit juice she'd taken out of the fridge and brought them to the table.

'So, we're doing this then. I'm going to Daadi's party with my family and we'll officially be a couple.' She added quotation marks with her fingers as she said the last four words.

'Yup, we will. Do you want me to come and pick you up earlier?'

She shook her head. 'No, I'll come with my family.'

'Great. So, how's the job hunt going?' Ibrahim needed more than a drink to cool his ardour down. Seeing her again made him question his own choice not to vocalise his attraction to her but he needed to stand firm. The mention of her father had worked brilliantly in tamping down the rush of desire that he'd felt and hopefully her talking about her career would finish the job off. He could hardly hang about and have dinner with her family with his tongue hanging out at the sight of Jiya.

A reminder that this was all very transient was exactly what he needed to put things into perspective.

'So, I got in touch with the contact you had given me and after a couple of emails back and forth, he told me to submit an application. I'm hoping to hear back from them soon but I'm not super keen with the package they have to offer.'

'Did you ask if they have any openings in any international offices?'

'Yeah, they do, in Sydney. It's not a terrible opportunity with four six-month placements in different departments but they don't offer much support in terms of relocation if you're not from around town.' She put on a hideous Australian accent at the end and Ibrahim groaned.

'Please don't do that again, darling. Your Australian accent stinks.'

She swatted his arm and gave him a pout.

'Jiya! Why are you hitting him like that?' Her mother had come in and went towards the sink.

'He's being mean.'

'He wouldn't know how. Ibrahim, why don't you join Yunus inside while Jiya helps me finish off dinner?'

Ibrahim recoiled at the idea of *joining Yunus* anywhere unless it was a matter of life and death. Even then he'd have to think about it. 'No, Auntie, I'll help you finish off dinner today.'

She looked as shocked as her daughter at what he'd just said.

'What? Can't I help?' He looked at them in confusion.

Her mother recovered first, while Jiya looked at him slack-jawed.

'Sure, you can,' her mother said. 'I just didn't realise you knew your way around a kitchen. All, if not most, of the boys I know only know how to fill a sink and empty a fridge, not the other way around. But then, to be fair, we mothers are the ones who are guilty of pampering them.' The last sentence seemed more for herself than him or Jiya.

Ibrahim busied himself by taking an ancient-looking apron off a peg on the back of the door and tying it at the back. 'Right, where do you want me to begin?'

He wasn't lying. He wasn't a Michelin-starred chef but he could take care of himself and put together some basics. It was more out of necessity than interest, but he also believed that no one was under the obligation of catering to his needs. If he wanted something, he should be able to do it for himself, even if it was baked beans on toast.

He made a big show of grating a cucumber for the raita and before long, he had Jiya's mother in stitches with elaborately told tales of his ventures in the kitchen.

Time flew as he pottered about in the kitchen with Jiya and her mother. They were enjoying his company and surprisingly, he was enjoying theirs. Jiya's mum told him about the first time she had come to England and how it had all felt to her. The adjustments she'd had to make in settling down here, with all her family in Pakistan, and no one to really help or guide her.

'My grasp of English was terrible, you know. Even now, after being here for over twenty-five years, sometimes this lot have to correct my pronunciation. I always get *vest* and *west* the wrong way around. They sound the same when I say them.'

She laughed along with him and Ibrahim was struck by the stark difference between Jiya's mother and his own.

Samina Ahmed and Farida Saeed had exactly the same starting points but were miles apart.

His mother had taken to the English lifestyle like a duck to water, only holding onto certain traditions she chose to or was forced to by her husband.

She wouldn't be caught in the kitchen cooking for the family like Jiya's mother was, or sharing self-deprecating anecdotes about her poor pronunciation and then laughing about it. She only wore traditional South Asian clothing for certain occasions and preferred spending her time socialising with women who were exactly like her.

The thing was, he actually had a decent relationship with his mother. Given what she was like, many people were surprised that she was a mother of five children. She didn't really give off major maternal vibes, and although she wasn't the kind of mother who would kick a ball with her kids or let them smear her clothes with their grubby hands, she wasn't neglectful of them.

She loved them in her own way and when that way was compared to that of Nasir Saeed, it was highly acceptable.

Dinner with the Ahmed family was a much more relaxed affair than the last time he had been here and he actually felt comfortable being around them, with the exception of Yunus Ahmed.

So long as the introduction to his own family went smoothly, Ibrahim was certain that this idea he was implementing really was the genius plan his brother had labelled it.

★

The morning of his grandmother's birthday, Ibrahim made his way to her room and saw all his siblings except the eldest gathered outside.

'Where's Zaf?'

'I'm here. Shall we?' Zafar came towards them just then, his wife following behind him.

They all went into their grandmother's room en masse and broke into the worst possible rendition of Happy Birthday they could. Deliberately.

It was a tradition they had among themselves and it tickled the old woman immensely, especially when Zafar, having the most melodic voice of them all, couldn't sing out of tune even when he tried.

'Zafar, my love, you have to work on it. You sound too perfect.'

'Happy birthday, Daadi.' He gave her a kiss on the cheek and the rest of them followed suit. She was being perfectly civil until Rayyan greeted her.

'Hello, handsome.' She winked at him and the tips of his ears turned pink, much to everyone's amusement.

'Happy birthday, Daadi.'

'So, where are my cardigans?'

He gave her a mock glare before handing her a wrapped package. 'The lady in the department store told me that these colours are all the rage among your age group.'

'Rayyan Saeed, are you going around telling people my age?' She was clearly horrified at the prospect.

'Umm, newsflash! Everyone coming today knows it's your big eight-o. But no, I didn't. I just wanted to see your reaction.' He gave her a rare grin and the old biddy chortled in delight.

'Rogue. Just like your grandfather.' She eagerly opened the packaging on her present and took out the collection of cardigans Rayyan had promised her.

'This is awfully heavy for cardigans. What's this?' She pulled out the book they'd had especially made for her with a collection of photographs of her with her grandchildren. Pictures from all their childhoods, teenage years and some more recent ones. There were a few particularly amusing selfies of her with various grandchildren, pulling faces or using social media filters. They had even included some messages for her to read alongside the photographs.

She looked up at all of them, her hand against her chest and her eyes shimmering with emotion. 'This is . . . I'm touched. This really is the most precious thing you could have given me. Whose idea was this? Zafar's?'

'Actually, it was Reshma's idea, not mine.'

'Thank you, my darling. It's very special and I'll always treasure it.' She gave them all a beaming smile and Ibrahim watched as her expression turned to one of mischief. 'But these cardigans!' She turned to address Rayyan. 'I will be the belle of the ball in them. Do you think I should wear one this evening?'

'They were only a cover-up for the real deal. You don't have to be so dramatic.'

'So, you *are* taking me to a club?'

'I'm out of here. See you this evening.' He gave her a kiss on the cheek and left the room like his arse was on fire, much to everyone's amusement.

'Ibrahim, is Jiya coming with her family this evening?' Ibrahim turned towards his grandmother as everyone else filed out of the room.

'Yes, she is. In fact, she's really looking forward to it.'

'I'm glad. It'll be nice to meet her family. She's such a lovely girl and I'm over the moon that you've been brave enough to stand by your own choice and be with the woman you love. I'm really proud of you.'

What?!

'I'll admit I was a bit worried after your disagreement with your father, but I'm so pleased about you and Jiya. Don't get me wrong, there's nothing wrong with being introduced to someone by your parents and having what your generation calls an *assisted* marriage. I think Reshma is an absolute gem, if only Zafar paused for long enough to see that.

'But for you, I know nothing else will do. You've always been a determined boy, wanting to figure things out for himself and having what you want on your own terms, so of course your life partner would be a determined woman of your choice.'

Ibrahim felt sweat trickle down his spine at his grand-mother's words. Where in the world had all this come from? He'd only come in here to wish her a happy birthday, for crying out loud. Not to have words like life partner, marriage and love – cue shudder – brought up.

She actually looked happy and Ibrahim was loath to upset her by telling her the truth of his feelings, especially on her birthday. Not knowing what more to say, he kissed her on the cheek and left the room, making his way towards the dining room.

Maybe some breakfast would chase away the gnawing sensation he was feeling in his stomach. But it seemed that fate was conspiring against him because the only occupant in the dining room at that point in time was his father, so he walked straight past it. *God give me strength!*

CHAPTER SEVENTEEN

Jiya

Expecting to feel horribly anxious about going to Ibrahim's grandmother's party this evening, Jiya was surprised to find that she was actually more excited than she was nervous.

Maybe it was because she had met most of his family and they had all been so nice to her. Or perhaps it was because the party venue was supposed to be a summer wonderland and from the pictures Ibrahim had shown her, it was going to be amazing and she couldn't wait to see and experience it.

However, if she was going to be honest with herself, she would acknowledge that some – or most – of her excitement stemmed from the fact that she was going to see Ibrahim. Again.

She had only seen him yesterday but she felt as though it had been a lot longer than that. He'd come to The Lounge after she'd finished an early shift and he had managed to duck out of work early.

They'd had a late, leisurely lunch and then he'd dropped her off home after a kiss on the cheek that had left her feeling on edge in a way she'd never been before. His lips had been soft yet firm as they'd landed on her cheek and she'd felt the urge to turn her cheek and have a taste of the kind of kisses they'd had twice before. Kisses that hadn't been repeated, much to her disappointment. Would kissing him again help to ease the mounting feelings in some way and help her reach for the elusive thing that felt just beyond her grasp?

In the end, she'd not turned her face and had let him move away, giving him a quick peck of her own on his stubbly cheek before leaving the car.

She had felt a subtle shift in their relationship over the last week. Her sense of guilt had slowly dissipated, although a niggle of it was still there whenever she spoke to her mother about Ibrahim and remembered that essentially, she was lying. However, the feelings she felt were no lie. They were very real and she couldn't say she knew what to do about them. She felt as though Ibrahim was there with her at times, feeling the same way, but then there were other times when she felt he might be holding a piece of himself back, confusing her a little.

How would he react if she told him that her attraction towards him was stronger? Would he agree or would he run a mile in the opposite direction? She had no experience of being in a relationship, fake or real, and she wasn't sure whether she should come out with her feelings or keep them locked up and stick to the plan.

They both had different ideas for their future and those ideas didn't align with those of the other. She needed to remember why she was doing what she was doing and she also needed to remember that Ibrahim had his reasons too.

Although, on the odd occasion, she had caught herself imagining what it would be like if she acknowledged her fledgling feelings to him and he reciprocated. Having a boyfriend was something she'd never done before and went against most of her mother's teachings. But this was a man her mother wholeheartedly approved of and so it was that much more tantalising to imagine what it would be like if they did take their fake relationship down that route of attraction. She couldn't help but wonder what would it be like, but would then think better of it and shake the feeling off.

The evening he had come over to personally invite her family to the party had been pretty hilarious, with Ibrahim actively avoiding being alone with her father, who made no secret of the fact that he wasn't a big fan of Ibrahim's.

Her heart had completely melted at the effort he had made to get to know her mother, and her mother had been like a completely different person with Ibrahim, opening up about things she had hardly shared with Jiya before.

Now she found herself standing in the car park while her mother finished adjusting Jiya's *dupatta* so the pleats sat just right.

While her mother was wearing a gorgeous bottle green *sari*, Jiya was wearing slim fit, cropped trousers made of midnight blue raw silk and a printed *kameez* that finished mid-thigh of the same fabric. The scarf with the outfit was supposed to be draped across one shoulder and as her mother pinned it into place, Jiya felt a swarm of butterflies take flight in her stomach.

She'd never felt such a keen sense of anticipation at meeting someone before now. The thought of seeing Ibrahim produced goosebumps on her arms and she couldn't help but fidget.

Tonight felt . . . different.

'Stand still or this pin will tear through the fabric and prick you in the process.' Her mother spoke with another pin clenched between her teeth as she worked. 'I did say let me do this at home but anyway, here, it's done. Let me see.' Her mother stepped back to inspect Jiya and gave a nod.

She pressed a finger at the corner of her eye and smudged the eyeliner that had come off onto her fingertip just behind Jiya's ear.

'Now no one can cast an evil eye over you.' Her mother had always done this whenever Jiya had got ready to go somewhere or before an important event. She wasn't sure if it was tradition or superstition, but she found it comforting when her mother did it, something she said had been passed down from generation to generation.

Jiya swallowed the emotion that suddenly clogged her throat and pretended to adjust the buckle of her high-heeled sandals to give herself a chance to get her various emotions under control.

In the last few weeks, a definite shift had taken place in her mother and while it pleased Jiya no end not to be at loggerheads with her, it also fuelled those moments of guilt she'd felt at not being entirely honest with her.

'Samina, I'd prefer not going in at all but if we must be here, can we get beyond the car park please.' Her father sounded as grumpy as he looked at the prospect of being here. 'Come on, it's this way.'

The four of them made their way towards the marquee that had been erected in the middle of a plush golf course.

Fairy lights intertwined with roses on trellises marked the path towards the entrance, filling the air with the scents of the fragrant flowers and lending the whole tableau an ethereal glow.

Soft strains of vintage music could be heard as they made their way into the marquee.

Jiya gasped at the splendour before her, not knowing which way to look first to take it all in.

On her left a bar had been set up, serving a choice of mocktails, soft drinks and whatever else anyone chose. Ahead of her, the marquee had round tables with an array of flowers arranged in elaborate displays in the centre with more fairy lights and tealight candles around its base.

A pathway had been cleared through the centre and further up it, Jiya could see that the back of the marquee opened up and the dance floor was out in the open, allowing people to dance under the sky. A long table was off to the side of the dance floor and that's where she spotted a few familiar faces.

Harry was the first to make eye contact with her, waving at her as he made his way towards her and her family. Jiya made the introductions, telling her family about Harry and how they knew each other. Her mother, as was her MO, was nothing but warm and friendly, and so were Jameel and her father. She was about to ask Harry where Ibrahim was when she felt a tingling sensation down her back and a split second later, she felt warmth dance along the right side of her body.

'You look ravishing. Like a midnight fairy wearing the night sky.' She turned and there he was, barely a foot away from her. He looked mouth-wateringly good himself in a tux, his jaw smooth and chiselled and his eyes bright, reflecting the fairy lights all around them.

'You don't look too shabby yourself; very James Bond.'

Before he could respond with more than his devastating smile, her mother saw him and he moved forward to greet her family, ushering them all towards his own to make the necessary introductions.

It was the first time Jiya had seen Ibrahim and all his brothers together and what a sight it was.

All five brothers were tall and broad and looked extremely dapper in their tuxedos although she thought Ibrahim looked just that much better – but then she was biased.

His sister-in-law Reshma looked stunning in a *sari*, like an striking jewel.

Ibrahim's grandmother and parents greeted her with all the warmth of a much-loved member of the family and were just as pleased to meet her own family.

'Jiya sweetheart, you look lovely, *Mashallah*.' Ibrahim's grandmother looked like a *Maharani* of a bygone era in a cream-coloured *sari* with gold print work on it. She had pearls around her neck and in her ears and even her fragrance was something exotic and expensive.

'Happy birthday, Daadi. May you have many more.'

'Thank you, my darling.' She turned towards her parents. 'You must be so proud of this delightful girl.'

Jiya stepped back as the parents and grandparent formed a little circle and found her brother chatting to Ibrahim and his brother Ashar. Harry came and stood beside her.

'Looking good, Shorty.'

'Thanks. I figured if I'm going to be standing next to your brother then I need to look the part.'

'Please. You could wear a bag for life and he'd still be drooling over you. Besides, when I said you look good, you were supposed to return the compliment.'

Jiya reluctantly pulled her eyes away from Ibrahim and looked at Harry.

'Well, I guess Baby Saeed scrubs up well after all. Did you do the bow tie up yourself?'

'Very funny. And no – Zaf did. Since these boring people are busy being boring, let's go get a drink.'

They made their way to the bar and Harry got them each an exotic-looking mocktail.

'So, how's it going?'

'How's what going?' She took a sip of the drink and relished the tart flavours bursting on her tongue.

'My master plan obviously. We've not had a chance to catch up, so I want deets.'

'*Deets*? How old are we, fourteen?'

'Hmm. Avoidance, I see.' He held his glass against his lips but didn't drink, his brow puckered in concentration.

'I'm not avoiding anything.'

'Denial. Ooh, this *is* serious.' His puckered eyebrows were now both arched and he had the expression of someone on the brink of discovering a top secret, his eyes twinkling with mischief.

Jiya rolled her eyes at him and turned to make her way back to where everyone else was. 'I'm sooo not doing this with you.'

'What does he want to do?' At Ibrahim's voice, Jiya just about stopped the drink from sloshing over the edge of the glass and onto his pristine jacket. He eyed Harry warily. 'You're dressed like an adult; do you think you could perhaps make an effort to behave like one this evening instead of being a plonker?'

'You know, I'm fast coming to the conclusion that you people simply have no respect for my genius. I helped the pair of you. Massively, might I add. And what do I get? Nothing but disrespect from the pair of you.'

Jiya giggled at him. 'You're such a drama queen and I love you for it.' She hugged him around the waist and after a moment he returned the embrace and gave her a lop-sided grin. 'And you're right. I owe you.' She reached up and gave him a kiss on the cheek. 'Thank you.'

His eyebrows first shot up to meet his hairline and then, catching his older brother's eye, he waggled them suggestively at him. 'You're most welcome, Jiya darling. Any time.'

Ibrahim shook his head but Jiya could see the amusement on his face when the corner of his mouth lifted in a grin.

'Now, if you don't mind, can I have a few moments with Jiya while you go and dazzle the guests who are now arriving in their masses.'

Jiya looked around her and sure enough, the venue was filling up fast and people were now milling around and socialising. Harry gave them a wave and made his way towards a small cluster of people and then it was just her and Ibrahim.

'Come with me, I want to show you something.' He took her glass and placing it on the counter, he took her hand and made his way out of an opening beside the bar.

'Slow down Usain Bolt, I'm in high heels.'

Ibrahim

'Yeah, I noticed.' That wasn't the only thing Ibrahim had noticed. Slowing his pace down for Jiya to keep up, he catalogued all the details he had noticed when Jiya had entered the marquee.

He'd had to look twice to make sure that what he was seeing was real. Gone was the signature ponytail; her hair falling just past her shoulders in soft waves instead. The fairy lights cast subtle shimmers on it and Ibrahim knew without a doubt that before the evening came to an end, he'd have run his fingers through those tresses at least once.

The colour around her eyes lent them a smoky and mysterious look and the eyeliner outlining the shape made them look even bigger. Her cheeks were a becoming pink, though that was probably natural rather than her make-up and the way her large dangly earrings kept kissing those rosy cheeks whenever she moved her head had a spike of lust lancing him straight to his core.

The short *kameez* and cropped trousers of her outfit made her look tall and slender and the high-heeled sandals she wore made him zone in on those delectable ankles of hers. There wasn't a single part of Jiya Ahmed that didn't demand his attention this evening, so much so that Ibrahim felt supremely conflicted about what he *should* do and what he *wanted* to do.

He should have been back inside that marquee with his family, greeting guests and making sure the evening ran as smoothly as possible. He should be spending time with his grandmother because it was her special day.

Seeing Jiya hug Harry and then kiss his cheek had pushed him to err on the side of want and here he was, pulling her along by the hand under the pretence of wanting to show Jiya something when he was the one who wanted to do the looking. And touching.

Never before had he felt such a strong sense of urgency. A deep need to get away from everybody and anything else and for it to be just him and her.

Ibrahim pulled in a deep breath to try and tamp down the riot of feelings churning within him, but all that did was fill his lungs with her scent. A woody and earthy scent with soft floral undertones. The scent of the summery evening and the abundance of flowers everywhere was mingling with Jiya's scent, a feast of fragrances for him to take in.

They came to a secluded spot, the marquee some distance behind them. The muted sounds of music and the slight hum of voices could just about be heard. They walked down a set of stone steps and were out of sight of anyone who happened to come out of the marquee and look in this direction.

'What did you want to show me out here?' Jiya looked around her, obviously finding nothing noteworthy out here except for plenty of grass and the peace and tranquillity offered by the solitude.

He stepped up close to her and held her face in both hands, lowering his own towards her slowly, until his lips were a breath away from hers.

'Nothing and everything.'

'Is that supposed to be cryptic or poetic?' Her voice was a soft whisper, her breath brushing his mouth as she spoke.

'Both. Neither. I find when I'm around you that's what I am, just a mass of contradictions. I shouldn't want this, but I do. Desperately.'

She was looking directly into his eyes now, her own were two deep pools of dark chocolate he wanted to drown himself in.

'Can I show you what *I* want?' Ibrahim felt a tingling down his spine at her words and not trusting himself to speak, he nodded, his forehead brushing hers.

Taking in a deep, audible breath, she closed the distance between them and Ibrahim felt every other thought, feeling and emotion melt away as her lips touched his.

CHAPTER EIGHTEEN

Ibrahim

A series of mini explosions went off in Ibrahim's body, alighting every nerve ending and shooting sparks in every direction. A fireworks display had nothing on the fireworks Jiya was setting off in his body.

He traced her face with his fingertips as their tongues duelled for dominance. She tasted tart and sweet, the perfect definition of Jiya herself and he couldn't get enough of her.

Her hands skated up his shoulders and back down, leaving a trail of fire in their wake. She deftly undid the button on his jacket and pushed her hands around his waist and down towards his backside.

The boldness she showed in her touches only fuelled the flames of his desire and unable to hold back from having more of her, he began moving his own hands downwards. He skimmed her neck and shoulders as he moved his mouth to trace the parts of her face his fingertips had just touched.

The cool silk of her *kameez* felt as impenetrable a barrier to her skin as a brick wall and Ibrahim was desperate to have a feel of her skin beneath the silk.

She dropped her head back as his lips descended to her neck, nibbling at the delicate skin there and then running his tongue over the tender spot. He moved his hands further down along her sides, past the indentation at her waist and down over her slightly rounded hips while his lips made their way back up from her neck to her ear lobe, her dangling earring scratching his chin as he moved.

His hands came up her torso and he brushed the undersides of both breasts with his thumbs, eliciting a shocked gasp from her lips which he cut off by crushing her mouth under his own.

He moved his fingers around her breasts, avoiding the peaks he knew she wanted him to touch, judging from the way she had involuntarily pushed herself towards him.

All of Jiya's actions were completely instinctive. He knew she wasn't sexually experienced but the fact that she felt she could be open about how he made her feel when he touched her like this made him feel ten feet tall.

'Ibrahim?'

'Hmm.'

'I . . . Ibrahim.'

'*Ibrahim* what, Jiya? Say it, what are you feeling?' Unlike her breathless whisper, his own voice sounded as though his throat had been coated with coarse sand.

'I don't know. I just . . . it all feels . . .' Unable to articulate her feelings, she rested her forehead against his shoulder, pulling in deep lungfuls of air.

This was all new for her and although he wasn't as much of a novice as she was, he had never before felt desire to such an extent that he'd practically dragged her from the party, leaving behind their families and all thoughts of what they should be doing and was instead in a secluded part of the venue, kissing and touching her like some out-of-control teenager.

Dramatic enough?!

He most certainly wanted to do more of what they were with Jiya and she didn't seem averse to the idea, but his timing and location could definitely be better.

Easing away from her slightly, he gave her a chance to step back from him. She moved her head back but didn't step away.

The setting sun cast a golden glow over her, highlighting shades of brown in her hair and making her eyes shine. Her cheeks were well and truly flushed now, the pink tinge visible on her neck too. Her lips were swollen from his kisses and as he was watching her, she pulled her lower lip between her teeth, sending another shaft of desire straight through him.

'You're killing me. And if we don't stop now, I will literally go up in flames.' Was that his voice, sounding heavy and gravelly?

She gave him a grin that was a combination of cheeky and shy and 100 per cent Jiya. It also told him that the haze of desire she'd been under was beginning to fade.

'What do you say we walk a little before we go back inside? We have some time, don't we?'

Jiya

She hoped her voice sounded less husky than it had earlier. The feelings that had consumed her moments before had been completely alien to her and while she was aware of what she had been doing, it had felt instinctive, as though a greater need had taken over her body and was calling the shots and she felt very much shaken by the intensity of it all.

Now all those feelings were rapidly being overtaken by a horrible sense of awkwardness, a feeling she'd never experienced in Ibrahim's company before.

In fact, she'd never even felt this awkward when her mother had presented her with unknown men she thought might make good husbands for Jiya. The perpetual stream of *Abduls*, as Harry liked to call them.

Straightening her *dupatta* and *kameez* so they sat as they should, Jiya took a few steps away from Ibrahim and looked over at the vast greens laid out before her. The summer evening made the whole place look so lush she was tempted to take her sandals off and walk on the grass barefoot. The soft beat of the music became audible again, along with the hum of conversation from what was probably hundreds of people in the marquee.

Ibrahim came and stood beside her, his hair back in place and his jacket buttoned up once again. He looked so incredibly handsome it made the breath hitch in her chest.

'Come this way, there's only the golf course on that side, but on this side there's actually a well-maintained garden that looks amazing.' He led her towards the garden, the pathway to which was lined with more flower-covered trellises and fairy lights.

The garden itself was surprisingly empty, even though it was perfectly visible from the open side of the marquee.

A small fountain took pride of place in the middle and it was surrounded by flower beds in full bloom, the cacophony of colours a feast for the eyes.

'This place is gorgeous.'

'That it is. Zaf comes here to play golf every now and then so he managed to hire it for today's event, but the details of today are mostly thanks to Reshma, I believe.'

'Really? I would have thought you'd have an army of event planners taking care of all the details. It's a pretty big gathering.'

'I think there is one of those too, but Reshma's overseeing everything. She's got a good eye for this sort of stuff so . . .' He shrugged his shoulders.

She sensed there was something he wasn't saying, but rather than push for details, she left it for Ibrahim to share if he wished. He spoke after a lengthy pause.

'She's actually not bad, you know, and if it wasn't for the way her and Zaf got married, I'd probably get along better with her. In fact, apart from my mother, there's no one Reshma can't get along with.'

'Your mum's great – why doesn't Reshma get along with her?'

'It's actually my mother who doesn't *want* to get along with Reshma. I told you that my brother's marriage was arranged, right?'

Jiya nodded, not sure where exactly Ibrahim was heading with this particular conversation.

'Well, since they've been married, my brother's not been the same and while I believe that it's because of that, my mum actually comes out with it. She openly holds Reshma responsible for ruining my brother's life by being married to him and making him miserable. She doesn't think Reshma's good enough for him and doesn't hold back in making her feelings known.'

'But then why did she agree with it in the first place? Isn't that how arranged marriages work? Everyone is supposed to be in agreement on both sides.' Jiya felt confused by the turn of conversation but she was now more intrigued than ever by the workings of the Saeed family.

The dynamics of the family were obviously more complex than she had first thought, especially when you included Ibrahim's somewhat contentious relationship with his father.

He went and sat down on a stone bench overlooking the fountain and the flower beds and she sat down next to him. There was a light breeze carrying the fragrance of the flowers around them and if it wasn't for the noise coming from within the marquee behind them, it could quite easily feel like they were the only two people there.

She knew they should really go inside. They had been outside for quite a while now and if they didn't go back in soon, someone might well come out looking for them but she didn't make a move to do so.

'My mother never agreed for Zaf and Reshma's marriage to take place. It was my father's decision and because Zaf agreed or accepted it – whatever way you want to take it – it was a done thing. My mother actually had someone else in mind for him. He was quite the catch, she would say – handsome, well-educated, a successful businessman, a well-connected family, whatever that means. And there was no shortage of beautiful women who would make him the perfect partner. She was pretty pissed off when my dad decided that Zaf would marry Reshma and he agreed, and she still is.' He laughed but there was no humour in it. It was an awkward and difficult situation to say the least.

'Zafar agreed to marry her; he wasn't forced. What about Reshma?'

Ibrahim looked slightly confused at Jiya's question. 'What about her?'

'Did she *want* to marry your brother?'

Ibrahim scoffed. 'Why wouldn't she? Have you seen my eldest brother?' The disbelief in his voice was so clear, he almost sounded offended by her question.

'I'm not saying your brother isn't great, I'm asking about how she felt. They're two completely different things.'

He shrugged his shoulders again, turning his face away from her and looking towards the softly gurgling fountain. 'I don't know. I've never thought about it or asked her how she felt.' He ran his fingers through his hair, but as always, it fell back into place perfectly.

'What I do know is that I don't want the same, or even a similar fate, as those two. I'm not going to just agree to marry someone my parents think will be the ideal partner for me and then spend the rest of my life tied down to a relationship I never wanted in the first place.'

'What *do* you want?' Since she'd started to get to know him, this was the first time they were having such an in-depth conversation about what Ibrahim might actually want for himself. They both knew what he didn't want, but it wasn't the same thing.

Sure, the timing could have been better, but now that he was finally opening up about his thoughts and feelings, Jiya was reluctant to call an end to the conversation and go back to join the party.

'And that's the million-dollar question.' He rubbed his chin and then moved his hand to the back of his neck, his confusion clear in his body language.

'I suppose I want them to get off my back with their own suggestions and their own ideas of who the right partner for me is and give me the time and freedom to figure out what I want and to choose someone for myself. I want—'

'There you are! I've spent ages looking for you both.'

Jiya let out a sigh of frustration at the interruption that meant Ibrahim couldn't finish what he had been about to say. She found that she was actually desperate to know his thoughts and for him to tell her what he was feeling. If Harry could have waited just a few more minutes, she might have found out.

'Why?' Ibrahim had lost the look of both longing and confusion on his face from earlier and was back to being the well-put-together, elusive and hard-to-read Ibrahim Saeed.

'Uh duh! They all want you back inside. Dad wants to get the party officially started and Daadi's playing the role of an "eighty going on to eight"-year-old to perfection. She wants to cut the cake first and then do anything else.'

Jiya stood up from the bench, her backside feeling sore now that she'd got up. As beautiful as the feature was, a stone bench was not kind to the behind, that was for sure.

She looked up to find Harry looking at her closely. A slow smile spread across his lips and she knew the weasel had seen something he shouldn't have.

He waved his index finger in a circular motion around her face like a magic wand. 'I hope you have lipstick in that titchy purse of yours. You need to reapply.' He moved his finger to wave it towards Ibrahim. '*You* need to wipe *your* lipstick off.'

'One of these days I'm going to seriously hurt you,' Ibrahim growled at his brother.

'Gracious as always, I see.'

Making themselves presentable, they followed Harry back into the marquee, leaving behind the sense of physical connection they had both found in each other's arms and the sense of emotional connection they had found with each other in the garden, and walked towards their families, who were all stood near each other.

At their arrival, everyone took their seats, while Ibrahim's father took the microphone and, after welcoming all the guests, he wished his mother well for her birthday. Ibrahim's grandmother had the smile of a Cheshire cat while her son waxed lyrical about her and everyone gave her a huge round of applause as she stood up to cut the cake.

Dinner was served, with entertainment from a wonderful string quartet and after being served course after course of delicious food, everyone had a chance to burn it off on the dance floor.

Of course, the family started the dancing off, as Jiya saw Ibrahim's brother, Zafar, take his grandmother by the hand and lead her to the centre of the dance floor. The rest of the brothers followed him and at Rayyan's nod, a smooth voice could be heard through the speakers, crooning a soft, mellow song to which Zafar swayed while holding his grandmother in his arms.

They waltzed a few steps when Ibrahim took over and twirled her ever so gently on the dance floor, straight into Rayyan's arms. For the next five minutes, all the brothers took turns in dancing with their grandmother – Harry being as flamboyant as could be expected – and when they finished, the entire marquee erupted in celebration at the sweet scene they had all just witnessed.

The rest of the gathering was then encouraged to join in and as the empty floor space was filled, the volume within the marquee of both music and cheering went up.

Jiya stood at the edge of the dance floor, clapping and cheering as people around her did the same while others joined in with the dancing. The tempo of the music changed to upbeat, lively tunes and before she knew it, she was tapping her feet in rhythm.

Harry came towards her weaving his shoulders and making her laugh as he waggled his eyebrows suggestively and before she could protest, he had grabbed her arm and twirled her onto the dance floor with him to join in with all the fun.

Jiya moved in time with the music and was loving every minute of it. She couldn't remember the last time she'd freely danced like this, or felt an immense sense of happiness with everything that had her wanting to express that feeling through movement.

Harry was still dancing with her and as she made eye contact with him, he raised his chin and lifted his eyebrows, alerting her a split second before she felt a tingling on the back of her neck.

CHAPTER NINETEEN

Jiya

Dancing with Ibrahim was like being on a rollercoaster. It was nerve-racking, exhilarating, and so much fun. She didn't want to stop but if she didn't, she'd have to be carried out of here because her feet were absolutely killing her.

Dancing in high heels was only for professional dancers and a professional dancer Jiya was not. Her feet throbbed and she really needed to sit down, but first she needed a drink.

'Let's go to the bar and grab a drink.' She had to shout at the top of her voice right in Ibrahim's ear. He looked back at her in confusion and yelled in her ear.

'What?'

Shaking her head at the silliness, she gestured a drinking action and pointed in the direction of the bar. He *'ohed'* in understanding and grabbing her hand, he cut a swathe through the dancers towards the bar.

He'd taken his jacket off and she could see the movement of muscles in his back as he walked slightly in front of her, weaving his way through the tables and chairs. She probably looked sweaty and dishevelled, her hair a bird's nest rather than artfully styled waves and her face shiny from all that dancing. He on the other hand, looked as delectable as ever. *So unfair!*

He grabbed two flutes from the bartender and handed one over, downing his own in one go. Jiya carefully sipped her own drink and savoured the ice-cold temperature of the liquid. Ibrahim was watching her closely, his expression inscrutable as he lifted his hand and brushed her hair behind her ear.

'Did I tell you how beautiful you look today?'

She arched an eyebrow and gave him a playful pout. 'And what about every other day?'

He rolled his eyes dramatically and she gave him a grin. 'Every other day you look like a complete troll so I'm glad you made an effort today.' She swatted him playfully on the arm.

'You better watch what you say to me, Ibrahim Saeed, that kind of talk could cost you.'

'Really?' He edged towards her, much like a wild cat hunted its prey, his head angled to one side. 'And what would that cost be?'

'Ladies and gentlemen, if I could have your attention once more, please.'

Ibrahim's father's voice boomed through the speakers once again as he spoke into the microphone. The music had faded out and everyone had turned to look at him.

'I've already thanked you all for coming and since you're all near and dear to the Saeed family, I wanted to take this opportunity to share some very important and happy news with you all. Now, where are they . . . Aha, there they are. Ibrahim and Jiya.'

Jiya looked at Ibrahim, his face mirroring the confusion she was feeling at being singled out by his father like that. She quickly placed her empty glass back on the bar next to Ibrahim's, tucking strands of hair behind her ears with both hands and then running her palms down her *kameez*. Glancing at Ibrahim, she saw him run his fingers through his hair and then smile at the people looking their way.

'Come here, you two.' Ibrahim's father motioned for them to come and stand beside him and Jiya could see her own parents standing beside Ibrahim's mother on the other side.

A shiver of foreboding went down her spine and her scalp prickled as she saw the expression on Ibrahim's older brother's face, completely in contrast to that of almost everyone else.

It's nothing, he's probably spoken to someone he's not fond of. Or maybe his shoes are killing him too.

She tried to will away the sense of unease she was feeling all of a sudden, but her gut was churning in a way that was hard to ignore.

She took some deep breaths to try and settle her nerves and she felt Ibrahim take her hand and squeeze it reassuringly. He must have sensed her unease because when she looked at him, he gave her a tight smile. He was obviously feeling some of the tension she was but he was trying to make *her* feel better.

'Now, I know we're gathered here to celebrate my mother's birthday and I have to say, we've certainly done that. Wouldn't you agree, Amma?'

Everyone turned as one to look at Ibrahim's grandmother, who was standing beside Harry on the dance floor and much to everyone's surprise, she let out a big cheer.

'There you have it.' He laughed out loud into the microphone, causing a horrendous feedback noise to reverberate through the entire space and making everyone wince. 'Well, I have a wonderful piece of news to end the evening with. Moments like these are what give any parent a great sense of pride and joy and that is exactly how Farida and I feel this evening, as do Yunus and Samina, the proud parents of this delightful young lady.' He gestured towards her.

What?!

'I'd like to take this opportunity among all our family and friends to announce my son Ibrahim Saeed's engagement to the lovely Jiya Ahmed.'

Ibrahim

A number of things were clamouring for Ibrahim's attention and he was finding it difficult to decide which one needed his attention first.

There was a persistent drumbeat in his head and the whooshing sound in his ears seemed to be in sync with it. Was it his thundering heartbeat or the sound of blood rushing through his body? Or maybe they were one and the same thing. Could everybody around him hear that whooshing sound?

His bow tie was slowly constricting his throat like a python gradually constricted its prey in its coils and he ran his fingers along the inside of his collar in an effort to loosen it, but it did little to allow more air into his lungs.

His palms felt ice-cold but clammy and, he couldn't be sure, but his right hand felt like it was in a vice slowly being squeezed until all he could feel were tiny pin-like pricks.

He turned to look down at his hand and saw a smaller one wrapped around it. Moving his eyes up the arm, he saw Jiya's face, white as a sheet, her eyes looking overly large and her jaw taut with tension.

The battling sounds in his mind receded enough to allow the deafening noise of clapping and cheering to penetrate the momentary fog that had clouded his senses. Jiya's mother came towards them from beside his parents and enveloped her daughter in a hug, causing Jiya to let go of his hand, the only lifeline he'd had after he felt like he'd been thrown overboard into rough seas.

Daadi came towards him, a beaming smile on her face, and stretching up, she took his face in her two hands.

'This is one of the best birthdays ever and a present I'm over the moon with. Thank you, my darling boy.' Unable to articulate any kind of response, he could only stare at her as she went towards Jiya and his mother came forward.

'I'm so happy, honey. Jiya is an absolute gem and I'm so proud of you both.' She kissed him on both cheeks, not needing any sort of response from him and followed his grandmother.

'Well son, how did you like my surprise? Got you, didn't we?'

As a child, Ibrahim remembered watching his grandmother put water on the cooker to boil. He had watched the water with all the fascination a young child has, as slowly bubbles began to emerge and then the water began letting off steam. Those bubbles would then get bigger and bigger until the entire saucepan began trembling slightly with the force of the boiling water within it.

Right now, Ibrahim felt as though his insides were doing what the water in the saucepan had done. He was seconds away from coming to a rolling boil himself and if he didn't get out of here, then carnage would most definitely ensue and as much as his father might deserve a blistering, Ibrahim would not make a spectacle of himself or his family for everyone to see.

Thankfully Zafar stepped up towards him. 'Dad, Jiya's father is there, perhaps you should . . .'

'Oh, yes, yes.' Clapping Ibrahim on the shoulder, his father went off. Ibrahim watched as his brother took charge, grabbing the microphone from where their father had left it, he switched it off and motioned for the music to be started again. Ibrahim, meanwhile, was feeling completely off-kilter.

Zafar grabbed him just below the elbow and gave him a slight shake. 'Did you hear me? Come with me, now.'

He led the way outside, through the main entrance and down a few corridors until they reached what looked like the empty club café. He'd obviously grabbed two drinks when Ibrahim hadn't been looking and thrust one of them towards him. Ibrahim took a gulp and felt the cool liquid slide down his throat, easing some of the churning in his gut.

Zafar didn't say anything and Ibrahim relished the silence after the intense noise in the marquee.

The door to the café swung open and his other three brothers came and stood beside him.

Despite feeling a toxic mix of emotions he couldn't yet fathom, a sense of calm came over him as he stood there with his brothers in silence. They didn't need words to understand each other but whenever one of them needed the others, they were there, supporting each other, being each other's rock.

After a few minutes, Ibrahim felt ready to speak. 'Any idea when he decided this? I saw him this morning and he said absolutely nothing about Jiya to me.'

Ashar, Rayyan and Haroon shook their heads and looked to Zafar.

'After you introduced Jiya's parents to ours and went off to God knows where, the four of them and Daadi were chatting. I didn't think much of it and since I was greeting guests who were beginning to come in, I didn't pay them any attention. After some time, Dad called me over and told me that since you and Jiya seemed set on being with each other and our family, and Jiya's family are happy with that choice, why don't we announce your engagement today?'

'And why the hell didn't you stop him?' Zafar levelled a look at Ibrahim and he immediately felt contrite. 'You did. Of course, you would have. Sorry.' He scrubbed a hand across his face.

'I did. I told him it was early days and that it would be a good idea to run it past you and Jiya first and see how you both felt about it, but you'd both done such a convincing job of wanting to be together that Jiya's mother thought nothing wrong with announcing an engagement and then allowing you both some time before having the wedding, if you needed it.

'Seeing my doubts, Dad asked me if I thought there was any reason why they shouldn't go ahead with it, other than the fact that I thought it was too soon. He asked if there was any reason I thought that Jiya wasn't the right sort of girl for you. What was I supposed to say? "Actually Dad, there is. She's pretending to be your son's girlfriend." I could hardly say anything without giving the whole game away.'

Ibrahim felt cold all over his body despite the lack of air-conditioning in the room. In fact, he felt sick thinking about everything since he'd walked off the dance floor with Jiya.

It was exactly what he had been trying to avoid from the start. His father had taken control and was now trying to orchestrate things to go exactly how *he* wanted them to go. All in the name of a fucking surprise.

'Shit!'

'He's only announced it, Ibs. It's not set in stone. Go and tell him you need some time and you're not ready to get engaged.' Rayyan, as always, tried to be the voice of reason. But right then, Ibrahim didn't want to hear reason.

'You think it's that easy, do you? He just announced my engagement in front of the entire fucking crowd and you think I can just waltz back in there and say, "Hang on a second, Dad, turns out I'm not as ready as I made out?" I told him that I see a future with Jiya, for Christ's sake.'

'Calm down please, Ibs, he's just trying to help.' Harry looked from him to Rayyan and then towards Zafar.

'Did Jiya know about this?' He turned to look at Ashar, unsure of what to make of his quietly voiced question.

'You what? When would she have known? She was with me the whole time.'

Ashar shrugged, his usual expression of bored indifference firmly in place. 'Just asking. No one knows who actually initiated the conversation between our folks and her parents. It might have been her mum and dad.' He shrugged again and Ibrahim felt an uncomfortable sense of foreboding snake down his spine.

Surely what Ashar was insinuating couldn't be right. Could it?

He had an uncanny ability to come at things from an angle no one else would consider. Was that what he was doing now?

'She knew what your deal was and your feelings about the whole thing, right?'

Ibrahim nodded in agreement. 'Yeah.' His voice was little more than a whisper as the cogwheels of his mind ran faster than he was able to keep up with.

The ringtone of Zafar's phone cut through the tense silence and glancing at the screen, he silenced the phone.

'Jiya wouldn't do something so underhanded.' Harry sounded affronted on his friend's behalf. 'Surely you know her better than that by now, Ibs?' He looked at Ibrahim but before he could respond, Ashar cut in again, his theory gathering momentum.

'So how do you explain the sudden change in the situation? One minute she's happy to focus on her own plans but needs a fake boyfriend, and then as soon as her parents are introduced to ours, boom, things change. Maybe she had a change of heart after seeing more of Ibs and all that comes with him.

'Our father might be a despot, but since when has he ever gone ahead with a decision of such importance so recklessly? Do you guys remember how long he took to finalise things for Zaf?'

The door to the café swung open again before anyone could respond to Ashar's acidic implications and Reshma stood there holding the door open. 'Daadi is asking after you all, wondering where you are. The sparklers display is about to start and she would like everyone to be there so she sent me to find you.' She looked at each of them in turn, the furrow between her brows deepening. 'Is everything all right?'

Zafar straightened up. 'Tell her we're coming.' After a slight pause, she nodded and left, the door swinging shut behind her. 'I think the best thing to do now is to go back in there and finish the evening on a high for Daadi's sake. It's her big day and I don't want anything ruining it for her. We'll have time enough later to figure out what to do about Ibrahim's situation.' He squeezed Ibrahim's shoulder and normally, seeing the support and understanding in his older brother's eyes would have helped ease the tension he was feeling constricting his chest.

Today, however, it didn't.

CHAPTER TWENTY

Jiya

Jiya stared down at the golden bangles. There was one on each wrist, a centimetre thick in width with intricate patterns carved into the gold. Ibrahim's mother had taken them off her own wrists and put them on Jiya's to welcome her into their family. They were pretty and delicate and Jiya felt their weight on her wrists like handcuffs, despite the fact that they were a bit big for her.

The evening had taken such a turn that it had left her mind spinning, leaving her unable to figure out which way was up. Snatches of moments and emotions were coming out at her and she felt she was watching everything happen around her as though she were sitting securely in a bubble.

She remembered holding onto Ibrahim for dear life because if she hadn't, she'd have collapsed in a heap with the shock of his father's announcement. Her mother had come towards her, beaming from ear to ear, and enveloped her in a tight hug, followed by Ibrahim's grandmother and mother.

Her brother had seemed genuinely happy for her when he'd come forward and hugged her and despite showing Ibrahim nothing but his grumpiness, she had seen her father pulling him in for a hug and then standing there with Ibrahim's father, chatting and laughing together.

If she'd expected anyone to object, it was her father. She had seen nothing but reluctance from him where Ibrahim was concerned but according to Jameel, their father wasn't against the match at all.

'There's no reason for him to really object, is there? He's just been playing the hard nut with Ibrahim but he's actually impressed by him; he's a decent guy, the kind we want for you. He was definitely surprised with the way the whole thing came out and that made him less trusting but he's quite happy with the match, especially now that he's met Ibrahim's family and knows how happy you are with him. Also, I'll let you in on a secret: Mum spoke to Auntie Nadia and she found out that Auntie Nadia has known of the Saeed family for a while and couldn't stop gushing about them. That helped ease any concerns they had. And I spoke to them too.'

She had looked at him in surprise then.

'You don't have to look so shocked, Jiya. I could see he made you happy so I had a chat with Abba and urged him to at least give Ibrahim a chance.' Her brother's thoughtfulness brought a lump to her throat but she didn't have the liberty to delve into the feeling any further because of the torrent of thoughts jostling that little kernel of hope in her mind.

They were sitting in the car on the way home now, her mother in the back with her while Jameel sat in the front passenger seat.

Things had taken a turn at lightning speed and she knew she needed to act sooner rather than later to put a stop to things.

'I still can't believe it, Yunus. Our little girl is all grown up and ready to settle down. Ibrahim is a wonderful boy and his family is so lovely. I can't thank Allah enough for this blessing.'

Looking out of the window on her side, she tried to tune out of the conversation going on around her.

Feeling horribly car sick left her with just enough energy to concentrate on taking deep breaths and keeping the contents of her stomach down. There was no point her saying or doing anything at that point in time to stop her parents. She needed to speak to Ibrahim first and figure out what exactly had happened.

'Hmm. I'll admit I had my doubts about the boy but his family seem to be very decent. You can tell by the way the children interact with their parents and their grandmother. Did you see their eldest son? If Ibrahim is anything like his eldest brother, I think our Jiya will be very happy.'

Jiya wished her parents would stop talking. God, they sounded so happy. How were they going to react when they found out that the whole thing had been a ruse? Her father had been furious when he'd first found out about Ibrahim being on the scene. She couldn't even begin to think how he'd react when he found out that they'd been faking it.

Her father jerked the car to a stop outside their house, yanking up the handbrake with a grating noise that Jiya felt deep in her skull. She staggered out of the car on her blistered, achy feet and pulled in a couple of deep breaths to help tamp down the rising nausea. Her head was pounding as though her temples were being bashed with a mallet on both sides in synchronisation.

She felt far too fragile for anything more this evening and despite wanting some answers from her parents, she knew she wouldn't be capable of doing anything more than taking herself to bed.

But first, she would take the torture devices off her feet. Thankfully the motion sickness had subsided and she only had the splitting headache to contend with.

She was making her way to the stairs, after mumbling a good night to her parents when her mother stopped her.

Jiya turned a frowning face towards her mother but any words of protest about being stopped didn't pass her lips as she caught her mother's expression. It was the same as when she'd come and hugged her after Ibrahim's father had made 'The Announcement'. Her eyes were openly brimming with emotion and she looked more than just happy. She looked content.

'I'm so happy, Jiya, I don't even have the words.'

She didn't know what to say to that. There was plenty she wanted to say about the evening, but feeling as she was, she knew there was no sense in saying anything contrary just then. Even if she had been feeling up to it, the expression on her mother's face and the emotion in her voice was enough to make her think twice.

'What's the matter? You look a bit pale.' Her mother put the back of her hand against her forehead in the age-old gesture of checking for a temperature. 'Was it the drive? I don't know why your father thinks he's a rally driver. Go upstairs and get ready for bed, I'll bring you something to help you feel better.'

Before Jiya could say anything, her mother had left her at the bottom of the stairs. The feeling of sickness had mostly passed and the headache, while still there, wasn't as intense. Now she was just left feeling confused and that dreaded feeling of guilt was creeping its way back to take centre stage.

Stepping into her bedroom, Jiya sat on the bed, looking through the window out onto the street. The light from the street lamp outside their house threw white light directly into her bedroom, often doing away with the need to light a lamp. There was enough light for her to see what she was doing, as she took her jewellery off and grabbed her face wipes. It always frustrated her that the make-up which took her forever to get right could be wiped off in a matter of minutes, leaving her looking like she was in need of a good dose of sunshine.

Moving the wipe systematically across her face, she tried to think of anything except for the minefield she would have to cross at some point and desperately wanted to avoid just then, but her mind was intent on stepping towards it anyway.

She had wanted to talk to Ibrahim before leaving the venue but she didn't get the chance. He had disappeared soon after 'The Announcement' and she had caught a glimpse of him talking to his grandmother but before she could get to him, he had disappeared again. What did he know about this evening's bombshell? How did he feel? And why hadn't he sought her out?

A light tap at the door broke through her thoughts and before she could respond, her mother walked into the room.

Classic Mum, don't wait to see if I'm decent, just charge in!

'Here. Tea and biscuits. Then take these two paracetamols – not with the tea for God's sake – and go to bed. And there's no need to stay up reading or Facegramming or whatever it is you kids do.'

There was so much Jiya wanted to say back to her mother just then but settled with 'Thanks Ammi, good night.'

As her mother closed the door behind her, Jiya reached into the clutch she had taken to the party and pulled out her phone, wanting to see if Ibrahim had called. There were plenty of *Facegram* notifications but nothing from him.

Jiya thought to message him but not having the energy to wait for a reply, she phoned him. It went straight to his voicemail so she put it down without leaving a message.

There was so much to sort through, she'd be better off tackling it all tomorrow, especially given that Ibrahim wasn't available to talk to right then. With that thought, Jiya finished off her tea and biscuits and after downing two paracetamols, she got ready for bed.

Ibrahim

Ibrahim pulled open the door leading out to the garden from what he and his brothers referred to as their den and pulled in a deep breath in an effort to clear his mind and ease the tension in his shoulders. Since earlier this evening, it felt as though a boulder had been placed on his chest and he was struggling to take in enough air.

'I'm not saying this to shit-stir or piss you off. I just think it's all a bit shady. I mean, how long have you known her?'

'I've known her for a lot longer and for the hundredth time, she's not like that.'

Ashar and Haroon had been going back and forth for a while now about what Jiya's motives were and what might have triggered this evening's momentous announcement.

'What do you know? You're a kid.'

'At least I'm not twisted.'

'Ashar and Haroon, that's enough. If you're not going to be constructive and help, feel free to leave.'

Cutting their eye at each other, they acknowledged Zafar's tired telling off.

'Ibrahim, have you heard from her?'

He went and sat on one of the deep leather sofas and took the steaming cup Rayyan held out to him.

'No. She called but I didn't answer and she didn't leave a message. I don't even know what to think, let alone what to say to her.'

He turned to look at Ashar. 'You think she might have engineered this whole thing? Don't interrupt Harry,' he held his hand up to stop their youngest brother from speaking in defence of his friend, 'I want to hear what Ash has to say.'

Ashar moved forward and rested his arms on his thighs, his bow tie dangling around his neck.

'You told her everything about how Dad was setting you up with a friend's daughter and you weren't interested in settling down. She told you about how she wants to finish studying and work. Even if we take into account that you mentioned the M word to Dad with regards to this bird . . .'

'Her name is Jiya.' Ibrahim had never seen Harry so serious before. As though anything against Jiya was a personal affront to him.

'Yeah, yeah, Jiya then. You mentioned marriage but then you told Daadi that you were still finding your feet. You even told us that she wasn't the kind of girl our old man would approve of but then what happened? She came and wowed him and he was more than happy to give your relationship his stamp of approval.

'Then, to top it all off, the first time our parents meet hers, our dad goes and announces your engagement.' He paused, letting them all ponder his words for a few minutes.

'Like I said before, maybe she had a change of heart. I mean, I could be wrong, but what if I'm not? What if she liked what she saw and decided that she'd rather have that than what you'd initially agreed with her? I wouldn't blame her – you're quite the catch, brother.'

Ibrahim let Ashar's words wash over him, thinking back to some of the moments he had referred to. None of what he had said was beyond belief; in fact, it was very much believable.

But could his judgement have been that wrong? Was it possible that Jiya was that ruthless?

'Believe me guys, Jiya's not like that. Bhai, you've met her, do you think she could be like that? That she would deliberately deceive Ibrahim?' Harry looked as bewildered as Ibrahim felt as he spoke to Zafar. Ashar spoke before Zafar said anything.

'She might have nothing to do with it and be completely innocent of anything but I find it's all a bit too convenient, isn't it?' He shrugged his shoulders, leaning back against the sofa.

'I think the best thing to do would be to talk to her. Rationally.' Rayyan came to sit beside Ibrahim. 'You'll never really know anything unless you speak to her. Ash might have a point, because a lot of what he's said is how things appear to have gone, but then she was with you or Harry most, if not all of this evening. At what point would she have agreed to or encouraged an announcement of an engagement?'

Ibrahim felt that boulder press harder on his chest and ran his hands through his hair and then gripped the back of his neck, staring up at the ceiling. 'I don't know. I don't fucking know!'

'Look, I've got nothing against her but I just think you should have a healthy dose of caution going forward.' Ashar looked directly at Ibrahim as he spoke, his cynicism crystal clear in his words.

The tightness in Ibrahim's neck was so intense it made his head feel like it weighed a ton. He had no idea what to make of both this evening and the discussion he'd had with his brothers – especially Ashar's words. But he needed to. He needed to make sense of what had happened other-wise the whole situation would gather momentum like a runaway train and the wreckage it would cause would be catastrophic.

He couldn't just give in and end up like Zafar, in an unwanted relationship. Or like his parents: together but just as comfortable apart. And in his case, a part of him would always doubt Jiya. He would always wonder how much of the whole debacle had been orchestrated by her and her family.

A long-forgotten feeling emerged from the recesses of his mind. The feeling of being cheated and duped into believing something that was nothing more than a smokescreen.

Graduating with a first-class pass, completing his Legal Practice Course and being at the tail end of his training contract, he had been on his way to becoming a qualified solicitor. He had been on top of the world, with the false optimism that nothing was beyond his grasp and whatever he wanted was at the end of his fingertips.

He had been in the enviable position of many of his peers because aside from his academic and professional accomplishments, his girlfriend had been one of the smartest women in their cohort and being a cosmetics model hadn't done her any harm. They were known as *the* power couple and he had taken for granted that none of that would ever change.

But boy had he got the reality check of a lifetime with that one!

The woman he had thought would be his partner in every sense of the word had been cheating on him behind his back and he himself had overheard her saying that she was only with him because of what she could get out of being associated with the Saeed name. 'Ibrahim is a rung on a very tall ladder. The main prize is way past him. If I had to do the same thing with someone his father's age, I'd do it in a heartbeat. The wealth and prestige that comes with him . . . there are few people who can achieve that and if I can get to it on his coat-tails then why not? Besides, it doesn't hurt that he's smitten with me.'

The feelings that had swamped him that day were as clear as if he'd only just experienced them. He had gone straight to the gents and emptied his stomach, the acrid taste of bile forever associated with betrayal for him.

Over time, he'd come to accept that not all women were like that. In fact, most women were not like that. But what if he'd found two who were?

Was Jiya like that?

Sure, up until today, he'd not seen anything to suggest she wanted anything more from him than they'd agreed. But the same thing had happened all those years ago. He'd never suspected a thing. He'd thought his relationship was the stuff of dreams, when in reality, it had turned out to be the ugliest of nightmares.

With all these thoughts clamouring for attention, Ibrahim stood up, his body protesting at the sudden movement.

He looked towards Ashar. 'You're right, I need to talk to her and see what she knows or says, which will obviously have to wait till tomorrow.'

'I think you mean later on today. It's three in the morning.' Zafar flicked his cuff back and stood up as well. 'Let's call it a night. I also think sleeping on it might help clear your mind and decide how to move forward. Just one word of advice. Don't act in haste.' He squeezed his shoulder and left the room, followed by Rayyan and Harry, whose shoulders were slumped.

Ashar stood up and came towards him. 'I know you all think I'm too cynical and see the world through jade-coloured glasses. But I care for you and I don't want to see you used or hurt. If she's innocent, then she'll have nothing to hide and will turn down this proposal straight away. You have nothing to be worried about because you didn't make her any false promises about engagements or weddings, did you?'

Ibrahim shook his head, his brain not fully comprehending anything anymore.

One corner of Ashar's mouth lifted in a semblance of a smile. 'Get some sleep, bro. You'll need your wits about you when dealing with this.' He slapped him on his back and left the room while Ibrahim stood where he was.

How had things spiralled so far out of control? He had actually thought everything was working out perfectly. So, when and where had things fucked up? And who was responsible for it?

CHAPTER TWENTY-ONE

Jiya

In all the weeks she had known him, Jiya had never seen Ibrahim look as solemn as he did then. His face was drawn and his jaw looked like it had been carved from granite.

Despite the summer sun beating down on her as they sat outside a small coffee shop, she felt an ominous shiver down her spine and placed her milkshake on the table and ran her palms down her thighs.

He kept his sunglasses on his face so she couldn't see his eyes, only her own reflection. Perhaps she should have worn her own sunglasses; at least they would have given her some sense of protection rather than feeling like all her thoughts and feelings were laid out for him to see while he kept his own well hidden.

'Did anyone say anything when you got home?'

He tilted his head ever so slightly at her question. 'About what?'

Ah! So, we're playing that game.

'Well duh!' Best to keep the tone easy. 'About the announcement your father made yesterday.'

'Why, did someone say something to you?'

Oh, for crying out loud! She just about stopped herself from huffing out loud and slapping her palm on the table at his sheer obtuseness. Time to take the bull by the horns.

'No, nobody said anything to me except my mother, who couldn't contain how happy she was. Although that's all she's said, nothing more. Since this morning she's been busy making phone calls and sharing the news with relatives and friends far and wide and I didn't know what to say to stop her.' Jiya shook her head, remembering how animated her mother had been on the phone to her sister. If only the whole thing had been genuine and not born out of a lie.

How would her mother react when she found out that she and Ibrahim had been faking it this whole time? She'd be devastated. Heartbroken.

She would have to answer questions from the very people she was phoning with news of Jiya's engagement, about why there was no wedding date fixed.

She looked up and saw that Ibrahim had taken his sunglasses off – thank God – and was staring at her with the strangest expression on his face. As though he wasn't sure what he was looking at.

'What? Do I have a milkshake moustache or cream on my face?' She swiped at her cheeks with her napkin but nothing came away.

'I have a question for you.' Again, that ominous shiver went down her spine and she straightened in her chair. She didn't know what to make of both his tone or his statement and she couldn't figure out what his expression meant either.

Swallowing down the golf ball lodged in her throat, she ran her palms down her thighs again. What on earth was she nervous about? She hadn't said or done anything to feel guilty about, so why was she? Yesterday's announcement had been his father's work, not hers. Of course, she wasn't clear on how exactly it had all come about, but surely, they should be working together to figure out what had happened last night and come up with a plan – together – for damage control. Instead, she felt she was being questioned as though she had committed some crime. He totally had that lawyer thing going on right now.

Well, she had nothing to be afraid of or feel guilty about so he could bring it on.

'Go ahead.' She leaned back in her chair after picking up her milkshake, trying to relax her taut nerves.

A corner of his mouth lifted but there was no humour in his expression. 'Before my father made his announcement, what did you and your family think was the future for our "relationship"?' He had lifted his fingers to emphasise air quotes and Jiya felt part shocked and part bewildered.

She had a sneaky suspicion where his line of questioning might be heading, but for the sake of their friendship and her faith in such a bond, she prayed to God that she was wrong.

In a clear voice she was super proud of, she answered his question.

'Before your father's announcement yesterday, I was under the impression that we are pretending to be boyfriend and girlfriend, each for our own reasons. As far as my parents were concerned – and I had thought your parents were in the same boat – they believe that we genuinely like each other. That we are *in love* with each other and want to spend the rest of our lives together.' She saw a smug expression come over his face and held her hand up to stall any comment from him. 'But . . . but they certainly hadn't come to the party with the intention of making anything official or even discussing our relationship as such. It was the first time they were meeting your family, for God's sake.'

'Could have fooled me.'

His tone was frostier than she'd ever heard it before and she could see the lines of tension bracketing his mouth. He was obviously as affected as her by the turn of events last night and was probably behaving the way he was – not attractive, but she could give him some leeway – because of that.

She tried to keep her voice as calm and even as she could. 'Look, we were both caught completely by surprise with your father's announcement last night and . . .'

'And I wonder who instigated the whole thing.'

Jiya curled her fingers into her palms and felt her nails biting into the soft skin. She also ground her back teeth together for good measure to try and rein in her temper, before she did something reckless like fly out of her chair and fold him in half for his ridiculous attitude.

'To be honest, I'm not sure myself what happened. I would have asked my parents if I'd had a chance but like I said, my mother was busy on the phone all morning and this afternoon you wanted to meet up. Did you manage to have a chat with your parents or Daadi? Were your brothers not aware of what your father planned to announce?'

He looked away from her at that and instead concentrated on the glass of iced water coated in droplets from condensation in front of him. 'My dad spoke to Zaf but only to inform him that he was about to make an announcement; he didn't say anything about whose idea it was. But it's funny isn't it,' he shrugged his shoulders and scoffed, 'you're hardly the kind of girl my father would normally approve of. In fact, he would never consider someone like you so I can't for the love of me understand how you managed to impress him enough to have him announce our fucking engagement.'

Jiya hoped to hell she had masked the hurt his remark caused. What the hell had got into him this afternoon? Her own patience with him was fast running out, especially with his attitude of wanting to lay blame somewhere, and judging by what he'd said so far, the contenders seemed to be her and her family.

Ibrahim

It took a considerable amount of willpower not to wince at the hurt that flashed across Jiya's face because of his words. He wasn't a bastard by nature, but he really needed to be sure about what had happened. Had she pulled the wool over his eyes as had happened once before and as Ashar had suggested? Or was she as innocent as she would have him believe?

He hadn't managed to get any sleep last night despite being dog-tired and as a result he'd had to take painkillers with his morning coffee to stave off the worst of a headache he could feel brewing. He hadn't seen either of his parents in the dining room for breakfast and when he'd asked after them, Reshma had told him that his parents and Daadi had gone to visit some relative. Something about them not being able to come to the party and *blah blah blah*.

Unable to get any answers from his own family, he had messaged Jiya, asking her to meet him at a coffee shop, hoping that she would have some information about what exactly had happened. So far, the only thing he'd been able to make out was that she had as much idea about the announcement as he did and she had yet to find out anything from her parents. Unfortunately, it wasn't enough to quieten the voices of doubt that were clamouring for attention in his overactive brain. If anything, those voices were getting stronger and louder in their suspicion of exactly what had gone down.

Was she that good an actress? Was all this confusion and hurt feigned for his benefit? Or was she genuine?

The rush of thoughts in his head was enough to trigger a stonking migraine but this thing couldn't be left to be picked up later or another day. He wanted answers. Now.

'I thought we had set things out pretty clearly, so where and when do you think this fuck-up took place? I certainly didn't ask my dad to make the announcement.'

Carefully placing her half-finished milkshake onto the table, she looked at him directly, the changing expressions on her face indicating that she'd come to some sort of decision or conclusion.

'If there is something you would like to ask me, or accuse me of, then do so directly. Stop beating around the bush.'

The bright afternoon sun cast a golden glow over her, and with her fierce expression she looked like a warrior princess. The deep chocolate of her eyes was clear and her lush lips were pressed in a firm line. The pull of attraction was ever-present and that pissed him off even more. How was his fucking libido not getting the message that there were bigger fish to fry here?

'All right. Did you engineer this whole thing?' The instant dimming in her eyes made his own gut clench but he ploughed on regardless. 'Maybe you started off thinking that you want to complete your course and get a decent job. But then going out with me, meeting my family and seeing the life we lead probably got you thinking that maybe you could tweak your plans. You could have something even better. My credentials are hardly shit.

'Besides, your ultimate goal has always been to get away from your family but it doesn't have to be a plush city office, right? My place would work just as well.'

She stared at him silently for a few moments, the hum from conversations from the tables around them and passing traffic were the only noises they could hear.

Ibrahim felt sick. Having to voice all those poisonous thoughts had the coffee he'd consumed swirling in his gut like a raging sea storm, threatening to come back up. His palms felt clammy and the muscles in his neck felt as though they were made of steel. He hoped to God he was wrong. He'd gladly go and give Ashar a leathering for filling his mind with all this shit, older brother or not.

But if he was being honest with himself, Ibrahim had to acknowledge that the only reason he was sitting here saying what he was, and using Ashar as a crutch, was because there was a part of him that needed to hear it refuted. He couldn't be the man who had been duped twice like this; wanted for reasons that had nothing to do with him as a person. It wasn't that he thought of Jiya as duplicitous. Well, up until then that thought had never crossed his mind, but after Ashar had spoken, the thoughts in his mind hadn't stopped and he was sure that the only way they would was when he knew what was true and what wasn't.

Jiya's quiet but firm voice pulled his attention back to the table. 'Is there anything else you'd like to add to that before I speak? I think it's best if we get everything out in the open all at once. No room for any ambiguity then.'

Ibrahim leaned forward, resting his arms on the table. 'I just want answers, Jiya. I want to . . . no, I need to know what happened.'

'Well, in that case, I hope you find my answers satisfactory, Ibrahim. Of course, I also hope you'll do me the courtesy of answering my questions too.'

CHAPTER TWENTY-TWO

Jiya

Jiya was absolutely sure she had never felt such intense rage before. There had been many times in her life when her mother, father or brother had pissed her off but this . . . this was in a category of its own. She was livid. Incensed. But the problem here was that it wasn't just anger Jiya was feeling. She was feeling hurt too. Actual physical pain at the things Ibrahim had just said.

Not in a million years would she have believed him capable of such cruelty. But then that just went to show how well she actually knew him. Or didn't, as was the case.

She didn't even know exactly how to answer everything he'd just said because her brain felt frozen at the accusatory tone of his voice. She couldn't believe this was the same man who she thought she might have been falling in . . . no, she wasn't. Nobody could feel such deep feelings in half a dozen weeks. And even if she was, such feelings could not be trusted. Especially when you – quite obviously in this case – didn't even know that person very well. At all, in fact.

Oh, I've been such a fool!

She should have known better than to rely on another to help her solve her problems. When had that ever been a sensible idea? She should have relied on her own ability to solve her problems rather than depend on the likes of Mr Ibrahim – *My Credentials Are Hardly Shit* – Saeed.

But how could she have known that such a thing would happen? He had seemed so . . . normal to her when Harry had introduced him. Never in her life had she come across someone who had switched on her so drastically – not even in school, and she had gone to an all-girls' school for God's sake. She'd seen it plenty of times in films, so it stood to reason that there were people out there that did this sort of thing. Like the man sitting opposite her.

Pulling in a deep breath and pasting a relaxed expression on her face, she leaned forward and clasped her hands together on the table.

'You're right.' She paused for a split second and was rewarded with a quirked eyebrow. The higher he rose, the harder he would fall and the greater her satisfaction would be.

'I started off thinking I would complete my MBA and then go on to work in a plush office. That plan has never changed. In fact, it is very much in place even now.' She could see the disbelief on his face but didn't let it deter her. 'Going out with you was purely for the benefit of giving me some reprieve from my parents trying to railroad me into getting married. You see, they're somewhat . . .' she shrugged, unsure about what words would be politically correct here, before he used whatever she said to throw back in her face. '. . . let's say *traditional* in terms of wanting to see their daughter settled with a husband. For them, that is the ultimate picture of parental duties carried out to the T. Neither of my parents went to university and nor has my brother so I've had to fight for some of the privileges you seem to have taken for granted.'

'I don't . . .'

'Please don't interrupt me. You've had your say, so now do me the courtesy of letting me finish.' Her anger

216

was gaining momentum and she relished the feeling it was giving her, as though she could take on the world and its dog right now.

'Where was I . . . yes, privileges. For me, getting an education and being able to work aren't just a given. My mother was a housewife and a mother at my age and her mother before that and so on and so forth. So naturally, they would think that I'd do the same. It's not entirely their fault I suppose, but I digress.

'You're also right in saying that your credentials aren't *shit*. They're quite impressive and they most definitely impressed my parents. You're an educated man, working hard for a living for the family business; no obvious vice like excessive drinking, gambling or womanising as far as anyone can tell. Even Auntie Nadia thought you were quite the catch when she found out about you.'

Jiya could tell that he was beginning to feel a bit uncomfortable at what she'd said so far because he was shifting restlessly in his seat. Well, that was just too bad because she wasn't quite finished with him yet.

'Humour me, Ibrahim, if I'm not the kind of girl your father would ever approve of, which I'm guessing is the reason you went ahead with this charade with me as your choice of candidate, what is it about me that impressed him enough to announce an engagement?

'Or could it be that *you* decided that rather than settle with some daughter of your father's friend, you would rather be with me. I mean you had my mother eating out of the palm of your hand and my brother got along with you perfectly well too. And let's be honest, *my* credentials are hardly shit. I'm actually as educated as you are and I've worked harder in that my father or older brother didn't set up a springboard for me. Whatever I've achieved has been through my own sheer grit, determination and bloody hard work.'

'Jesus, Jiya! Don't hold back, will you?' He looked as surprised as she felt at the bite in her words. She had never realised she was capable of being just as cruel as he had been. But fighting fire with fire wasn't a bad thing. It was self-preservation.

'And why should I?' Jiya dropped all pretence of having a civilised conversation with Ibrahim and gritted her teeth. 'Why the hell should I hold back? You sat there and had the audacity to question my integrity and point a finger at my family's and my intentions. What's the matter, Ibrahim, you can dish it out but you can't take it, is that it?

'I came here hoping . . . thinking that we would moan and complain; laugh about what happened last night and then deal with it. Together. The last thing I expected was for you to turn around and accuse me of trying to trap you into marriage.'

Jiya stood up, unsure whether she'd be able to keep a lid on her anger long enough to not start getting louder. She was still aware that they were in a public place and the last thing she wanted was to make a scene with him and add embarrassment into the mix. Or further embarrassment anyway. He'd probably think she did it on purpose.

'Thank you, Mr Saeed, for proving to me that men like you have no integrity and should be avoided like the fucking plague.' She slung her bag over her shoulder and then opened it to pull out a tenner. She slapped it on the table and placed the milkshake glass on top of it. 'I'd hate for you to think I'm out for whatever I can get.'

He rolled his eyes and looked the other way, his expression one she could only label as belligerent. Jiya turned to make her way through the tables placed outside the coffee shop but at the last minute, she turned to face him.

'Oh, and another thing. When you realise how wrong you are – and trust me, that will happen – do me a favour, will you? Don't call me or try and meet me. OK?' She didn't wait for any response, turning away before her tears broke the bank and gushed down her cheeks. She was proud of herself for not crumbling or breaking down under his verbal assault or when delivering her own put-downs, but her energy had just dropped from twenty per cent to two per cent and she needed to get the hell away from him, pronto.

Disbelief. Hurt. Rage. Jiya didn't know which emotion got top billing.

She pumped her legs harder, avoiding collisions with people with the practised ease of a city girl, as she made her way to the bus stop where a double decker had pulled up, the orange indicator flashing like a beacon.

Making her way to the top deck of the bus, Jiya sat right at the front, the large windscreen giving her a clear view of the route the bus was taking. Sitting at the front also meant that nobody could see her face as she wiped away more tears that didn't get the memo. *Ibrahim Saeed isn't worth a single tear!*

She felt her phone vibrate in her bag and pulled it up to see a missed call from Harry. A message notification lit up the screen a moment later asking her if she was all right. She sent back a quick message to let him know that she was fine and would catch up with him later.

Just because his brother had proved to be a royal arsehole, it didn't mean that she would let it impact her friendship with Harry. He hadn't given her any reason to cut ties with him. Yet. Who knew, maybe he'd turn out to be like his older brother at some point.

As soon as she thought it, she realised that she wasn't being fair to Harry. He had always been a good friend and in introducing her to his older brother, he had been trying to help her. Ibrahim's behaviour was his alone to own. Harry had nothing to do with it until and unless he proved otherwise to Jiya.

It was always better to have some caveats in place.

She knew that now. She had just learned it the hard way.

Going through her previous conversations with Ibrahim, she tried to recall if he had shown any signs that he was the king of morons. But she kept coming up blank. All she remembered now was how her feelings for him had gradually been morphing into something else.

But there was no point in going over any of that.

The thing she needed to concentrate on now, was what to do. What was she going to tell her family? How was she going to move forward with anything? And what about the persistent pain she was feeling deep in her chest since leaving that Godforsaken coffee shop?

She decided she needed to walk off some of the restlessness building up within her before she could go home. She wiped away her residual tears and pushing the stop button on the pole behind her seat, she got off the bus a few stops before the one she needed.

The sun was still shining and plenty of people were out and about soaking up the late afternoon heat.

An ice-cream van was parked a few feet ahead of where she was walking and a wave of sadness enveloped her anew, enough to make her slow down to match the pace of a snail, as memories of buying an ice cream with Ibrahim and spending a similar sunny day together washed over her.

Is this what would happen to her now whenever she saw something? Would it trigger memories of moments shared with a man who didn't deserve a single thought? Would she forever miss out on things she had loved way before meeting him because it might make her think of him? Miss him?

No. Hell no!

Swiping at her damp cheeks – again – Jiya hiked up her chin and joined the queue snaking from the ice-cream van's window.

She would not let thoughts of *him* change anything. She would still do whatever she liked without thinking about *him*. She wouldn't let *him* have such power over her or her actions. She would buy a Flake 99 right now and enjoy every single lick and bite of it.

Taking the loaded cone from the ice-cream man, Jiya took a big mouthful of the ice cream as she started walking again. The generous bite gave her brain freeze and she sucked in her cheeks and clenched her eyes shut as the sensation skated down her spine.

So much for showing him.

By the time she popped the last bit of wafer in her mouth, it tasted like sawdust had coated her tongue and she was feeling sick.

She needed to get her reaction under control for long enough to make it to the safety of her room, although her mum usually just walked in so the bathroom was probably a better bet.

The house was silent as Jiya let herself in. The kitchen was visible from the front door and she couldn't see her mother in there. Closing the front door as softly as she could, she made it up three steps when her mother came out of the dining room and came and stood at the bottom of the staircase.

'You're home. How was my favourite son-in-law-to-be?'

Jiya turned to look at her mother and seeing her face broke the last vestige of control Jiya thought she'd had on her emotions. She felt her lower lip tremble and before she could fully register what had happened, she was in her mother's arms sobbing like a baby.

'Jiya? What's happened? Are you hurt?'

She tried to get words out of her mouth but all that came out was a pathetic gurgle, followed by more sobbing so she settled for shaking her head in answer.

Her mother led her into the front room and sitting back on one of the numerous sofas scattered around the room, she held Jiya close to her chest and let her cry, rhythmically rubbing her back.

After a couple of minutes, when she thought the worst of it was over, her mother moved her head back and peered down at Jiya's face, pushing stray strands of now damp hair away from her forehead, her own expression calm but curious.

'Here, blow your nose.' She handed Jiya a tissue and the small gesture set her off again.

After another few sobs, Jiya pulled in a breath and hiccupped.

'Now, do you want to talk to me before, during or after a cup of tea? We have the rest of the day because your father and Jameel won't be back until late.'

Giving her mother a watery smile, Jiya burrowed into her arms again, mumbling as she did, 'During and after.'

Placing a plate of pakoras on the coffee table alongside two mugs full of tea, her mother came and sat on the sofa next to Jiya and began adding sugar to the teas.

'I made a mistake, Ammi.' Her voice was barely more than a croak as she addressed her mother. She expected her mother to sigh dramatically and start a monologue about how trying a child Jiya was to her but all she did was nod once.

Unable to bear the guilt, she picked up a pakora and jammed it into her mouth.

Her mother placed the plate between them both and dipping her own one in the bowl of chutney, she asked, 'What kind of mistake?'

Over the next hour, the entire plate of pakoras and two rounds of tea, Jiya told her mother everything. She started off backwards, talking about what had happened at the coffee shop earlier first and then moving onto the fact that she hadn't been all that honest about her relationship with Ibrahim.

Her mother didn't say anything; she just sat there quietly listening and nodded her encouragement every now and then for Jiya to carry on.

When she had finished telling her mother everything about her fake relationship with Ibrahim – leaving out the bits where they had occupied themselves in less fake activities like kissing – they both sat in silence for a few minutes. She felt somewhat relieved but the feeling of guilt was there in the form of a rock settled at the bottom of her gut.

Her mother sat there quietly, absorbing everything Jiya had just said. The only sounds in the room were the ticking of the clock on the wall and the low hum of the radio from the kitchen, which was always on.

'Why did you think you needed to do that?'

CHAPTER TWENTY-THREE

Jiya

Jiya swallowed the lump in her throat. She hadn't expected her mother to congratulate her or praise her for what she had done but she hadn't expected such a softly voiced question either. If she was being honest with herself, she had expected a lengthy complaint about what a disappointment she was as a daughter.

'Jiya? I asked you something. Why?'

Pulling in a breath, Jiya felt her chest expand. She'd been deceptive enough to last her a lifetime. She didn't want any more lies or falsehoods. She needed to be honest with her mother. About everything.

Looking at her mother directly and with a firm voice, Jiya plunged ahead.

She spoke about her feelings of inferiority and lack of importance in the family. About her dreams and the fact that she felt her parents never understood or appreciated them. Her desperation to prove herself as someone worthy of their attention and unconditional love in ways besides marrying a suitable boy.

'I want to be important to you for who I am, not because I can marry someone and you get to tick that off your list. I'm not saying I want to be more important than Jameel, that's not the case. But surely there are times when you can tell him he's wrong because he blatantly is and I'm not. Or, as childish as it sounds, I can sometimes have the last chocolate bourbon instead of always giving it to him.

'I know how precious he is to you, Ammi, and I know why. But why aren't I precious to you? You just want to send me away with a husband and that's it, job done.'

Jiya looked at her mother, who looked somewhat stunned, until her face fell and her eyes softened, filling with tears.

Putting her arm around Jiya's shoulders, she pulled her in for a tight hug and kissed the top of her head.

'You *are* precious to me, so much more than you know.' Her voice was such a soft whisper and since she was speaking into Jiya's hair, she could hardly hear what her mother was saying, but the feelings in those words were crystal clear. Her mother meant what she was saying.

'I'm sorry, my love, for not telling you how important you are. I . . . I suppose I have no excuse for it.' She eased away from Jiya but pulled her hand and clasped it between her own two. 'Except, I was never raised that way myself. My parents, even until today, have never said they love me. It was just something I never questioned; I simply didn't know to. I didn't realise that even though you know you love your child immensely, you should express those feelings to them. I guess you could say it's a modern concept for us.'

Jiya looked at her mother closely, seeing her emotions clearly on her face; though whether that was because her mother had let her guard down or because Jiya was looking more carefully, she didn't know.

'I know it was different for you, Ammi.' Jiya spoke as she huddled back into her mother's arms and they leaned back into the sofa.

Her mother scoffed. 'That's putting it lightly. I didn't even see your father until our wedding preparations were well under way, and that was only around thirty years ago. I never thought I had any other option. In my family it was more important that the boys were educated than us girls so I was just pleased to be able to write my own name out.

'That's one of the reasons I wanted you to at least get your O levels.'

'They're called GCSEs, Ammi.' Jiya rolled her eyes and giggled. Her mum was so solidly stuck in the seventies, it was hilarious.

'Yes, yes, GCEs. And you've done more than that. You've done so much and I'm sorry for not saying it before but I am proud of you. So much. I thought you knew that but if I've never said it, how could you.'

Jiya felt a lump in her throat again and before she could hold them back, tears rolled down her cheeks unchecked. If she carried on blubbering like a baby, she wouldn't be able to see a thing tomorrow, her eyes would be so swollen.

Her mother silently handed her a tissue and she noisily blew her nose. 'Does Abba think the same?'

She smiled at her. 'Your father is as tight-fisted with his words as his mother was with her purse; may her soul rest in peace. But never doubt that he loves you and is very proud of you. You're the first girl in our family who's got a degree, I think that's amazing. I'm just annoyed at myself for not saying it to you sooner, thinking that if I raised you how I was raised, everything would be fine. I should have appreciated the fact that times have changed, our country has changed and just because my parents or your father's parents did something a certain way, it doesn't make it right or necessary for us to do the same.

'I'm also annoyed at you.'

The quietly voiced chastisement caught her by surprise and she sat up to look at her mother fully. 'Why?'

'Firstly, because you lied and it doesn't matter what era you've been raised in, a lie is a lie and that's not how I've brought you up.'

The guilt that had become a permanent resident within her bloomed throughout her body, making her lower her eyes from her mother's and start crushing the used tissue in her hand.

'While I can understand that you felt you couldn't come to us and you thought we would push you into marriage, lying is wrong, Jiya.'

'But . . .'

'No buts. I don't like the fact that it took that boy to upset you for you to be able to talk to me.'

Jiya watched as the now shredded tissue made a pile beside her. Could it really be that simple? Should she just have spoken to her mother? But, she had before and it hadn't done anything. In fact, they'd just argued and butted heads, with her mother complaining and Jiya getting frustrated with her lot in life.

'What was the second thing?'

'Huh?'

'You said firstly, so what was the second thing that annoyed you?'

'Oh, yes. Yesterday, at the party, I spoke to Ibrahim's older brother's wife, though I can't remember her name.'

'Her name is Reshma.'

'Yes, Reshma. Such a lovely girl. She told me something interesting.' Her mother looked at her pointedly and Jiya racked her brain trying to think about what Ibrahim's sister-in-law could have told her mother. *Please don't let it be about the kissing.*

Her mother didn't let her squirm for long. 'She told me that she thought it was wonderful that you were applying for jobs in the city, but wouldn't it be amazing if you were able to work abroad if you got the chance after you had finished your course. You've never said anything of the sort to us.'

Jiya felt her cheeks heat up as her mother confronted her with that particular revelation. Her gut twisted at the thought of how unfair she had been towards her family, barrelling ahead with her own plans and ideas without even informing them. Her mother must have been caught completely off guard when Reshma spilled the beans.

'So, when were you planning on talking this idea through with us?'

'I'm not actually pursuing anything abroad, Ammi; I didn't think you or Abba would agree. I have been applying for jobs in the city but nothing's come through yet. I was going to tell you but . . .'

'*Oh Allah!* The fault is mine. Look, Jiya, so much of what you've done or are doing is completely new for us. Do you think anyone before you has done waitressing in our family?'

Jiya shook her head, somewhat stunned at her mother's response.

'Let your father and brother return and then we can see what they say about your plans. I know your father's friend – your Uncle Tariq – his niece went and worked in Dubai for six months. If she can manage, I'm sure you'll do even better. I've been wrong in not trusting your ability to do things and instead focusing blindly on doing what has always been done, before thinking about whether or not it even works for you. I've probably wronged Jameel too.'

Jiya's heart clenched at her mother's disparaging words about herself.

'No, Ammi, don't say that – you're the bravest woman I know. You've come here and made a life for yourself, Abba and us, despite not knowing at times whether or not you were doing the right thing. You've always put our needs first, over and above anything for yourself. And maybe I should have told you before now that *I'm* proud of you.'

She saw her mother's eyes shimmer with unshed tears and flung her arms around her, holding on tight.

They'd both spent so many times at odds with each other, Jiya thought, without stopping and trying to understand each other and more of that blame lay at her own doorstep. She should have stopped and thought about why her mother said and did what she did and communicated her thoughts with her. How else would her mother know what was going through her head? Wasn't communication the magic key to success in every relationship?

Neither of them realised how long they had been sitting there chatting and it was only when they heard a car door slam right outside, did they both move. Her mother gasped when she looked at the clock. 'Oh my God, look at the time. Jiya, come and help me finish off dinner. Those two will come in here and bring the roof down in no time unless we feed them.'

Jiya looked out of the window and saw her father and brother huddled over the boot of the car. 'Ammi?'

Her mother turned and looked at her questioningly.

'Will you tell Abba everything we've spoken about?'

Her mother's expression cleared and she ushered for Jiya to go to her. 'I will.' She placed a hand on her shoulder and gave it a squeeze. 'And I'm absolutely sure he won't be any more annoyed than I was.'

Jiya gave her mother a tremulous smile and they both made their way towards the kitchen. 'Of course, how he'll feel about Ibrahim is a different thing entirely.'

Ibrahim

Ibrahim pressed the ignition switch and the bike roared to life beneath him. He could feel the thrum of the engine through his whole body as the bike vibrated with suppressed power. He pulled his helmet down, secured his gloves and grasping the handlebars, he moved the kick stand and tapped the gear shift with his foot. Crouching low over the bike, he navigated it onto a stretch of open road and as the engine warmed up and he felt it ready to go, he changed gears and pulled on the throttle. The bike flew forward effortlessly, gliding on the tarmac smoothly.

The roar of the powerful engine drowned out some of the persistent noise that had taken residence in his brain since everything had gone to hell a couple of days ago. He still hadn't managed to reach his parents, who had seemed to vanish. It was strange how whenever he'd wanted to avoid his father, he had always found him never too far away. Yet now, when he wanted to talk to the old man, he was out gallivanting. Again.

An approaching curve in the road had Ibrahim slowing down enough to take the bend safely. He was supremely pissed off but not enough to put himself and others in danger by being a dick on the road. Besides, he was a lawyer for crying out loud. Breaking the law so flagrantly would do him no favours. Sure, he was driving a bit over the legal limit, but he knew when to rein it in.

Taking out Ashar's bike gave him the chance to blow off some steam and clear his head and all while he was by himself. He didn't need any more thoughts or nuggets of wisdom or cynicism – take your pick – from his well-meaning brothers.

Seeing a good stretch of empty road ahead of him, he picked up speed again, crouching low as he accelerated.

After Jiya had walked out on him – he still couldn't believe that she had, especially that stunt with the ten-pound note – he had gone home and holed himself up in his room for the rest of the evening, only coming down around midnight after his empty stomach had started grumbling loud enough to wake the dead.

He couldn't even say what he'd spent the evening doing or thinking about because his thoughts weren't any clearer today than they had been yesterday. He'd ended up having a shitty night and then oversleeping. He'd gone into work and then had been practically frog-marched back home by Zafar because apparently, he *looked like shit*. At least his looks matched how he was feeling.

He hadn't left home with any destination in mind, letting the bike and the road take him wherever it went but it seemed a small part of his subconscious knew exactly where he needed to be. He followed the signs and after a few miles, took the exit.

He followed the road for the nature reserve and parklands he had visited often many years ago but had stopped when the rigmarole of life had taken over.

Pulling the bike to a stop in the expanse of gravel-covered ground that was used as a car park, Ibrahim made his way towards one of the trails.

The reserve was a few miles outside of London but being there, a person felt lightyears away from it. There were no sounds of traffic, horns or sirens. The peaceful silence was only broken by the sound of nature. Birds twittering and chirping, calling out their tunes. The rush of the breeze through the trees every now and then.

He paused and closing his eyes, he pulled in a deep breath of air mingled with the fresh scent of the soil and the woody scent of the trees. He felt the protest of muscles around his chest as the air pushed against his ribcage and his back.

He followed the trail as it wound through trees and slowly ascended up a small hill and then made its way down as it fell in line with a small stream. An elderly couple in walking boots, armed with walking poles and robust-looking rucksacks, walked past him, the lady eyeing him suspiciously before walking on.

He'd eye himself suspiciously too. He was wearing a busted old pair of biker boots, jeans and a T-shirt that had seen better days under a weathered leather jacket. But he wasn't there for a serious or leisurely hike.

Coming to a small clearing beside the stream, Ibrahim made his way towards the water and lowered himself onto a conveniently placed boulder, smoothed from decades of use.

The vista before him was as breathtaking as always: the clear rush of water over pebbles, the majestic stands of trees with their myriads of colours against the glorious backdrop of the blue sky. Wispy clouds scudded across its surface and it made Ibrahim think of those pointless geography lessons, where he remembered learning about clouds but right now couldn't identify even one of them in the sky, except to say that they looked like scattered balls of cotton wool. Some whole, and some pulled apart. Some of them resembled waves as they rode the sea.

He pulled out his phone and took a picture of the clouds, zooming in and out until he was happy with it, moving onto the trees to capture the different shades of green amidst the blue above and the brown below.

Before he knew it, he'd stood on the boulder and taken dozens of photographs, before moving several paces to the left and then right to capture different angles. Of course, the quality of these would be absolutely shite compared to photographs taken with an actual camera. The kind he had boxed away, sitting on top of the cupboard in his bedroom.

When was the last time he had pulled out any of his cameras and immersed himself in the joy of capturing moments like he used to?

Heaving a sigh, he plopped down on the boulder again and started flicking through the photographs he'd taken, discarding a few as he went and favouriting the ones he'd upload later. He was swiping his thumb across his screen a split second faster than his brain processed the image and suddenly he was looking at a picture of Jiya.

His heart skidded to a stop before kick-starting again in a jerky rhythm that had his breath hitching in his chest.

He remembered the day he had taken this picture. She'd been pestering him in her playful way about his photography and then urging him to get back into it, even if he started by using his mobile phone. He had taken his phone out and started taking pictures of her, at which she had giggled and tried to bat his phone away.

He wasn't any closer to figuring out what to think or what to do about what had happened. All he knew was that he'd never felt such intense despair before. It felt as though a vital part of him had been left behind somewhere and he didn't think he could carry on without it.

But did he want that part back in his life if it turned out it was all a sham? Of course not. So then why did he feel as if his life would remain forever stagnant as it was, with nothing to bring him that sense of completeness he had experienced just a few days ago?

CHAPTER TWENTY-FOUR

Ibrahim

Ibrahim rode back home well within the speed limit and parking the bike in the garage – after having topped up the tank – he made his way into the house. It was quiet and he couldn't see anyone as he made his way into the kitchen. He filled a glass with water and stood by the windows, taking in the view of the garden.

It was strange how despite seeing it every day, he'd never stopped to pay much attention to it. Paying closer attention to it now – his inner photographer really was making its presence felt – he could see the spectacular palette of colours in the flower bed in the centre of the garden, the contrasting greens of the various trees, the perfect backdrop of the sky. He saw movement from the side of his eye and found his brother's wife walking along the flower bed along the side, pausing every now and then to do something with the flowers.

Normally, he would have left her to it and moved on, but today something compelled him to go out.

'Hey.'

She turned abruptly, a startled look on her face and one gloved hand on her chest. She looked behind him and then back at him. 'Hey?' Her voice and face were both confused.

'Sorry, I didn't mean to scare you. I saw you from the window so I just . . .' Not knowing what else to say, he went quiet. How long had he known Reshma? Yet he could probably count on one hand the number of times he had actually spoken to her. Like, a proper conversation.

Unbidden, Jiya's question from the day of the party came to him.

What about Reshma? Did she want to marry your brother?

If he was honest with himself, he'd been too busy blaming her for marrying his brother to bother with her or think about things from her perspective.

She gave him a tentative smile. 'That's all right. I just wasn't expecting anyone, that's all. But I suppose it's too nice a day to stay indoors.' She turned back to the flowers for a few seconds and then turned back to face him. 'Are you all right?'

'Yeah. Why wouldn't I be?' It was an answer given on autopilot, without any thought and she obviously knew that, judging by the slight lifting of the corner of her mouth.

'How's Jiya?' Ibrahim stiffened at the mention of Jiya. He hadn't called her or seen her since she'd walked out of the coffee shop and she hadn't got in touch with him either.

He wasn't sure how much Zafar would have said to Reshma, so he shrugged in response. 'I've not spoken to her since the party.'

She gave an acknowledging nod and then there was awkward silence again.

The warmth of the sun, the scent of the flowers and the fresh air eased away some of the tension that was creeping in again in his shoulders. What would it take to stop this dreadful gnawing in his stomach?

He needed to find out, for the sake of his own sanity if nothing else, what had happened on the day of Daadi's party. Who had instigated the announcement of his and Jiya's engagement? Once he found out, he could put the whole sorry situation to bed.

Whatever the outcome, he probably wouldn't be seeing Jiya again. The thought made his stomach drop anew, and not in a pleasant, anticipatory kind of way. If it turned out that she or her family had pushed for the engagement, he'd never be able to trust her again. It would be the death knell on . . . on what? Their relationship? He didn't even know exactly what they had.

What he did know was that even though it had only really been a couple of days since he had seen her or spoken to her, he felt a gaping hole in his life already. How was it possible that she had taken up such a huge amount of space in his life in such a short space of time?

'Would you like to talk about it?' Ibrahim whipped his head so fast to face Reshma, he felt his already tense muscles screech in protest. His face probably mirrored the confusion he was feeling and it must have looked seriously unattractive because Reshma actually took half a step back away from him.

'You don't have to, of course. I just thought that maybe if you spoke about whatever was bothering you, it might help you figure things out because you seem to be quite stressed since your engagement was announced.' She gave him a small smile and gestured to the space around them. 'Coming out here was a great idea. There's just something about being out among nature which unravels our thoughts, simplifies a few things or just makes them that much more bearable.'

She moved a few steps further away and without any conscious thought or intention, Ibrahim followed her and fell in line with her small steps. She wasn't wrong. Going to the nature reserve had definitely helped and being out here wasn't dissimilar.

'Jiya's not really my girlfriend; we were pretending.' Ibrahim turned to look at Reshma's reaction to his words and to give her credit, she did bloody well. The only sign of her shock was the slight widening of her eyes.

Before he knew it, he had told her everything. Even – embarrassingly enough – that they had been seriously attracted to one another and how much he had wanted to explore that attraction but hadn't. He told her about Jiya's family, her issues with them, her dreams about her MBA and working, some of which she already seemed to know, probably through speaking with Jiya.

They had walked the length of the garden a few times and of an accord, they both went back into the kitchen as he carried on speaking, settling down at the small table with drinks and some finger food she had pulled out of the fridge – and he carried on talking.

He didn't even realise when he had started talking about himself. His own fears about losing control to his father and spending the rest of his life being miserable because he hadn't put his foot down. As soon as the penny dropped, he felt a stab of remorse.

Way to go, son! Disrespect the woman who's actually offered you a chance to offload your woes without any fucking judgement.

He stopped speaking and looked across at her, her expression one of understanding and empathy, rather than pissed off – which he definitely deserved.

'Sorry, I didn't mean to—'

She shook her head, a smile breaking out on her face. 'Don't. You don't have to apologise for how you feel. I can't speak for your brother and maybe another time, we can have a heart to heart about my story, but this is about you.

'I know it's not easy when we want something different to what our parents want for us; it's usually just their protective instinct or tons of experience compared to their children that drives their wishes. However, sometimes children know more than they're given credit for. They also have the benefit of moving with time a bit better than the previous generation and being more clued up about current times. Unless of course we're talking about Daadi.' She gave a little laugh and Ibrahim rolled his eyes at the mention of his grandmother.

'You can't use her as an example for anything. The woman's a maverick.'

'She certainly can be. What I'm trying to say is that it's never clear-cut and one will usually feel like they're compromising. But sometimes, you can actually both be on the same page. It could be that your parents genuinely like and approve of Jiya as a partner for you and rather than be against your choice – like you expected your father to be – they accept it.

'I'll accept that announcing your engagement like that was a shock but I think he was showing you his support in his own way. Maybe you need to come to terms with the fact that there could be times in life when you and your dad might have the same thoughts about something. It's all right if sometimes our choices coincide with those of our parents.'

How had he never noticed how perceptive she was? With her tentative smiles and gentle cajoling, in a single afternoon, she had prised his thoughts and fears out of him and was calmly making everything seem so unbelievably simple, but so real. She was talking to him, about him, but was she also thinking about herself and Zafar?

Before he could ponder on that thought anymore, she spoke again. 'Although the fact that she wasn't really your girlfriend changes things a bit. This is something you'll have to figure out and answer for yourself.'

Ibrahim scoffed at how simple she made it all sound. 'And how exactly am I going to do that?'

She shrugged her delicate shoulders, an open smile on her face which he had never seen before. 'By answering some questions. Honestly.' She emphasised the last word.

He eyed her sceptically. 'Such as?'

She wriggled forward in her seat, her eyes bright with enthusiasm. 'Does she make you laugh?'

'What?! How's that going to help me?'

Tilting her head to the side, she gave him a look of reproach, which instantly reminded him of *her*. 'You need to do this properly—'

'I will, I will. Yes, she can make me laugh.'

Reshma's smile was back in place. 'OK, good. What can't you talk to her about?'

Ibrahim leaned back in the straight-backed kitchen chair, balancing on its back legs as he pondered the question. What hadn't he spoken to Jiya about? They'd spoken about work, home, family, education, politics, their dreams. Hell, he'd even told her about his love for photography and not even his parents knew the extent of that.

He couldn't actually think of anything. There was no topic he hadn't or couldn't talk to Jiya about.

He looked across at Reshma who was grinning. 'Nothing, right? OK, last question.' She was looking at him intently, her face now completely impassive. 'How would you feel if you never saw her again?'

Ibrahim slammed the chair down with such a loud crack he was surprised the wood didn't splinter, and braced his hands on the table. He immediately felt a trickle of unease snake down his spine and his gut clenched so painfully he felt as though he'd been winded and was going to bring up whatever he'd just eaten.

How was it that having only known Jiya for such a short period of time, the thought of never seeing her again could have such a visceral impact on him? His throat went dry as the thought went through his head again, Reshma's soft voice echoing in his ears. He grabbed the glass in front of him and gulped down the juice in it without tasting a thing.

His pulse was pumping as though he'd sprinted a mile, pounding a tattoo in his temples.

'I'm sorry, Ibrahim, I didn't mean to upset you like this.' He lifted his head to look at her. Her brow was furrowed and she looked worried.

'You didn't.' Was that his voice? It sounded as though he hadn't spoken in over a week and his throat was coated with broken glass. To be honest, it felt like that too.

Ibrahim cleared his throat and gave his head a slight shake. 'You didn't upset me, I'm fine.'

Feeling fidgety, he got up and paced to the sink with the excuse of filling his empty glass. He heard her quietly voiced statement just as he turned the tap off and froze.

'You love her.'

He turned to look at her and she smiled at him knowingly. 'I think you've fallen in love with Jiya and judging by what I've seen of her, I wouldn't be surprised if she felt the same way about you.'

'I've known her for what? A couple of months, if that. How can you say that?'

'Oh, Ibrahim.' She shook her head as though disappointed with what he'd said, standing up and walking towards him. 'So how long do you think you need to know her before you can fall in love with her?'

He shrugged his shoulders, feeling distinctly uncomfortable with the turn of the conversation. 'I don't know.'

'That's because there's no definite answer. There's no set time frame from some rule book or "How to" guide about love. Love is a feeling; sometimes it develops over a longer period of time and sometimes it just hits you right here,' she pressed a finger against his chest, 'with a bang and you feel as though it's been there the whole time.

'When you're alone, ask yourself the same last question I asked you and answer it, honestly. And then, ask yourself if it's worth losing the person you love because of some ideas that might not even make sense to you a few months or years from now.'

Ibrahim felt the strangest sensation where Reshma had just prodded him. Like something had cracked in there, while at the same time it felt like someone had shaken a bottle of a fizzy drink really hard and then opened the lid. He couldn't contain those feelings, which were pouring out of his chest and working their way through his entire body.

Could it be that simple? Was he really in love with Jiya? Had his father announced his engagement to Jiya as a show of support, accepting his choice?

What about all that poison you spewed towards her at the coffee shop?

His heart sunk at the memory. He had said some pretty harsh words to her. In fact, calling them *pretty harsh* was putting it mildly. He had been downright nasty, insinuating all sorts of crap about her and her family.

He ran both hands through his hair as all those words went through his head on a loop. 'It doesn't matter how I feel, Reshma. I've cocked things up with her pretty badly. I said some seriously offensive things to her, both about her and her family.'

'Hmm. Well, you're going to have to figure out how to make it up to her then, aren't you?'

241

'She categorically said to me that I shouldn't call her or try to meet her again. She's pretty headstrong, she's not going to budge.'

'This is the part where you have to come up with a grand gesture.' At his confused expression, she elaborated, 'Something big that blows her socks off, shows her how important she is to you, how much you love her and makes her forgive you.'

'Yeah? And how am I going to do that exactly?'

'You know what, Ibrahim, I think I've helped you enough. I'll leave you to figure that one out.' Smiling at him, she gave his arm a little squeeze and left him standing by the kitchen sink, wondering how the hell he was going to come up with a gesture grand enough for Jiya to forgive what was most likely his own gargantuan fuck-up. He really needed to speak to his dad and get to the bottom of this. If he was wrong, he had a shitload of grovelling to do.

'Oh, and Ibrahim?' Reshma stood in the doorway. 'Thank you for this afternoon. I'm pleased you felt able to speak to me and I really hope everything works out for you.' She turned and walked away.

God, I hope so too.

CHAPTER TWENTY-FIVE

Jiya

Putting the last of the dishes away in the cupboard, Jiya was just closing the dishwasher when her phone pinged with an email alert.

She had spent the days since her falling out with Ibrahim in a state of fog. Wavering between anger and deep sadness and much to her annoyance, lately the bouts of sadness were more frequent than the moments of anger. She would remember him at random moments because of random things and would feel a sharp, stabbing pain right in the middle of her chest. She didn't feel like doing anything and could see the looks of concern on her family's faces.

She looked at the email notification. It was from someone she didn't recognise and it wasn't a forward or a circular. This had been written directly to her.

Not bothering to wait before she could open it properly on her laptop, she opened it up on her miniscule phone screen.

It was from someone called Carter James from a firm she might or might not have seen, given that she'd trawled through hundreds of firm websites in the last few months.

Jiya read the whole thing through once and her heart screeched to a halt. She went back to the top, her halted heart now firmly in her mouth, and started again.

This Carter James had received her *resumé* and was keen to have a chat with her.

'Deep breaths, Jiya! Deep breaths. And now I'm talking to myself. Great!'

'What are you mumbling about?' She hadn't even heard her mother come into the kitchen behind her and jumped at her question.

'Nothing, I'm just reading an email.'

'On your phone?'

'It's a smartphone, Ammi, albeit a titchy one. You can get emails on it too. I showed you how to, remember?'

'Who's emailing you on your phone then? Is it Ibrahim?'

Jiya gritted her teeth at the mention of his name. He was currently Public Enemy No. 1 in the Ahmed household and her parents had insisted on knowing if he got in touch with her again.

After the heart to heart with her mother, where Jiya had told her about practically everything, her mother had told her father and brother and they had all sat together and discussed things, a complete first for them.

Her mother had also told her father everything about Ibrahim and though he hadn't said anything to her, she knew he wasn't happy with how she had gone about things. With hindsight, she saw that she hadn't exactly handled things maturely and maybe if she had been a bit more honest and open with her parents, things might have turned out differently.

But then you wouldn't have shared those good times with him either, would you?

She suppressed that treacherous thought before it could go any further. She was not going there!

Seeing her be less than her usual exuberant self, her family had taken to being much more alert about everything to do with her. Her brother was constantly trying to make her laugh, especially when their mother egged him on and her mother had taken to making a boatload of pakoras regularly and saying she had a sudden craving for them, when they both knew that they were expressly for Jiya.

To help alleviate her heartbreak and guilt-induced sombre mood, her usually stoic father had surprised her by bringing her a bagful of chocolates and declaring that they were going to do a movie night. He'd stuck on a prehistoric black and white film which she had been sure she would hate but given the effort he had made, she hadn't had the heart to refuse his choice and had persevered. She was pleasantly surprised at how much they had both enjoyed the quality time.

Her father wasn't demonstrative by nature but just sitting beside him and making her way through the chocolate stash together with him in silence had comforted her immensely. But his side hug and soft kiss on her forehead as they'd sat there during the end credits had helped her more than all the chocolate he'd bought. With her family's love and support as her lifeline, she felt like she might actually be able to get through the unending grief she'd been feeling since that dreadful day at the coffee shop.

During the few discussions they'd had, her family had peppered her with plenty of questions about working in the city for a 'corporate shark' – her father's words – instead of starting a business of her own. They had completely surprised her by asking why she hadn't pursued any placements abroad if she was interested in them.

Of course, there had been a whole list of rules and conditions, but they had agreed that if she got the opportunity, she should definitely accept it. Jiya had been completely surprised given that she had believed the whole time that the opposite would happen when her parents found out about her plans and she'd said as much.

'Your mother and I had a pretty lengthy chat, Jiya, and we realise that we've not been entirely fair with you. We've not shown confidence in your ability, which you've earned many times over. I know this seems like a complete turnaround but your aspirations are important to us so we want you to grab opportunities with both hands when they come your way.'

Jiya had practically squeezed the life out of her father after that as he laughed and patted her on the back.

She had their permission and their enthusiastic blessings to make her dreams come true, something that had seemed impossible to her not so long ago.

And if there was a small part deep within her chest that still ached at the thought or mention of Ibrahim, she was ignoring it, especially when something she had coveted for as long as she could remember seemed to be within reach.

'No, Ammi, the email isn't from him. It's from someone in a company in America. He received my CV and liked what he saw. He'd like me to do an interview and a few online bits and pieces and if I'm successful, I could be selected for a placement.'

Despite feeling new depths of misery since she'd had the falling out with Ibrahim, she felt a kernel of hope and excitement at the new possibility. This was the opportunity she had wanted for such a long time. It's what she had worked super hard for and she totally deserved it.

So why wasn't she feeling an all-consuming sense of euphoria? Why did that feeling of hope and excitement feel . . . muted? Why was it that despite trying her damn hardest, she couldn't ignore him or the fact that he wasn't there to share this moment with her?

'*Ya Allah*, thank you. This is good news, yes? So, why don't you look happy?' Her mother looked at her closely,

246

and since Jiya had promised herself that there'd be no more secrets, she answered her honestly.

'This is great news and I am happy, just not as happy as I thought I would be.'

'What are you unhappy about?' Her father came in and her mother gave her an understanding look before, true to form, she bustled over to put a pot of tea on.

She told her father about the email. 'If I'm successful, I could be there in a matter of months, if not weeks, starting this placement. I'm excited, but scared too. What if I muck it up?'

Her father sat down at the kitchen table and heaved a great big sigh. 'From what I know of my tenacious daughter, she only mucks things up when she really puts her mind to doing so. Don't go in with the intention of mucking it up and you won't.' He shrugged his shoulders, as though pleased with himself about that little titbit of wisdom as he reached for a plate of sweetmeats.

'What sort of advice is that, Yunus?'

He ignored his wife glaring at him and looked at Jiya. 'Seriously? I think it's perfectly normal to feel a little nervous or anxious about doing this. It's a big step, but you're ready. You have been for a long time. You're a smart and resourceful girl and can come up with some pretty harebrained schemes to get what you want,' he raised his eyebrows at her knowingly and Jiya grinned at him sheepishly, 'so some time abroad will be a doddle for you.

'But if you're really concerned, take your mother with you. It'll give me a break.' He whispered the last bit and Jiya giggled, her nerves melting away under the reassurance her parents offered her.

'I heard that. You wouldn't last more than a week without me, Yunus Ahmed. You don't even know where the stock of teabags is.'

'She's right, Abba. I think I'll just have to let you keep Ammi and manage without her abroad.' He shook his head in defeat and Jiya and her mother laughed at his feigned distress.

This is what she had wanted and missed. This level of comfort and ease. Though now when she thought about it, maybe it had always been there, but just not as open or as often. And she was just as much to blame because she had chosen to focus on what she didn't have rather than what she did, which was a loving family, who were willing to step out of their comfort zone and what they considered normal in order to support her and her dreams.

But while Jiya felt really pleased about the change in her family dynamic recently, the persistent dull ache constantly with her reminded her that all was not well in her life.

She had spent enough hours over the last week thinking – as painful as it was – about her time spent with Ibrahim and how she felt about it all.

In the beginning, she had fought tooth and nail to stop those thoughts from entering her mind and circling around like a pack of hyenas circled a carcass. She had lost. The thoughts she desperately didn't want to think about stormed through her brain regardless, tearing their way through her body and splitting her heart wide open.

In the end, the only thing that had brought her some comfort had been acceptance and owning the fact that he had indeed been a part of her life. Once she had accepted that, the thoughts – though still painful – had become bearable. She found she could even smile at some of the memories.

If she was being honest with herself, she had enjoyed every moment of being with Ibrahim Saeed. Well, of course, apart from the last time when he'd accused her of trying to trap him into an unwanted engagement. In pretending to be together, she hadn't even realised when she'd fallen—

If you're all about ownership and acceptance, then don't hold back on this, Jiya Ahmed!

She left her parents in the kitchen while they chatted and made her way upstairs, somewhat in a daze as her brain had frozen on that one thought.

She had fallen in love with him. Deeply.

She had no idea when, where and how it had happened, but there it was. As clear as a bell. And somehow, that made it easier to remember the good times but even harder to remember the hurt he had inflicted.

'Ammi? Abba? Ammi? Where are you guys?'

Two days later, Jiya ran down the stairs as fast as she could, her heart bumping within her chest as though it was going to beat right out of it. The spark she had thought had fizzled out under the crushing weight of a broken heart was flickering back to life as she raced through the house. She found her parents in the dining room and her mother stood up as soon as Jiya came through the door, her expression anxious.

'I got it. They offered it to me at the end, didn't even wait.' Her voice was barely above a whisper. She should have been shouting from the rooftops, that was more her style, but her voice was just about audible. Her parents heard her though because her mother came forward and crushed her to her chest, while her father beamed back at her.

'I knew you'd get it. You're a star and you probably shone right through the computer screen all the way to America,' her father said in an uncharacteristic display of pride, patting her on the shoulder.

'Well done, Jiya. I'm so proud of you,' her mother gushed.

Her brother ambled in from the front room. 'What's all the fuss?'

'Your sister got offered a placement at the American company she applied to.'

Jiya could hear the pleasure in her father's voice and felt tears gather in the corners of her eyes. How was she going to leave them behind now when things were so great between them?

'No, don't you dare start having second thoughts, Jiya!' Her mother held her face in both her hands. 'You need to do this. For yourself and because we all want you to do this too. You'll be doing something no one has done in our family, let alone a woman. Before, I used to lament that people will insult me and my daughter because she can't make a plain naan. Now people will look up to my daughter because she's achieved something no one in our family has before her.' Her mother dabbed at her eyes with the corner of her *dupatta*, her feelings open on her face for everyone to see.

'Ammi, it wasn't just my hard work. It's the support you and Abba have given and the fact that you're not just letting me, but you're actually encouraging me to pursue my dreams. You're both the best.' She wrapped her arms around her mother's neck and gave her a loud kiss on the cheek. Her brother came and ruffled her hair, messing it up and then darting to the other side of the dining table before she could get him.

Leaving them all downstairs, Jiya bounded back up the stairs. She had to tell Harry because he would be so happy for her. She had missed him this last week. Although they had texted each other a couple of times, it just wasn't the same, it felt stilted. She'd hate to lose him as a friend but she was hoping that their friendship was stronger than that.

He answered on the third ring.

'Miss Jiya Ahmed! Tell me you have good news.'

'How did you know?'

'Here we go again. How long before you actually believe how much of a genius I am?'

'I'm not touching that with a barge pole right now,' she muttered. 'They offered it to me straight after the interview. Can you believe it?'

'Of course, I can. You're brilliant so there was no way you wouldn't have got it. So,' it sounded as though he was settling down somewhere, 'when does the ball start rolling on this gig?'

'Not sure, I'll get the details in the next few days but they said that I could go to the New York office a few weeks earlier to help settle in and find my feet before work begins. I reckon it'll probably be within four to six weeks though. And check this, they'll help with getting me a flat, or apartment actually. I just hope it's bigger than a cardboard box. I've seen some of their flats on TV and some of them are so small it's a joke.'

'What are you up to tomorrow? Let's meet up. I better cram in as much of your sweet little mug as I can before you fly out.'

'Fine, but we'll do a picnic. I haven't had a proper picnic yet this summer. Also, you'd better come out to New York when I'm there – that's non-negotiable.'

'Sweetheart, that'll all depend on the size of your shoebox *apartment*. See you tomorrow at the usual picnic spot then.' And with that, he hung up.

Ibrahim

Walking out of the kitchen, Ibrahim paused as he heard his father's bellowing laugh from down the hallway.

Bingo!

Following the sound of his voice, he found his father on the phone in a small room beside the dining room, which was often used as an office.

He looked at Ibrahim quizzically as he took the chair opposite, acting as nonchalantly as he could, placing his cup of coffee on a coaster in front of him just so and then leaning back in the chair to look at his father.

The look of confusion on his face gave him some comfort, although it was nothing compared to the emotional seesaw he had been on. He probably looked a state too, with stubble on his cheeks, uncombed hair sticking up at all angles because he'd run his hand through it at least a hundred times already and a T-shirt that had seen better days.

'Right, I'd better go, I've got the groom-to-be sitting here waiting to talk to me. Give the family my regards.' He swiped his thumb across his phone screen as he leaned forward on the table.

'Everyone's full of praise about Amma's party, but the engagement announcement is what everyone wants to talk about.' His father laughed as though supremely pleased with himself while Ibrahim continued to sit there and look at him, making a conscious effort not to grind his teeth into powder.

He'd let anger and frustration dominate too many conversations already, so it was absolutely fundamental not to lose his cool with his father just then, even if this meeting was completely out of the blue. He'd like to see how his father liked being on the receiving end of an ambush.

'Are you happy, son?'

Ibrahim didn't answer his father's question and instead asked one of his own. 'What made you announce my engagement at Daadi's party?'

His father's brow furrowed slightly, whether at his tone or the question, Ibrahim didn't know. 'We wanted it to be a surprise and your Daadi was more than happy for us to make that announcement at her party.'

Ibrahim sucked in a deep breath willing the question he both wanted answered and didn't want answered to push past his lips. What would he say if his father acknowledged it all as his own idea? Or worse, what if Ashar was right and the whole thing had been orchestrated by Jiya and her family?

'That was the first time you were meeting Jiya's family, wasn't it?' His father nodded as he began getting distracted by the pile of unopened post on the table in front of him. 'So, how did they agree to an engagement so soon after meeting everyone?'

His father looked up at that. 'Eh? I'm not sure I understand what you're getting at, son. We all discussed it and everybody was in agreement that since you and Jiya are so happy together and have expressed the desire to spend the rest of your lives together, why wait?' He shrugged, as though the whole thing were of no account. 'Now we just need to set the date for the actual engagement party.'

'Who brought it up first, you or them?'

'Brought what up, Ibrahim?' His attention was back on the envelopes in front of him.

'Look at me please, Dad. I need to know whose idea it was. Who suggested announcing mine and Jiya's engagement at the party?'

His father looked so confused, it would have been funny if Ibrahim's heart wasn't in his throat just then.

'It was your mother's idea.'

Ibrahim felt the bottom of his stomach fall out and a burning rush worked its way up his throat at the same time.

What? His mother?!

Ibrahim couldn't believe it. The person he hadn't thought of even once in all this drama turned out to be the one who had set this whole thing in motion. Wow.

She hadn't once said or done anything to suggest that those were the lines she was thinking along, so when and how had this all happened?

'Your mother spoke to me after you had brought Jiya to come and see the family, telling me that Jiya is a lovely girl with all the qualities and attributes we would want in our son's wife. I was certainly sceptical before that, but after meeting the girl I had to agree, she really is lovely. Seems like you've followed your old man in terms of choosing the best for yourself, eh?' His father guffawed, not catching Ibrahim's look of utter disdain.

'Anyway, we both agreed that we're happy for you to settle down with Jiya but I thought we were going to wait to meet her family properly after Amma's party. Your mother though, had other ideas. After you had introduced us to her family that day, she told me that it was the perfect opportunity to announce the engagement if Jiya's parents agreed. Of course, your mother can be very persuasive when she wants to be, so she spoke to Yunus and Samina and they were both happy to announce an engagement. Amma was over the moon with the idea.'

Ibrahim was stunned. This was so far off what he had believed to be the truth. He couldn't even get his head around it. *His mother?!*

And the things he'd said to Jiya. He dropped his head into his hands and groaned.

'What is going on, Ibrahim? That's hardly the reaction of a man on the cusp of pledging his life to the woman he loves.'

When he had free brain space, he'd wonder about his dad's choice of words and phrases, but for now he had other things to focus on.

'Was there no one who disagreed or questioned that decision?'

His father leaned back in his chair, playing with the letter opener in his hand. 'Zafar did. He thought it was a bit sudden but then he's always been a protective brother over you all.'

Of all the things, his discovery today was the last thing he expected and the surprise of it all had rendered him speechless and left his brain frozen. He couldn't figure anything out beyond the fact that he'd screwed up. Royally.

His father was eyeing him curiously, running the letter opener across his hands like some shady bad guy in an eighties film.

'Why wouldn't Mum wait or at least talk to me about it first?'

His father stopped playing with the letter opener and put it down on the table softly, his brow furrowed once more. 'Because she blames me for what's happened with Zafar. She didn't want me to choose someone for you and have you end up being miserable like she believes your older brother is, so she absolutely insisted we let you choose your partner for yourself. She wanted to show you that we support your decision. As for not talking to you . . .' He shrugged, his attention once more on the letters. 'It was supposed to be a surprise.'

Ibrahim sat there, stunned for a few moments, and only the loud ringing of his father's phone jolted him out of the stillness that had taken over his mind and body. He picked up his untouched, now cold coffee and made his way back to the kitchen to dump it.

She was innocent. In all of this, neither she nor her family had said or done anything to warrant the disgusting allegations he had thrown their way. And the irony of it all was that his mother – the driving force behind the whole bloody palaver – had shared the same concerns as he had. She had done what she had to avoid his father taking control and saddling him with someone, like he had done with Zafar. Just as he himself had concocted the whole charade to avoid his father's matchmaking.

And look at what had happened.

What the fuck have I done?

CHAPTER TWENTY-SIX

Ibrahim

Ibrahim could feel Harry's eyes boring into the side of his head but resolutely ignored him. After finding out about his argument with Jiya, in a completely out-of-character moment, his younger brother had come up to him, told him how disappointed he was with him and hadn't said a single word to him since then.

Normally, Harry couldn't go more than twenty-four hours without harassing each and every one of his siblings. He hadn't realised how much it would bother him, but bother him it did. He already felt shitty after his argument with Jiya. His conversation with Reshma had thrown him for a loop, and his father telling him that it was all actually his mother's doing was something he still hadn't quite processed entirely – and he had yet to tell his brothers – and to top it all off, his brother was giving him the cold shoulder. And he hated it.

His mind was a minefield and every thought had the potential of blowing his equilibrium to pieces. What he needed to do was get away from everything and bit by bit try to make sense of his thoughts and feelings and what was going on. Maybe then, he'd be able to come up with some idea about how to move forward and what he ought to do next. He needed answers if he wanted some semblance of normality back in his life.

And then there were his feelings for Jiya. Did he love

her? Or was his mind playing tricks on him? How would he know one way or the other?

There were times in the past couple of days when his mind had been so deeply troubled, he'd decided to bury himself under a mountain of work. There was never any shortage of it in the office, something or other always needed doing so he had focused on that, hoping that some answers to the multitude of questions in his head would organically present themselves if he let them be.

He had been falling into bed absolutely knackered but not tired enough that his mind didn't wander towards thoughts of a certain brown-eyed beauty and how haunted those eyes had looked the last time he'd seen them.

'Harry, you're doing it wrong, mate,' Ashar pointed out mildly. 'You're supposed to look him dead in the eyes. Or is this some new spin on the staring game where you just look at the side of your opponent's head, although how they would catch you blinking when they're looking the other way is a mystery.'

Ibrahim carried on ignoring them all. If Harry had something to say, he needed to just come out with it rather than being dramatic as usual.

'What's going on, Harry?' Zafar asked from across the room. They had all gathered to watch the football because miraculously, all five of them had been free that day.

'Nothing much. I'm just bummed about a really good friend of mine moving to New York.' The disappointment in his voice was clear for everyone to hear, but it was laced with annoyance.

Ibrahim slowly turned to look at Harry, his blood freezing in his veins in slow motion. Did he mean . . .? Of course, he did. He couldn't be talking about anyone else like that.

'When?' His voice was little more than a croak and he swallowed a couple of times, hoping it would help the words come out clearer.

'Which friend? Do we know him?'

'It's a she, bhai, and yes, you've all met her.'

'Jiya? She got her placement in New York? That's fantastic,' Rayyan joined in. His brothers were talking as though he wasn't even in the room. As though none of this affected him.

Ashar let out a sardonic laugh. 'Oh, I bet she did. Not that any of us should be surprised by that little nugget of information; she's clearly determined. She used our brother to get what she wanted because had it not been for him, she would never have managed it. Ibrahim sorted it all out for her. I think the least she could do is send him a thank you note.' His voice was dripping with condescension.

The blood that had frozen in his veins a moment ago rushed back in full force, bringing heat into his face. 'You're wrong.' His voice was still croaky, as though a toad rather than a frog was lodged in his throat.

Ashar turned to look at him from the recliner he was lying back on. 'You what?'

'I said you're wrong.'

Much better. Now he sounded more like himself. Strong and determined.

'All I did was give her a few names and email addresses – *if* this opportunity is from a contact I gave her. She did the rest by herself. All of it.'

'And what was that, bat her eyelashes and . . .'

Before he had registered what he was doing, Ibrahim had lunged for Ashar, grabbing him by both sides of his T-shirt and pulling him up.

'You ever, *ever* talk about her like that again, and I'll knock seven fucking bells out of you. Do you hear me?' He slammed him back into the recliner, his heart pounding at double the rate.

He felt a hand on his shoulder pulling him back and he went with the momentum as Zafar sat him back down.

Rayyan pointed a finger at Ashar. 'What the hell is wrong with you? You don't talk like that about anyone, no matter what. We all know how angry you are about the world and women after . . .' He paused because they all knew that Ashar's history was a complete no-go area, 'but that doesn't give you the right to be disrespectful about someone else. Are you listening to me, Ash?'

'Can't you all see how she's got him in fucking knots? Since he started this stupid fake relationship with her, he's not been himself. He was so busy trying to keep Dad off his case that before he knew it, she had pulled the carpet from under him.'

'Well, she's out of his life now and soon she'll be out of the bloody continent, so you guys never have to be bothered by her again.' Harry's voice was laced in steel and his eyes were hard and intent as he took it in turns to look at Ashar and then at him.

Ibrahim's heart lurched and he felt physically sick.

She was going. She was leaving everything here to go to New York.

She was leaving *him*.

How would you feel if you never saw her again?

Why did that thought fill him with terror?

Why did it feel as though he couldn't get enough air into his lungs and as though his heart was going to stop beating any second now?

Ibrahim closed his eyes, trying to steady his breathing while the sound of his brothers bickering faded into the background.

Her beautiful eyes twinkled as she smiled at him, her ponytail swishing behind her head. Her gorgeous, happy face slowly morphed into the expression she'd had the last time he'd seen her. Her eyes full of anguish rather than mischief. Her lips pressed together in a firm line rather than lifted up at the corners. Her face ashen rather than glowing with vitality as it usually did.

When you realise how wrong you are — and trust me, that will happen — do me a favour will you? Don't call me or try and meet me. OK?

What had he done? And how the fuck was he ever going to fix it?

As the silence around him penetrated through his churning thoughts, he looked up to find four pairs of eyes trained on him, their expressions filled with concern. Well, except for Harry, whose face was shouting 'I told you so' loud and clear.

He was also the first one to speak, lifting a finger up to stop him before he said anything. 'Don't even bother asking for my help with anything. You don't deserve it.'

Ibrahim turned to look at Zafar. 'It was all Mum's idea. The engagement announcement at Daadi's party.'

They all looked as stunned as he'd been with that revelation. 'I've been meaning to tell you guys but my head's been all over the fucking place. I spoke to Dad, ready to rain fire on his head when he told me that the whole thing was Mum's doing. Jiya, her parents and even he had nothing to do with it. Mum got it in her head that because I was happy with Jiya and had said I was serious about her, they should announce our engagement that day. Dad said that one of the reasons was that she wanted to stop Dad from choosing someone he liked but I didn't. She didn't want me to be miserable like Zaf is.'

They all looked towards Zafar, who had sat back down rubbing a hand along his jaw and then the back of his neck, his expression a mixture of confusion and frustration. 'I think it's high time we set this thing straight. My relationship with Reshma is . . .' He ran his hand through his hair and before he could finish his sentence, Ashar spoke.

'Let me guess – "complicated"?'

'You know, Ash, when the situation is already a shit fest, you don't always need to add your two-pence worth on top and make it worse. It would be really nice if on the odd occasion you showed some fucking understanding or compassion for the other person.

'I was going to say that my relationship with Reshma is ours to deal with. With all due respect, it has nothing to do with anyone else and it should certainly have no bearing on how you all conduct your own relationships.'

Zafar turned to look at Ibrahim. 'You need to figure out where you stand with Jiya and make a choice based on that, free from any other preconceived ideas you have in your head. Whether I'm happy with my wife or not shouldn't be the driving factor for our parents in deciding to announce your engagement given that their interference was the primary bloody reason for this whole charade, except this time it's our mother rather than our father doing the interfering.'

Standing abruptly, he made his way towards the door, leaving the four of them staring after him. He turned to face them just before leaving, 'Decide what *you* want, Ibrahim, then go for it. The only reason for you choosing to be with or without Jiya, should come from you, no one else.'

The only sound in the room was the commentary from the football game on the screen. Ibrahim felt as though his mind had split itself into two.

One part saw his entire situation as though it was a huge knot which could never be undone without cutting parts of it away. But how did one choose which parts to cut away? And surely, if any part *was* cut away, the length would be lost. It would never be whole again.

The other part of his mind saw everything as though it were crystal clear. He needed to answer the ultimate question, much like Reshma had said when he'd spoken to her about everything. All the other stuff didn't really matter. If he loved Jiya and wanted to be with her, then nothing else mattered.

Perhaps once he'd honestly answered that question, everything else would fall into place. The knot might well undo itself and none of it would need to be cut away.

And the honest answer was that he did love Jiya. With his heart and soul.

It hadn't been something he'd actively tried to do and he couldn't even say when exactly it had happened, but it had. He'd fallen in love with Jiya Ahmed and now the thought of losing her made his blood run cold. She was planning on leaving and going to the other side of the Atlantic.

That had always been her dream but that had been before all this. Before they had pretended to be boyfriend and girlfriend. Before she had snuck into his heart when he hadn't been looking. Before he'd had a taste of her lips and a feel of her beneath his hands.

God, just the thought of her made his blood fizz. But how did she feel?

Oh, she was definitely attracted to him, he was sure about that, but had he killed that attraction with his harsh accusations? Fuelled by his own anger and frustration at the situation he had found himself in, he had been unforgivably cruel to Jiya, so it was perfectly plausible that the attraction she had felt towards him might well be over.

He had to find out. He had to go to her and tell her how he felt and he hoped to God she would give him a chance to prove that what he felt for her was genuine.

'Harry—'

'No.'

'Cut him some slack, Harry. The man is in uncharted territory. Hear him out.' Rayyan was grinning at him as he spoke while Ashar was looking at his phone pretending not to listen.

'When is she leaving?' Ibrahim could hear the anxiety in his voice.

'I'm not too sure but it will be sooner than planned. Maybe even as early as this week. Things seem to have fallen into place pretty quickly for her and an opportunity opened up sooner so she's taking it. She'll be leaving a bit earlier to check out accommodation and sort out some other stuff.'

That hardly gave him enough time to figure out what he needed to do. He'd have to act fast if he wanted the chance to prove himself and his feelings for Jiya. To ask her to give him another chance. He couldn't imagine not being with Jiya. He had to make this work.

Jiya

Closing the zip on another of her suitcases, Jiya huffed out a breath, blowing away loose tendrils of hair from her damp forehead. Today was one of those days where the heat made a person sticky and uncomfortable and would be best spent in the garden, but here she was, packing away things she needed to take with her to New York.

264

Her mother had been helping her but at the sound of the doorbell, she had gone down and had yet to come back up. Her mother was able to fit double of what Jiya did in her suitcase, so she really needed her to come back up here and help her.

She sat back on her bed and glanced around the room. While she couldn't believe that her dream to go away and work abroad was finally coming true, she couldn't seem to reconcile how she was feeling with how she had thought she would feel when such a moment came.

She was excited and proud about this opportunity but at the same time there was a sinking feeling in her gut and she had a sneaky suspicion that she knew the reason for it.

She felt a lump in her throat as she remembered the way Ibrahim had spoken to her, as though she were some money-grabbing opportunist out to get whatever she could. Why was it that her mind couldn't forget what he'd said and her heart couldn't forget how he'd made her feel?

She felt a familiar prickling at the corners of her eyes and lying back on her duvet, she closed her eyes, willing the tears to stay back because if they came, she wasn't sure they'd stop. She felt so full of sorrow that she'd probably drown in a deluge of tears if she let it come.

Keeping herself busy had helped keep her mind off him for the better part, but something or other always triggered thoughts of him. She couldn't even say it was when she least expected them or wanted them because both those things were untrue. She knew thoughts of him were never far away and the really sad thing was that a part of her wanted to remember him. She didn't want to forget him. How could you love someone and then want to forget them? Yeah, he'd been an absolute dick to her, but that didn't diminish her feelings. She still loved him. A lot.

Wiping away the few errant tears which hadn't got the memo, she sat up, and spying her open suitcase, decided to get her mum to come back up and help her. She didn't have enough energy to mope *and* pack. There was time enough for moping on her flight and when she got to America and time beyond that, if she never got over it.

CHAPTER TWENTY-SEVEN

Ibrahim

Not much of a boy racer and being on a countdown, Ibrahim had roped Ashar in to drive him to the airport. Harry had jumped into the back for a front row seat to watch him grovel after informing him that Jiya was leaving later today.

'It's the least you can do for me after the shit storm you instigated. I have to see her before she goes, Ash.'

'Mate, I never said she *was* guilty. I said she *could* be guilty. There's a subtle difference between the two.'

'If you say so, Shitlock Holmes. Now move your arse and take me to the airport. I need to make it before she—'

'Yes, yes, you need to get there before she goes. Which airport are we going to?'

'Heathrow. And if you don't hurry up, I swear to God I'm going to knock you into next week.'

Ashar had grinned at Ibrahim as he'd taken his time getting to the car and then paused to put his driving gloves on.

'Are you fucking kidding me?!'

'Ibrahim, do me a favour, son, shut up and let me do my thing. What time does her flight leave, Harry?'

'At five o'clock, I think, so she'll probably be checking in soon.'

'Plenty of time. Buckle up, folks.'

Ashar had long ago mastered the art of speeding through the streets of London. He knew exactly where the speed cameras were and he navigated the roads like a Formula One driver navigated a track, provided the cops weren't prowling the streets.

Ibrahim often admired the way his brother handled a car but at that point in time, he didn't want to see any show of skill. He just wanted him to drive hell for leather and get his monster of a Porsche to the bloody airport before the flight to New York was boarded.

They had managed to get onto the motorway quite swiftly and Ibrahim began to relax. Asking Ashar to drive him had been the right move because however long Ibrahim took to make a journey, Ashar almost always did it in significantly less time. Hopefully today would be the same.

'Oh shit.'

Ibrahim looked ahead at his brother's expletive and saw all the brake lights of the cars in front of them gradually come on. He looked further up and saw a car rammed into the side of another and winced.

'What's going on?' Harry pushed forward to have a look. 'Oh shit, that's ugly.'

Ashar put his hand behind Ibrahim's head rest and looked behind them before indicating left and pulling across the lanes as the traffic edged forward.

'I'm going to take the next exit and see if we can detour.'

'That'll take you ages. Aren't you better off staying on the motorway?'

'Mate, this will take us at least another forty-five minutes to get through, it's a complete bottleneck. Trust me.'

Ibrahim's head was spinning like a top, all sorts of different thoughts vying for attention.

Would he get to see Jiya before she left?

Would she want to see him?

What would he say to her?

Was he even in any position to say anything? He'd said such harsh things to her, they didn't even bear thinking about. All because his own demons had come to party in his mind and his brain had decided to take time off just then. He'd acted like an absolute idiot and if he was honest with himself, he wouldn't give himself another chance after the things he'd said to her, so he shouldn't be surprised if she didn't.

But that didn't stop him from hoping and praying.

Praying to God that they'd make it to the flaming airport. That she'd not have left and that she'd give him a chance to at least apologise, if not make it up to her.

You don't deserve her.

It was true. He didn't deserve her.

No man behaved like that with the woman he loved. Love was about trust. It was about caring. It was about honour.

He had shown none of those attributes.

He hadn't trusted her; he hadn't shown her any care or consideration and he certainly hadn't acted honourably.

So how could he claim to love Jiya?

The best thing she could do was follow and live her dreams in New York. Away from him and the vitriol he had dished out.

'Hey Romeo, we're here. The pair of you can get out and I'll go and park up.' Swerving into the drop-off point, Ashar let them out and just as Ibrahim was about to shut the door, he heard the most cynical of his brothers wish him luck.

'Go and get her, mate. And try not to cock it up.' He winked at him and then moved off, leaving Ibrahim standing there before he turned to see which way Harry was heading.

They raced through the door towards the departures desks but couldn't see any familiar faces.

'Are you sure it was this terminal and at this time?'

'That's the third time you've asked.'

'Sorry.'

They were nearing the end of the desks and heading towards the entrance to the departures lounge when Harry called his name and pointed.

He saw Jiya's parents and her brother standing together a few feet away and turned to look towards the winding queue that made its way into the departures lounge.

It was empty.

He was too late. She'd gone.

He'd missed her.

The last chance he'd had to say how sorry he was and to tell her how much he loved her and he'd missed it.

A keen sense of loss came over him that made it hard to breathe.

The noise around him came in bursts of loud and quiet. His hands felt clammy and the churning in his gut told him that he was moments away from being sick.

If only he had come to her sooner. If only he hadn't acted like a fool.

Closing his eyes and dropping his chin to his chest, he hauled in a deep breath, hoping to calm the rising acid in his gut.

There was no point in going over 'if onlys'. Nothing ever came of it.

The memory of her perfume teased his senses and he held off from howling in pain. After everything he'd said to her, this was what he deserved. It was only fair that she followed her dreams and he was left behind with ample time to think over what a fool he'd been.

He felt a hand on his shoulder slowly turn him around and he looked down into chocolate brown eyes.

It was Jiya. She was here. She hadn't left.

Without any further thought, Ibrahim pulled her into his arms and crushed her against his chest as tight as he could, fearing that if he didn't, she might disappear and the crushing sense of loss would finish him off.

'I thought you had left.' He could hear how gravelly his voice had become and marvelled at how in a matter of weeks the woman in his arms had turned him inside out. He felt as though all his emotions were on display for everyone to see.

'You're squashing me.' Her voice, though muffled, was music to his ears.

'Get off my daughter right now!'

Ibrahim eased back, but didn't take his arms off Jiya. He saw her father had made his way towards them, followed by the others.

'How dare you come here?'

'Uncle Yunus.' Ashar was making his way towards them, and before Jiya's father could respond, he'd slung his arm around his shoulders as though they were good old friends, and was slowly guiding him away, talking just loud enough that only he could hear him.

Harry had moved Jiya's mother and brother a few steps away and he could see him charming Jiya's mother, though Jameel was looking daggers his way.

As much as they could be a pain in the arse, he loved his brothers to pieces and he'd tell them as much, just as soon as he'd told Jiya all he needed to.

She was watching him closely, her eyebrows slightly furrowed in that cute way of hers and her lips slightly parted. Her hands were still at his chest and he could feel the reverberations of his own heartbeat against them. It was as though his heart was finally beating properly after its staggered staccato since she'd walked away from him.

His lips curved up slightly as her hands moved down from his chest gradually, as though she were savouring the moment. She covered his hands at her hips with her own and pulled them away, taking a step away from him and breaking the contact between them.

'What are you doing here, Ibrahim?' The flatness of her voice cut him to the core. The exuberance and excitement that usually laced it was gone.

'I . . . have you got a few minutes?' He ran an unsteady hand through his hair.

He could see her giving his request thought but after a few seconds, she gave him a curt nod and giving her mother a quick wave, she led him to a small grouping of seats on one side.

They sat beside each other, just a few inches separating them, but he felt as though they had miles between them already.

'I wanted to apologise.' Her posture stiffened, her hands curling into fists as he watched.

'I'm pretty sure I was crystal clear when I told you not to bother coming when you realised how wrong you were. My word obviously means nothing at all to you, Ibrahim. You didn't believe me then and now you've disregarded my feelings about seeing you and have turned up anyway. Just as I'm leaving.'

'I know what you said, Jiya, but I couldn't stay away. My head was all over the place when my dad announced our engagement and I . . .'

'Don't, Ibrahim.' Her voice was firm. 'Don't you dare try to excuse what you said to me. I'll accept you were surprised and that the announcement caught you completely off guard but the same thing happened to me too. I didn't turn around and point a finger at you and question your family's integrity. There's no excuse for the stuff you said to me.'

She was right. There was no excuse. What he'd said was unforgiveable and he told her as much.

'So why are you here then?'

Ibrahim tried to swallow down the shards of glass in his throat. 'Harry told me you're going to the States. You've been offered a job and you're leaving.'

He saw her expression change to one of disbelief. 'Have you come to tell me that it's thanks to you I get to go? Because it isn't.'

'What? No. God, no. I only said it because that's what prompted me to come here. I don't get any credit for that, it was all your hard work, I know that. I . . . I just had to see you before you go and . . .' He swallowed again but the bloody shards of glass were ever present. 'And say how sorry I am. I know I messed up and it doesn't matter who said or did what that led up to what I said to you. The fact of the matter is that those words came out of my mouth and I'm responsible for them.

'The irony is that deep down, I knew as soon as I said those things to you that they were untrue. You're one of the most honest and genuine people I know, who would go out of her way to help others. You would never cheat anyone. I let my own fears overcome my common sense. My fear of being conned as I have been once before and the fear of losing control of my life and who I allow into it or out of it.

'And here's another irony: I didn't even realise when you became such an integral part of my life and now that

273

I have realised it, I'm losing you all over again. You're going away.'

He huffed out an exasperated sigh as the sorrow of what he'd said pierced his heart anew. He bowed his head, his arms resting on his thighs as he thought of how to say what he wanted to say to her.

He was normally so good with his words, especially with his line of work. So why was he struggling so much right now?

That's because the stakes have never been so high.

'Why is it so hard?' he whispered, more to himself than to her. Why was he saying everything else when the only thing worth saying was the one thing he wasn't telling her.

'What's that?' Ibrahim wasn't sure if Jiya had said those words in response to him or if his mind had conjured them up because he wanted to hear them. Because he wanted her to ask him what he had to say.

He looked up at her but she looked blurry. He shook his head and that helped clear his vision.

He pulled in a shuddering breath and it came out in a whoosh as he felt her fingers on his cheek. As she ran her fingers across it, he realised that it was damp and unable to hold it back any longer, he whispered the words to her.

'I love you.' Her slightly softened expression hardened again and she dropped her hand. 'I know I don't deserve to even say those words to you, but if I hold them in any longer, I swear I'll go crazy. Not that I've not been going mad since before this. I feel like I've been on a bloody never-ending ride, and instead of slowing down and coming to a stop, it's just getting faster and faster and I . . . I just . . . I wish I had another chance with you.'

'I agree. You don't deserve to say those words to me.' He felt his heart plummet down to the ground and the pain nearly made him double over but before he could, Jiya carried on. 'You didn't just hurt my feelings that day; you broke my heart, Ibrahim. Every word you said to me that day has been branded on my heart.

'I've done nothing but try to be honest with you about everything, so the fact that you didn't trust me is something I still can't get my head around.'

It was as though the feeling of losing her was manifesting itself physically within him.

'How do I know you won't switch on me like that again if you had another chance?'

He didn't really have an answer to that because the fact of the matter was that there was no way he could convince her with words. He needed the chance to prove himself through actions and that was impossible because she was leaving.

CHAPTER TWENTY-EIGHT

Jiya

Ibrahim's shoulders were drooped as he sat there and Jiya felt her heart turn over.

This man had shown her nothing but confidence and assurance in all the time she'd known him. She couldn't think of a time when he hadn't been sure of himself, but today she had seen a complete turnaround. He looked so lost.

He had said he loved her. Could she believe that? Surely if he had loved her, he wouldn't have said all those nasty things to her?

Her mind went through a reel of the moments she had shared with Ibrahim that had made her smile and her heart feel lighter. There had certainly been a strong attraction between them and she knew she had feelings for him. Was it possible that his feelings were just as strong as hers?

But what difference did any of it make? She was sitting here, at the airport, ready to board a flight to New York, where a bright, shiny new opportunity awaited her.

She had woken up today thinking that she would put her interlude with Ibrahim firmly in the past and move on. She hadn't heard from him after that dreadful meeting in the café and she hadn't got in touch with him either.

She had been equal parts nervous and excited about her upcoming trip and if there was any sense of loss about leaving her family behind when they had finally found a really great place with each other, or about Ibrahim because . . . well, because; then she was going to try not to let it show.

After drinking practically a bucket of coffee, she had got to the airport and raced straight for the ladies. It was on her way back that she'd spotted Harry chatting to her parents and brother and assumed he'd decided to come at the last minute to see her off.

As she'd neared the four of them, some deeper instinct had made her turn and look to her left, where she'd seen Ibrahim, standing apart from everyone, looking desolate.

His anguish had been coming off him in waves and she'd felt compelled to walk up to him. She'd never thought she'd see him there.

When he'd wrapped her in his arms, completely unexpectedly, she had been torn between pulling away and pressing up against his chest even more, savouring the scent and feel of him.

What a pushover. After everything that's happened!

When her father had come storming towards them, she was sure he was about to deck Ibrahim. It was a good thing his brother had stepped in and God knows what he'd said to her dad but whatever it was, he'd lost the look of rage and had instead started talking – albeit with super animated gestures – to Ashar.

Harry was still chatting to her mum and she saw her brother – who had been spitting nails after she'd exacted a promise from him that he wouldn't go after Ibrahim – was making his way towards their father and Ashar.

She turned back and looked at Ibrahim. The man who had made her feel so alive when she'd been with him and so many of her favourite moments in the last few months had been spent with him. Moments filled with joy and exhilaration. Anticipation.

He was also the man who had caused her an untold amount of hurt and anguish and plenty of sleepless nights to go with it in a very short space of time.

As she watched him, he pulled in a deep breath and looked up at her, his eyes clear and focused. There was a determination in them which hadn't been there moments earlier, as though he had come to some momentous decision.

'During the first year of my degree, there was a girl on my course. Her name was Anushka. You remember? The woman we met at the restaurant that day.'

His change of subject came out of nowhere and though it had baffled her, she didn't say anything and just nodded, remembering the polished woman who had made her way to their table and the fact that she had sensed there was a story there. She had forgotten all about that until now. His voice was low as he spoke, but it had lost the earlier waver in it.

'We hit it off really well and before long we started seeing each other. We did practically everything together and our mates called us the "it couple".

'I thought that was it – she's the one for me. I told her everything about my family and even introduced her to my brothers. I had bought an engagement ring and thought I'd propose after we'd both qualified.'

He turned his face forwards; his arms were resting on his thighs again and she could see the line of tension in his jaw reach his temple. She felt a mix of emotions: wanting to keep her distance and wanting to gather him up in her arms and ward off the pain she knew he was feeling.

'We were at a party together when I overheard her talking to some of her girlfriends. She said that her biggest achievement from her time at university was picking a ripe peach called Ibrahim Saeed.'

Jiya had been expecting him to say something about how the relationship hadn't ended well but the moment still made her gasp softly.

'It turns out she realised pretty early on who I was and which family I came from. My father had recently bagged a pretty big real estate project and she knew that my family was already reasonably well off. Zafar had started earning a name for himself and she thought that aligning herself with me would work wonders for her prospects. She had done her due diligence, I'll give her that,' he said with no humour in his voice.

He looked at her again and she could see that remembering that moment of his life hurt him even now. 'I was just a convenient means to an end for her. She never loved me. She loved what I came from and she wanted that for herself. The fact that I was besotted only made it easier for her.'

She couldn't hold back and placed a hand on his knee.

She spoke after a few moments of silence. 'Thank you for telling me; I know it couldn't have been easy. I'm really sorry that you went through what you did. No one should be made to feel the way that woman made you feel but you can't be suspicious of every other woman you come across in life because of her. I'm not Anushka, Ibrahim. I've never once done or said anything to give you that idea. Have I?'

He huffed out a laugh. 'You're as different from her as they come. The truth is . . .' he paused.

'Look, Ibrahim—'

'Let me say this please, Jiya. As hard as it is, I need to.'

She nodded her head, a small kernel of nervousness taking root in her tummy.

Ibrahim

After days of feeling like he was wading through treacle, Ibrahim felt as though he had been pulled through it by an invisible force and suddenly everything had become clear. As though he were standing in his favourite spot on the nature trail and taking in a big deep breath, breathing out all of his doubts. Well, some of them at least.

In this moment of clarity, he knew what he was going to say.

The funny thing was, it had been his own words that had helped clear his foggy brain, and the answer now seemed blindingly obvious.

He wanted Jiya. He wanted to spend his life with her and have the chance to tell her every day how much she meant to him. He wanted to spend time discovering different things about her and with her. Moments of pure joy which he knew deep within he'd never find with anyone else.

He loved her.

But loving someone wasn't just about you and what you wanted. It went so much deeper than that, and it was from that depth Ibrahim got the strength to say what he had to.

He ran his hands across his face and then down his jeans before slowly taking Jiya's hand in his.

He gave her a tentative smile as she relaxed her hand and he gave it a gentle squeeze.

Yes. This was definitely the right thing to do.

'I'm going to start again actually and, hopefully, a bit more articulately than I did before.' Her eyebrows couldn't be any closer together if she tried and she was biting her bottom lip furiously.

'The things I said to you at the café were inexcusable and I have no justification. There is nothing I can say to make any of it remotely acceptable or understandable. For what it's worth though, Jiya, I really am sorry. I should have had faith in you and as new as it was, I should have had faith in what was blossoming between us.

'The thing is, I do love you, Jiya, more than I had realised, and it's taken me a lot longer than I'm proud of to realise this.'

Her eyebrows relaxed as her features softened, so he ploughed on.

'And it's because I love you, I'm going to say goodbye.'

Her frown was back at express speed as she slowly shook her head.

'I'm not going to ask you to give me a chance or say any of what I had thought I would say before coming here. You should go to New York and fulfil your dreams. Do what you had set out to do and show everyone how brilliant you are.'

Ibrahim swallowed the lump in his throat which was fast making it hard for him to speak. He certainly believed everything he had just said to Jiya but that didn't necessarily make it any easier to actually accept. That was something he would probably be spending the rest of his life doing.

He lowered his head slowly and gave her a soft peck on the cheek, pulling back before the sensation could fully register. He gave her hand a final squeeze and then slowly let it go, the pain of doing so intensifying.

He stood up but she stayed sitting. His brothers and her family were standing a few feet away, watching them but pretending not to. Except her father, who was crystal clear about the fact that he was watching him like a hawk.

'You just said you love me.'

He looked at her and nodded, surprised to see annoyance on her face.

'So how can you let me go so easily? If you love me, why aren't you asking me to stay and give this,' she waved her hand between them a few times, 'another go?'

He hoped his smile didn't look as pained as it felt. 'Who the hell said it was easy, sweetheart? You want the truth? It's killing me, but I can't and I won't ask you not to go or change your plans because the simple fact of the matter is that I don't deserve that. Besides, this is what you've always dreamed of doing, Jiya. You should take this opportunity with two hands and fly with it.

'I do love you and I always will, but surely that's more of a reason for me to let you go where your dreams are taking you?'

As hard as it was for him to say what he was, he knew it was the right thing to do. After the things he had said to her, he couldn't expect to be a part of her life or think he had the right to ask her to change her plans for him. Besides, even if she were open to doing something like that, would he want her to? Would he want her to decline such an opportunity knowing what it meant to her? No, not in a million years.

Knowing that gave him a strange sense of peace with his decision. There was still one thing he needed to hear from her though.

'Do you think you'll ever be able to forgive me?'

After watching him silently for a few minutes, she stood up abruptly. 'You know what? You're right. This is an incredible opportunity and it would be a shame to waste it, right?'

He swallowed down the ever-present lump in his throat and nodded jerkily. She obviously wasn't ready to forgive him and it should have come as no surprise really. As his grandmother often said, 'You reap what you sow.' It was time to face his actions with honour and integrity.

They made their way towards the others and Ibrahim apologised to Jiya's parents and brother for everything. Her parents weren't very forthcoming with their forgiveness but her brother took the hand Ibrahim had extended.

'You can thank my sister for the fact that you're still in one piece, Saeed. It doesn't matter how much I get on her nerves or she on mine, you hurt my baby sister and I can't say I'm OK with that or ever will be, but if she's happy to talk to you civilly then I'm willing to as well. I trust her judgement.' He winked at his sister and Ibrahim's regard for Jameel went up another few notches as he got what Jameel wasn't saying. His courteous manner was more for her sake than Ibrahim's.

He stood back as Jiya hugged everyone; her mother sobbing noisily while her son tried to comfort her. She hugged Harry and gave Ashar an awkward wave and then came and stood in front of him.

He wasn't sure how much longer his resolve would hold so he rushed to speak first.

'All the best, Jiya – don't work too hard out there.'

'Thanks for coming and for sharing what you did with me. I know it couldn't have been easy.

'Look after yourself, Ibrahim. And when you can, try and figure out what you really want, and then go for it.' She stood on tiptoes and gave him a kiss on the cheek which he felt deep in his soul.

She smiled at him and he felt a dull ache in his chest as his heart cracked in two.

Sucking in a breath, he smiled back at her and then she turned away and was walking away from him, weaving her way through the barriers and onto a new phase of her life.

Despite his sadness, he was happy for her. Jiya had worked hard and if anyone deserved a break as big as this, it was definitely her.

It just sucked that the opportunity of a lifetime for her and his own blind foolishness had taken her away from him.

CHAPTER TWENTY-NINE

Jiya

Jiya looked out at the scenery through the floor-to-ceiling windows of the conference room. It was a corner unit – apparently a big deal – and provided a stunning view of Central Park. As clichéd as it was, she was really pleased that the office she had spent the last three months working in had the classic New York feature a stone's throw away. As a non-local, the cheesy, touristy attractions always appealed more.

Had she made the most of it? You bet she had.

She'd done all the things she had seen on the countless television series and films she had seen, from walking around Central Park to getting into one of the classic yellow cabs. She'd been a spectator at some college games, getting sucked into the cheery atmosphere with her tour guide colleagues and saying things which always cracked them up.

'You know in England we play a similar sport but without any helmets or pads. It's a bruising game with no timeouts, but the scoring is completely different. You score tries, conversions and penalties rather than touchdowns, although funnily enough you do sometimes touchdown with the ball to score a try.'

They had all laughed at her description of rugby and then proceeded to try and explain the rules of American football to her, which she still didn't quite understand.

One of the things she'd found particularly amusing was how much everyone loved her accent. Had she made more of an effort to put one on? Uh, yeah! But it was all part of the fun.

Fun which stayed outside her shoe box-sized apartment.

All the emotions which were being suppressed during her working hours amplified themselves when she was by herself. The sense of loneliness. Being away from her family and friends. The feeling that despite having done what some people could only dream of doing, she still felt as though something integral was missing.

She was doing well at work and had learned so much. She was checking in with her mother practically every day and video-calling a few times a week to see the others. Harry had been in touch as well, and she'd even spoken to Reshma and Daadi once when Harry had been with them.

But the person she had been both avoiding and wanting to speak to every minute of every day hadn't called and she hadn't called him either. The last time she'd seen him or spoken to him had been at the airport when she'd flown to New York. Harry had dropped a couple of hints but she hadn't dared to pick up on them.

In the last three months, she had gone over her last conversation with him more times than she could count. With the enforced distance between them, she'd had time to give what he'd said and done plenty of thought and she had come to the conclusion that despite how much his words had hurt her, she could now understand why he had reacted the way he had.

During one of their regular catch-ups, Harry had told her more about what had happened at their end after his grandmother's party. It had helped many things fall into place for her and she now felt she understood Ibrahim a little bit better.

But she had no idea where they stood.

Was there even a 'they'?

She remembered that he'd asked her if she had forgiven him at the airport and she had deliberately not answered his question. His hopeless expression had told her what he thought her answer was. But it wasn't because she wanted to be cruel. She didn't. The truth was she hadn't been entirely sure of her answer at the time. So much had happened and he'd said so many new things to her which she hadn't been able to process properly at the time.

Now when she thought back, she could see exactly why she'd avoided answering his question. She'd been afraid.

A small but strong part of her couldn't drop the idea that he could do the same thing to her again. Why would she risk her heart and feelings again? Where was the sense in opening yourself up to that kind of hurt again? It would show that she hadn't learned anything and Jiya had no intention of letting *that* happen.

He hadn't wanted to stop her and he never said anything about having a long-distance relationship. She hadn't felt brave enough to initiate any such thing herself.

She had given into a false sense of security by keeping her own feelings locked back that day and with a false front of bravado, she had bid everyone goodbye and walked towards the departures lounge.

But running away from reality didn't mean it ceased to exist. It was still there, waiting to be addressed. Besides, wasn't taking risks a part of life?

Risk was there every step of the way. She had taken a risk when she'd decided to have a fake relationship with Ibrahim, just as he had with her.

She'd taken a risk coming out here to New York. It could have ended up being a complete nightmare. Thank God it hadn't, but the risk had been there, hadn't it?

And then there was the risk Ibrahim had taken on *her;* laying his feelings bare and telling her about his own vulnerabilities. That had been a massive risk on his part.

He'd risked his heart but she'd been too afraid to do the same.

'Jiya, I'm so sorry to have kept you waiting.' Her boss, Carter, came hurrying into the conference room, stopping her train of thoughts in its tracks. He placed his devices on the table and came to stand beside her.

'Beautiful, isn't it? This view never gets old.'

She pushed aside her thoughts which had unwittingly put a mirror up in front of her and focused again on the view in front of her. 'It is lovely. A spot of tranquillity in the midst of a city that never sleeps.'

He gave a deep chuckle and motioned to the table and chairs behind them. 'Absolutely. Come and sit. I've been on my feet all morning and my old legs could do with a rest.'

He was exaggerating. He was in his mid-thirties and could keep going for days without stopping, something she'd witnessed herself.

'How're things going?'

Jiya couldn't stop the confusion she had been feeling since he'd asked for this meeting, completely out of the blue this morning, from showing on her face and replied to his question cagily. 'Fine, thanks.'

He let out another chuckle. 'I don't mean anything by that, honestly. I didn't call this meeting to scare you. Before I say anything though, I want to tell you that you've been doing remarkably since you've joined our team. Your work ethic is unquestionable, you get along with everyone, you're a great team player and your progress has been absolutely mind-blowing. I'm over the moon to have you here. What are your thoughts? How have you found being here?'

She let out the breath she hadn't realised she'd been holding since his first question in a great big whoosh. He was happy with her; she was doing well and she felt pleased. When she said as much, Carter responded with a quirked eyebrow and her tummy somersaulted.

She could never see that particular gesture and not think of *him*.

'Hmm. I got a phone call at stupid o'clock this morning. Apparently Zaf Saeed thinks nothing of time zones.'

His elongated mention of Zafar's name, courtesy of his American accent, had her sitting up straighter in her chair.

'You know Zafar Saeed?' she asked.

He smiled at her as he leaned back in the chair, his arm resting on the table.

'I've known Zaf since college. We studied together when I was in the UK, became good friends and have kept in touch over the years. We also help each other out professionally from time to time.

'In fact, he found out that you were on my team and told me that he knew you. Small world, eh? I think he doesn't know that it was his brother, Ibrahim, who had actually sent your resumé over some time back. He saw pictures on my account from one of our events, I think. He was very complimentary about you although he did point out that he'd not seen you work in a professional capacity. I can now say that having seen you in a professional capacity, you are worth your weight in gold and I told him as much. And before you ask me, neither he or his brother had anything to do with you getting this job. It was all your hard work and a sprinkling of right place, right time with your resumé landing in my inbox.'

Jiya sat there open-mouthed, stunned with what she'd heard. She'd had no idea that Ibrahim's older brother had been complimentary about her? After her fallout with his brother?

And Ibrahim? He had sent Carter her CV?

He had done all this and not said anything to her?

'Anyway, this morning Zaf asked how you're getting on and if you're enjoying your time out here. I told him what I've just told you and he was both pleased and impressed. He's wondering if you're ready to go back because if you are, he's got an opening in his team and if you're interested, he's keen to have a chat with you about it.'

Watching her sit there imitating a landed fish, Carter poured her a glass of water and pushed it towards her.

She clutched the glass to her like a lifeline and tried to sort through all the words that had just poured out of Carter, trying to make sense of them. Before she had managed, he spoke again.

'Look, Jiya, you're a star and I'd love for you to stay here and watch you go from strength to strength. But I'm well aware that that is not what your long-term plan is. It can't be easy for you being here without any friends or family; you're probably missing them like crazy. And I've got a feeling that you're getting close to the point of wanting to go back home. Or have I got this completely wrong? Tell me I'm wrong and you want to stay.'

Jiya tried to swallow the lump in her throat at the mention of her family and friends. At the mention of Ibrahim. But she struggled. And then she felt the telling prickle of tears in the corners of her eyes. She saw the look of alarm cross Carter's face and let out a cross between a laugh and a sob, as a tear rolled down her cheek.

He scrambled for the box of tissues on the sideboard at the other end of the room as Jiya gave up the fight to stop the tears.

He pulled out three tissues in succession and held them out to her.

'I'm so . . . sor . . . sorry. I don't know why—'

'Don't worry about it. My niece has a similar reaction to me and she's only six months old.' Jiya giggled and she saw Carter's tense shoulders relax.

What was the matter with her, blubbering like that in a meeting with her boss? It felt as though her brain had powered down and the only thing in control of her were her emotions, which had already been rioting just before Carter had walked into the conference room.

'Take the rest of the afternoon off and have a think about what you'd like to do next. You have a lot of things to think about and I don't think deciding something like this on the spur of the moment is a great idea. If you'd like to stay here, I'm more than happy to have you, you know that. But if you'd like to go back, then an opportunity with Zaf would be something I'd definitely encourage you to consider. Obviously, he's not as good as me, but . . .' He shrugged his shoulders and gave her a crooked smile.

Jiya did as Carter had suggested and took the rest of the afternoon off, which happened to be a Friday, and the weekend to sift through the myriad thoughts circling in her brain. Thankfully there had been no more crying jags but her energy levels had definitely taken a battering.

Carter had told her before she left that he was willing to extend her contract if she chose to stay and the company would take care of all the legalities for her to stay on. He'd also sent her the details Zafar had sent him about the opening on his team in London.

Staying in New York had been amazing, each day bringing with it a new sense of adventure and excitement. But if she were being honest, it was beginning to lose its glow because she was starting to miss all that was familiar. She had no one to share jokes in the moment with and sometimes her British humour fell flat on those around her.

Working in London would mean being back home, with her family and friends and everything familiar to her. There was even the possibility of a job but where did that stand given her current situation with Ibrahim?

If she was offered and accepted the role, that would put her in the same building as him and they were bound to come across each other, especially given that her boss would be his eldest brother.

Deep down, she knew what her decision was when it came to choosing between staying in New York and going back to London. She was incredibly proud of herself for having achieved what she had but she was now ready to go back home.

As for the job, she would definitely have a chat with Zafar. Jiya wasn't one to look a gift horse in the mouth, but before she decided anything, she needed to take the risk she'd avoided taking three months ago.

She needed to show the same courage she had when striking out on her own when it came to telling Ibrahim how she felt; something she hadn't been brave enough to do despite the fact that he had.

If it so happened that she was too late and he'd moved on and wasn't interested, well, at least she would know where she stood with him. She could then move forward, with nothing holding her back. Except perhaps a broken heart.

CHAPTER THIRTY

Ibrahim

Ibrahim watched people walk past, bundled up in coats to ward off the autumnal chill and huddled up in his own jacket. It was windy, he was feeling cold and miserable and was mentally berating himself for giving in to his brothers and coming out with them.

To be fair though, it was hardly Arctic weather and the fresh air was welcome after having been cooped up inside for most of the week working.

'I'm going to get a coffee. Anyone want anything?' Rayyan looked at each of them in turn. Ashar agreed and went with him to get the drinks.

'I'm glad you decided to come out. You've been working non-stop recently.' Harry walked beside him along the South Bank, which wasn't too busy thankfully.

'Hmm.' He hadn't wanted to come out and he most definitely hadn't wanted to come here.

It was impossible to come here and not think of Jiya.

He'd tried his best to come to terms with the choice she had made but it had been nothing short of a Herculean effort on his part. Countless times he'd picked up his phone to call or message her but hadn't in the end.

Like a lovesick teenager, he'd go through the reel of photographs he had of her every night and hope that she'd make an appearance in his dreams. How sad was that? He didn't think he'd ever get over her.

His family had decided among themselves that they were going to pretend that the whole fiasco had never happened. His parents and grandmother never brought Jiya up, even though he knew that his grandmother had occasionally been in touch with her.

His brothers never mentioned her either, all of them making a concerted effort to try and keep things as casual as they usually were between them, although they all seemed to be making an extra effort with him this past couple of weeks. Maybe he'd been more miserable with them than he'd realised.

They came to a stop further along the path and as Harry took out his phone and began tapping at the screen furiously, Ibrahim turned to look out across the river. The trees were at the stage of heralding the changing season and he pulled out his phone to capture a few shots.

He'd been doing more photography in these last few months, sometimes going out and occasionally pulling his camera out at home and seeing his surroundings through his camera lens. The immersive nature of it helped him to step out of his own mind for that short period of time and he felt a small semblance of peace during and after.

He couldn't say his broken heart had healed – that probably wouldn't ever happen – but he had moved forward in other ways. Aside from the photography, he was happy with work, striving for a better work–life balance and he had even managed to come to peace with issues that had previously tainted his thoughts and relationships because of their darkness. He acknowledged now that he had given them more power than they had ever deserved. He knew that what had happened with Anushka was on her, not him.

And as for Zafar's marriage influencing his thoughts; he could now appreciate that it was for his brother to make of his marriage what he wanted it to be. What Ibrahim chose to do had nothing to do with that, really. And after getting to know Reshma better over the last few months, he had a feeling that his older brother had more issues of his own to resolve than he let on.

He pocketed his phone as he watched a small boat making its way along the river. Someone came and rested their elbows on the railing beside him. It was Reshma, with Zafar standing beside her.

He smiled at her. 'What are you guys doing here? I thought you had somewhere else to be?'

She didn't say anything. Instead, she lifted her eyebrows at him and nodded her head in his direction. He looked at her blankly and then at his brother, who shrugged.

She shook her head and then pointed behind him.

Rolling his eyes, he turned to look behind him, saw Jiya and then turned back to look at Reshma.

His heart leaped into his throat as the penny dropped; his breathing laboured as though he'd just tried to sprint run a mile.

He didn't want to turn back and look again, afraid that he might have imagined her standing there but he didn't have to. In typical Jiya fashion, she came and stood in front of him.

She was *actually* standing in front of him; all five foot two inches of her.

'Am I dreaming?' His brothers and sister-in-law laughed out loud at his whispered question and Jiya gave him an impish smile.

'No, you're not dreaming.' God, that voice. How he'd been longing to hear it.

He cleared his throat, hoping his voice would come out normally. Just because she was back and standing in front of him didn't mean what he wanted it to mean.

She had made her decision at the airport before leaving and he didn't feature in her plans for her future. She hadn't forgiven him for the way he'd behaved with her and he needed to respect her decision.

'It's so good to see you. How are you? How's the job in New York going?' That was good. Two perfectly normal questions in a normal tone of voice.

He looked at Zafar and Reshma, who both smiled at him and then with Harry, they walked away in the direction Rayyan and Ashar had gone earlier.

Jiya

Despite feeling nervous herself, Jiya couldn't help but find Ibrahim's confusion really cute. She could see how shocked he was but he was trying really hard to behave normally with her.

She gave him what she hoped was a reassuring smile and turned to look at the others – who were all in on her secret – as they walked away, waving and giving her a thumbs-up.

She looked back at Ibrahim, who was still staring at her in wonder, something which boosted her confidence a little.

Once she'd decided she was coming back to London, she had spoken to Carter, who had said that he had guessed that would be her choice but he was happy for her. She had completed another month working in New York after that and had been surprised with a big leaving party from her colleagues, who were now friends.

She had got in touch with Zafar and had a long chat with him about the role on offer, which she had decided to respectfully decline in the end.

'With all due respect, Zafar, I want to do this bit on my own steam. Maybe you can headhunt me in a few years' time,' she'd added cheekily.

'I had a feeling you might say that and so did Carter, the smug arsehole, when he found out that I know you and want you to join my team.'

She had managed to get a role with a subsidiary company of the one she had worked for in New York after having a chat with Carter. It was based in London and he thought it would suit her perfectly. She was due to start the following week and was pretty excited about it.

She had got back to London a couple of days ago and while she had wanted to meet with Ibrahim straight away, she had waited. It had been Harry's idea to surprise him like this today and they'd all agreed with it.

Her family had been over the moon to have her back and while her parents were sceptical about her plan of action where Ibrahim was concerned, they understood why she had to follow through with it and supported her decision. Her brother was in on the whole plan today and she had also found out that he'd been keeping in touch with Harry and had become good friends with Ashar while she'd been gone.

Her relationship with Jameel had seen a huge change since she had come clean about everything before going to New York and they had become very close, Jameel sharing some of his own insecurities with her when he had come to see her in New York, which had been eye-openers. She had no idea that her accomplishments made him feel inadequate and it brought home to Jiya furthermore that for her relationships with her family members to flourish, she needed to put in as much effort as she expected of them.

She had also found out that Harry had been in touch with Jameel on the day she had flown out to New York so that Ibrahim didn't miss out on seeing her. He said it was because he wanted to see him grovel but she knew her brother better now. He did it because he cared.

'Shall we go for a walk?'

Ibrahim looked unsure at her question and Jiya didn't want the awkwardness to linger any longer. 'Or we can stay here, I don't mind.' Gathering her resolve, she decided to cut to the chase. 'When I was leaving to go to New York, you asked me a question. Do you remember?'

He huffed out a laugh completely lacking in humour. 'There were so many things I said and plenty more I wanted to say but didn't. Which question are we talking about?'

He didn't look as miserable as he had that day at the airport but there was still an air of sadness about him which made her feel wretched.

'You asked me if I'd forgiven you.' He looked away from her at her words and faced the river. 'I *had* forgiven you, Ibrahim. I was just too much of a coward to admit my feelings at the time so I left things as they were. And *I'm* sorry about that. I should have been as brave as you were that day and told you how I felt. How I still feel.'

He turned away from the railings and faced her fully. 'Don't, Jiya. You have nothing to be sorry about, so please don't apologise. For anything. Tell me more about New York, is it everything you hoped it would be?'

Both Zafar and Harry had told her that he still felt guilty about what had happened and hadn't quite got over it. Hadn't got over her. She just hoped she could now show him what they could have if he could move on from what had happened.

He seemed keen to change the subject and keep things casual so Jiya started that way. 'New York was great. Carter, my boss, was really helpful and supportive and the team was really nice as well. I managed to complete my last few MBA assignments out there and now I'm just waiting to find out how I did. I did all the typical touristy things in New York, but I got kind of lonely by myself and really missed everyone here. There was no one out there to share the experience with or who I could share things with at the end of the day. Like my boyfriend.'

She saw his expression change from interested to crest-fallen. 'I really missed my boyfriend.' She whispered the words as she reached for his hands, which were fisted by his sides.

He shook his head slowly as he spoke. 'No, Jiya, trust me, you can do so much better than me. I don't deserve you.' He tried to pull his hands away but she didn't let him.

'Let me say what I have to say, please, Ibrahim. Then we can decide whether we deserve each other or not. What do you say?'

She held her breath as she stood there, the breeze buffeting her, hoping that he'd give her a chance. He jerked his head once in a nod and she let the air trapped in her lungs out.

'Thank you.' She squeezed his hands but didn't let go, needing the contact. She hadn't realised how much until she'd held his hands, the contact grounding her in a way she'd missed these past four months.

'That day at the airport . . . no, I'm going to go back further, so bear with me. I'm not going to go over what happened when your dad announced our engagement and what happened after that.' She felt him try and pull away again but held on. 'I want to talk about what happened before that, Ibrahim.

'I know we started something fake, seeing each other because of a wacky idea, but you and I both know that what we felt and what our relationship evolved into was not fake. It was as real as you and I are. We took the time to get to know each other, sharing things with each other that we hadn't really told anyone else before. Thoughts and feelings which we wouldn't share with others but which we picked up with each other, sometimes without saying much. We were happy and getting on so well, on our way to discovering something just for us. Something neither of us had ever expected or thought we wanted.'

His jaw was tense and she could feel the stiffness in his hands but she carried on.

'I've never felt this way about anyone before. What we had was special and I don't want us to lose it because of a mistake you made or because I wasn't brave enough to tell you how I feel.

'I love you, Ibrahim. I should have said this to you that day at the airport, even before you said it to me, in fact, because that's the truth about how I felt. I should have also told you that I had forgiven you. We had a misunderstanding and after you told me about Anushka, I understood why you reacted the way you had.'

'No.' This time when he pulled his hands away, she couldn't keep a hold of them and they slipped away from her grasp as he took half a step back. 'You were right that day, Jiya. My actions were inexcusable and—'

'It was a misunderstanding, Ibrahim; a mistake. We're humans, that's what we do. You can't spend the rest of your life feeling guilty about it and letting it be an anchor keeping you pinned down. Answer me this – do you love me?'

She could see the shimmer of tears in his eyes and felt her own eyes prickle with emotion. She felt the shuddering breath he hauled in and then her heart skipped a beat as he shook his head.

'You don't?' Her voice was little more than a whisper.

After what felt like ages but was only seconds, Ibrahim took a step forward and cupped her face in his hands. 'I don't think I'll ever stop loving you, Jiya.' He rested his forehead against hers, his breath warm on her cheeks and Jiya felt her heart settle back into its rightful place.

'I *do* love you, sweetheart; so much. Not seeing you or hearing your voice for these last four months has been nothing short of torture for me. It's as though there's a large rock sitting on my chest and no one except you has the strength to move it. My bold, brave and beautiful Jiya.'

The tears that had been hovering at the edge rolled down her cheeks and she sniffled. 'I love you too and the last four months have been really hard for me as well; knowing you were just a phone call away but not being able to hear your voice. I wanted to see you as soon as I got back and waiting till today was so hard.'

'Please don't cry, Jiya, I can't bear it.' He swiped his thumbs across her cheeks.

'I'm not crying. I just . . . *I* can't bear the thought of not being with you, Ibrahim.' She cupped his face in her hands, making him move his from hers and looked into his tear-filled eyes. 'Please can we forget what happened and start again? Misunderstandings are part and parcel of life. We can't punish ourselves because of them forever. Besides, you're punishing not just yourself by not being with me, you know?'

She felt his hands land softly on her hips and he let out a soft, beleaguered sigh.

'I messed up at the first hurdle, Jiya. I let all my insecurities take over and just reacted. I still feel like I don't deserve you.' She let out a frustrated growl and he gave the softest of chuckles. 'But if I'm getting another chance with you, I'll take it.' He pulled her closer and she moved her hands down to his shoulders. 'Let's do what you said. Let's start again. Nothing fake going forward. Just you, me and our very real relationship. What do you say?'

Jiya felt a rush of warmth through her body and she threw her arms around Ibrahim's neck as she squealed. 'Yes, yes, yes. A thousand yeses.'

His arms came around her waist as he held her against him before he moved his head back a fraction and quirked an eyebrow at her. 'Only a thousand?'

'Millions. Billions. Countless in fact.' She buried her face in his neck and let all her doubts and fears melt away as she felt a feeling of elation and completeness fill her being. 'I love you so much.' His chuckle was stronger this time.

'I love you that much more. And I only need one yes, Jiya. Just one and just you. Only you, my love. Only you.'

Acknowledgements

I'd like to thank my family for pushing me to believe in my dream – I love you.

Rhea and Sanah – thank you for bringing this story out in the world. Your enthusiasm and excitement for it has helped me more than you know!

Thank you, Virginia Heath – my friend and mentor. Your encouragement from the very beginning of my writing journey has been invaluable; I have learnt so much from you.

A big thank you to Essex Writers United for the fun gatherings and ace feedback. A special shout out to Kelly Stock, Lucy Morris and Virginia Heath – our writing retreat was where this story really took off and I had the best time.

Thank you to the Romantic Novelists' Association for being a marvellous place for writers.

Hannah, Layla, Louisa, Naomi and Sarah, you ladies are superstars and have been there from the start of this crazy journey – thank you.